AN UNGODLY VISIT

"Great God in Heaven!" Rose said, barely above a whisper.

She had heard the screams of terrified children and had come running. She arrived at the schoolhouse door at the same time as Brother Samuel. They saw Charlotte clutching sobbing children before a room full of swarming rats.

Rose wasn't afraid of rodents, or most small animals in small enough numbers. But rats were not her favorite, and these were far too many. Three scrawny gray rats scurried past and fled outdoors. What looked like at least a dozen more scrambled around the classroom. Their fur was matted and streaked with dirt, their eyes feverish with God knew what diseases. Rose shuddered. She dared not think where they'd come from. A wrinkled and dirty burlap sack lay just   en end faced towa

Other Sister Rose Callahan Mysteries by
Deborah Woodworth
from Avon Books

DEATH OF A WINTER SHAKER

A DEADLY SHAKER SPRING

A SISTER ROSE CALLAHAN MYSTERY

DEBORAH WOODWORTH

AVON BOOKS  NEW YORK

This is a work of fiction. Names, characters, places, and incidents either are the product of the author's imagination or are used fictitiously. Any resemblance to actual events, locales, organizations, or persons, living or dead, is entirely coincidental and beyond the intent of either the author or the publisher.

AVON BOOKS
A division of
The Hearst Corporation
1350 Avenue of the Americas
New York, New York 10019

Copyright © 1998 by Deborah L. Woodworth
Published by arrangement with the author
Visit our website at **http://www.AvonBooks.com**
Library of Congress Catalog Card Number: 97-94415
ISBN: 0-380-79203-6

First Avon Books Printing: May 1998

AVON TRADEMARK REG. U.S. PAT. OFF. AND IN OTHER COUNTRIES, MARCA REGISTRADA, HECHO EN U.S.A.

Printed in the U.S.A.

WCD   10   9   8   7   6   5   4   3   2   1

To my father, James R. Woodworth,
with love

ACKNOWLEDGMENTS

For their skill and friendship, I am grateful to my writers' group: Mary Logue, Marilyn Bos, Becky Bohan, Peter Hautman, and Tom Rucker. I also want to thank my editor, Patricia Lande Grader, and my agent, Barbara Gislason, for their insight and support. Always and forever, I am grateful to and for my family—most especially, Norm.

AUTHOR'S NOTE

The North Homage Shaker village, the town and the county of Languor, Kentucky, and all their inhabitants are figments of the author's imagination. The characters live only in this book and represent no one, living or dead. By 1937, the period in which this story is told, no Shaker villages remained in Kentucky or anywhere else outside the northeastern United States. Today one small Shaker community survives, Sabbathday Lake, near Poland Springs, Maine.

Deborah Woodworth
1997

ONE

We buried her this afternoon, my sister, my heart. Mother Ann opened her arms wide to carry her to God, and the angels appeared, crowds of angels, sparkling and chanting. They swooped down to reclaim one of their own. They knew she was pure in her soul, even if the brethren doubted. I watched them today. I saw the smug looks on her sisters' faces, the vengeful gloating. The vipers break their vows with every thought. The brethren are no better, with their secret faces like judgment carved in cold stone. Mother Ann knows the soul of her child. They do not. Especially him. He tried not to show anything, but I could see. He killed her as surely as if he stopped her breath with his own hand.

SISTER SARAH BAKER SMOOTHED THE DOG-EARED paper and skimmed the passage again. Bold handwriting slashed across the page. She'd lost count of how many times she had read it. Creases had already cut into the yellowed paper since Caleb had slipped it to her a few days earlier.

With a tired sigh, Sarah edged her plump body off

her bed. She had done what she'd been instructed to do, even though it took the better part of the night to find the right moment, when everyone was deeply asleep so she wouldn't be missed from her retiring room or caught in the act.

Sarah glanced in the small mirror hanging from a wall peg and straightened her stiff sugar-scoop bonnet over the cap that hid her hair. She didn't bother to primp before her reflection. She knew she wasn't pretty, not the way she remembered her mother looking during those first blissful six years of Sarah's life. She frowned at herself. It was a wonder Caleb had even noticed her.

No time for self-pity right now. Dawn would arrive soon. She had kept the journal page with her during the trying night to remind her of why she had agreed to do what she was doing, but now she needed to return it to its hiding place in the sewing room. Her simply furnished retiring room held no private spaces. She was afraid someone might find the paper, even hidden in her own little-used journal.

Sarah folded the page into quarters, then slid it under the kerchief that crossed over the bodice of her long, loose work dress. She heard it crinkle as she slipped into her long Dorothy cloak. The sound was somehow soothing. Sarah hadn't even asked Caleb where it came from, just some old Shaker journal, that was enough for her. The passage had the ring of truth. It was written by someone who had been there. Someone who knew who had killed her mother.

Sarah slipped through the always unlocked door to the Sisters' Shop. The weak dawn light barely penetrated the curtains covering the large windows. The ground floor was divided into two rooms opening to a central corridor, which led to a staircase. After breakfast, other sisters would arrive to work in these rooms, if their hands were not needed for kitchen or laundry rotation or for planting. At this early hour it should be empty.

As the nervous knots in Sarah's stomach loosened, exhaustion dragged at her like sacks of flour tied to her ankles. She pulled herself up the staircase, sliding her hand along the smooth oak bannister to propel herself along in the dark. She cried out as she tripped and her shin hit the sharp edge of a step. With a flash of temper, she grabbed her long skirt and yanked it well above her feet. No need to worry, at this hour, about brethren coming along and catching a forbidden glimpse of her legs, and she was tired enough to fall and break one of them.

Sarah reached her personal domain, the sewing room, which occupied the entire top story of the Sisters' Shop. She felt safest in this room, with its piles of soft, finely woven fabric surrounding her like comforting blankets. On the way to her own sewing table, she smoothed her hand over a length of dark blue wool spread out on the cutting table. She sank into her work chair and flipped on her small lamp.

The sewing tables had deep drawers built into their side, rather than their front, so that sewing sisters could open them without bumping their knees or crawling under the pull-out workboard. Sarah dropped to the floor facing the drawers. She pulled out the second drawer, held it on her lap, and drew the journal page from behind her kerchief. The comfort of habit made her unfold it one more time and begin to read.

A click, like the opening of a door, jerked her head upright. She held her breath and listened. A soft creaking sound reached her, followed by another click. A door opening, then closing again.

Feeling underneath the drawer in her lap, Sarah pried two tacks from the wooden bottom. With shaking hands, she tacked the journal page to the drawer bottom, then shoved the drawer back into its slot. She sat unmoving, alert. No steps creaked. If someone had entered the Sisters' Shop at this early hour, she—or he—must have stayed downstairs. It was probably just a sister arriving early for work. Still, it would be best to check. As sewing-room deaconess, she felt a responsibility for the whole building. She picked her way down the familiar staircase, avoiding the areas that squeaked.

She squinted into the open doorway to the weaving room. Old Sister Viola sometimes couldn't sleep, so she would trudge over in the dark to weave or simply to card wool by lamplight. But nay, the looms were still. Silhouetted against the curtains, they looked to Sarah's overheated imagination like those medieval implements of torture she used to scare herself silly by reading about as a kid.

Quashing old memories, she checked the opposite room, where the sisters spun and dyed their wool. Ever since Wilhelm got his brainstorm about going back to the old ways and being self-sufficient, the decades-old spinning wheels had been dragged out of storage one by one, dusted off, and repaired.

Skeins of freshly dyed yarns looped over pegs on a strip of wood which encircled the quiet room. In the gloom the skeins all looked to be shades of brown, but Sarah knew there were soft yellows and rusts and even some bright colors to please the Shakers' customers in the world. There was no one in that room, either. If her heart ever stopped clattering like a sewing machine, maybe she could still return to her retiring room and catch a short nap before breakfast.

Maybe she could even skip breakfast, if Eldress Rose didn't . . . A floorboard creaked inside the spinning room.

"Who is it? Who is here?" Sarah barely had breath to get the words out. She strained to see into the dim room. *I'm overtired, imagining things,* she thought, steadying herself on the doorjamb. She turned to leave.

The blow struck the back of Sarah's head a split second after she registered a footfall behind her. The impact did not fell her. She twisted toward the source of the attack as black confusion spread its fingers through her brain. She felt no pain. If there was no pain, could it be a dream?

The second blow caught her in the stomach. She called out Caleb's name, or thought she did. All she heard was a buzzing monotone. Whether it came from the room or from inside her own head, she couldn't tell. She couldn't even gasp. Her lungs refused to take in air. In her last moments of awareness, Sarah felt arms fumbling to break her fall to the floor.

TWO

Sister Rose Callahan, newly appointed eldress of the Kentucky Shaker village of North Homage, dragged open her eyes to darkness. She groaned and sat up in bed, sweeping a mass of unruly red hair off her forehead. Wearily tossing aside the light bed-clothes, she slid her long legs over the side of the bed. She shivered and crossed her arms as the cool air of early spring penetrated her long-sleeved cotton night-gown. The cracked-open window of her second-floor retiring room framed only black buildings in black air. No sign of dawn. She fumbled for the light on the plain wooden table next to her bed. Her small clock read three-thirty.

Rose padded barefoot across the cold pine floor to her east window. The Trustees' Office, in which Rose stubbornly still lived and worked despite her recent change in status from trustee to eldress, was located at the far west end of North Homage. Her corner retiring rooms, including a sitting room and a bedroom, looked east and south over the entire village.

At first she saw nothing that could explain why she'd awakened. All windows were dark in the Center Family Dwelling House, directly across from her, and

6

in the Children's Dwelling House, to her right just across the unpaved road running through the center of the village. Then she heard something, like faint, short cries.

She eased the window open farther and leaned her head and shoulders out into the crisp night air. She squinted at the buildings that lined the central path all the way to the fields beyond the orchard at the east end of town. Each building was dark and still.

A movement caught her eye, straight down the path near the new barn. She opened her eyes wide, as if it would help her penetrate the darkness. A bright spot of light hung suspended in the darkness. As the moon emerged from behind a cloud, Rose could distinguish an arm extended from the light. Someone was carrying a lantern. Since the Society's beagle-spaniel, Freddie, wasn't barking wildly, it must be one of the brethren out checking on the animals or getting an early—very early—start on the chores.

Relieved, Rose turned back to her small bed, which looked warm and inviting. But as she slid between the rumpled sheets, she heard the sounds again. This time she recognized them. The alarmed cries of animals. She ran back to the window. Just beyond the barn, white dots that could only be sheep roamed free in the fields. They should have been in a small pasture near the barn, surrounded by sturdy slatted fencing. A few sheep had reached the lawn around the Laundry building and were no doubt making quick work of the newly sprouting Kentucky bluegrass.

At the high-pitched whinnying of a startled horse, Rose squinted at the barn's front door. It stood open. She was certain it had been closed just minutes earlier.

She could see several shapes now flowing out the barn door and wandering around. Two certainly were horses trotting in confused circles. No brethren would be chasing animals out of the barn at this hour.

Rose came close to cursing. Someone must be out there now, letting the Shakers' animals loose and maybe even stealing their horses. The village owned only four horses, which they needed now more than ever, with spring plowing in full swing. Where was Freddie? Why hadn't he barked to alert the brethren to an intruder?

Rose yanked her nightgown over her head. Her long navy work dress hung where she'd left it the night before, buttoned on a hanger latched over a wall peg. She pulled the loose-fitting dress off the hanger and forced it over her thick mane of hair without undoing the buttons. No time for stockings or a cap. She slipped her bare feet into her black work shoes and ran.

As Rose arrived, panting, at the barn, Elder Wilhelm Lundel's unmistakable figure burst from the front door of the Ministry House, just across the pathway from the barn and Laundry. His white hair stuck out in spikes. A stocky, muscular man, he lumbered toward the sheep, waving his arms above his head.

Several of the brethren came running from the Center Family Dwelling House, including Brother Samuel Bickford, a tall, gaunt man in his mid-fifties. He slowed to a walk as he neared the alarmed horses and spoke to them soothingly, calling each by name. At the sound of his voice, a pinto named Rainbow stopped prancing and ducked his head toward Samuel's outstretched hand.

With the horses under control, Rose took time to look around. All four horses and the village's few dairy cows had been led, pushed, or frightened out of the barn. They would never have exited so quickly without encouragement and someone to open all their enclosures and the barn door.

With his usual calm efficiency, Samuel secured the horses in the barn while the other brethren herded the cows back home. Samuel emerged from the barn carrying a spare board, which he nailed to a broken length of white fencing. He opened the gate and began gently shooing in the nearest sheep.

Wilhelm, on the other hand, ran at the sheep, shouting as if he could shame them into returning. They scattered in terror.

Rose scooped up a bleating spring lamb and plunked him inside the hastily repaired fence. He bounded away to search for his mother.

"Well? Does this convince thee that the world is our enemy?" Wilhelm's white hair hung wildly around his weather-toughened face, and his labored breathing pumped his barrel chest.

"Wilhelm, this is surely an accident. Fences break." She doubted her own words, but with Wilhelm it was best to downplay any episode he might turn into an excuse for a crusade against the world.

"Fences are not thy specialty, are they? Anyone can see this fence had help getting broken," Wilhelm sneered. "Look, look for thyself." Wilhelm longed to revitalize the declining Society, and his plan for doing so hinged on returning to the old ways, such as saying "thee" instead of "you," to set the Shakers apart from the world. He had convinced North Homage Believers to switch back to nineteenth-century dress, but most resisted changing their modern speech into archaic patterns that confused and frustrated them.

Wilhelm led the way to the break in the fence. The upper wooden slate was smashed inward. The wood showed several round indentations, as if splintered with a hammer blow from outside the pasture. No hammer or other implement lay nearby.

"Is it thy opinion that the sheep so yearned to roam free that they smashed this wood with their hooves from the outside? Someone from the world did this, of course, someone who hates us."

"Wilhelm, these dents could have been here for years. They probably have nothing to do with the break in the fence. I'm sure this can all be explained rationally." Rose felt a pang of guilt over her unwillingness to let Wilhelm be right. His suspiciousness triggered her own stubbornness.

"And what about the other incidents, eh? What about all the food stolen from our storehouse?" Wilhelm's blue eyes glittered with the victory of a scored point.

"Just a half dozen jars of raspberry preserves, for goodness' sakes," Rose said. "It was probably just a hungry child, maybe even one of our own. We don't lock our doors, after all. We always grow and cook extra to share with the hungry. Somebody probably thought we wouldn't mind."

Rose became aware of the quiet. A silent group had gathered around Wilhelm and her. The first light of dawn slivered through the sky and illuminated the circle of faces. They were concerned faces, even alarmed, watching their spiritual leaders argue.

* * *

Rose frowned as she ran her fingertips over the damaged fence rail. She had hustled everyone off to breakfast and returned alone to examine the damage. She admitted to herself that Wilhelm was right. The splintered marks were fresh. One of them had cracked through the white paint, exposing unweathered wood.

She squinted at the dented wood. What would have made such a mark? A hammer? Perhaps a shovel?

The heavy barn door stood open a sliver. Rose slipped into the cool dimness that smelled of hay and manure and fresh-cut wood. The barn was still under construction in some areas.

Rose quickly found what she was looking for—a hammer that lay close to the door as if tossed hurriedly inside. She picked it up. A bit of white paint stuck to the head.

A faint noise startled Rose and she dropped the hammer. It thudded softly on the dirt floor. She heard the noise again—a wheezing sound, somewhere between a snore and a whimper. It seemed to come from behind a stack of hay bales.

Rose's first impulse was to run out of the barn, back into the spring sunshine. But she stopped herself. Maybe this was a derelict, hungry, tired, perhaps injured. She couldn't just leave him.

The hay bales were taller than she was. With one shaking hand, she steadied herself against the coarse wall of hay and edged around toward the sound. She peeked behind the bales. The Society's guard dog, Freddie, lay on the dirt floor, his legs splayed unnaturally. His eyes remained closed as he whimpered again.

Whimpering herself now, Rose sank to her knees and cradled Freddie's mottled face and floppy ears in her lap.

"Freddie, come on, boy," she urged. "Wake up. Let me know you're all right. What has happened to you?"

Freddie's limp body twitched. He showed no other sign of having heard the pleading of one of his favorite mistresses.

Rose knew she could carry thirty-five pounds, even of awkward, gangly weight. Getting Freddie off the ground and herself upright presented more of a challenge. She eased her arms under his body and pulled him onto her knees. She stumbled to her feet, clutching the dog about his middle while his legs flopped helplessly.

Whispering words of comfort to the unconscious animal, Rose cut across the grass to the Infirmary. She reached the doors just as Sister Josie Trent, North Homage's only nurse, returned from breakfast.

"He's been drugged," Josie concluded after a gentle examination. The Infirmary Sister had just turned eighty, but her fingers were as quick and sure as ever.

"That's my guess, anyway. I'm not a veterinarian. What sort of cruel nature would do such a thing?" Josie's normally cheerful many-chinned face flushed with anger. "I'm hopeful he'll come out of it, but nothing is certain. He is in God's hands."

Freddie's breathing had quieted somewhat. He lay on a long wooden examining table surrounded by shelves filled with bottles and boxes. Freshly packed round tins of Shaker herbs were stacked in precarious columns on a small oak desk.

"Could the drug have been an herb, do you think?" Rose asked.

"What you mean is, could one of us have done such a thing? I certainly hope not, but I can't really say. Poor Freddie is only a small creature compared to us. And his physiology is different. Who's to say how a large dose of valerian might affect him, for instance." Josie stroked the dog's long, silky ears. He didn't respond.

"I can't believe a Believer would want to do this, or feel it necessary to use such a large dose. I'll keep him here and watch over him. Good heavens, what can that be?" Banging and clattering in the outer waiting room sent Josie bouncing for the door, Rose close behind.

The waiting room seemed crammed with Believers, all chattering at once and swirling like leaves in the spring wind. Samuel and another of the brethren whipped through the anxious crowd into one of the sickrooms. Between them, they carried Sarah. Sister Charlotte scampered behind them, supporting Sarah's lolling head. Once pure white, Sarah's cotton indoor cap was streaked with blood, as was the triangular kerchief which covered Charlotte's shoulders and crisscrossed over the front of her bodice.

Her rescuers eased Sarah onto a narrow bed. With deft, plump fingers, Josie removed the cap. The bleeding began again as she pulled the fabric away from the scalp.

"First off," Josie said, "she'll need stitching up. Charlotte, fetch my bag from the corner, would you?

Thanks.'' She doused a sewing needle in alcohol and
began to stitch quickly. Most of the Believers who
had crowded in the room averted their eyes. They
were hard but careful workers, and all had taken a
vow of nonviolence. They rarely hurt themselves, and
they viewed violent injury with horror. Rose was
tempted to look away as well, but she sat on the edge
of the bed and held Sarah's hand, searching her face
for signs of pain.

"What happened?" Rose asked, without shifting
her gaze from Sarah.

Samuel stepped forward and squatted next to Rose
by the bed. "We don't know for sure. When Sarah
didn't show for breakfast, Charlotte went to check on
her. Found her in the Sisters' Shop, out cold at the
bottom of the stairs."

"She was alone in the shop?"

"Yea, as far as we could tell. We figured she'd
tripped and tumbled down the stairs. Took a mighty
bad crack on the head from hitting a step, that's all
we could figure."

Rose frowned. Sarah's injury was on the lower
right side of her skull, toward the back. She tried to
imagine what type of fall would cause a wound in
that spot. Perhaps if Sarah tripped and twisted sideways in an effort to catch herself? Rose made a mental
note to check the steps at the Sisters' Shop as soon
as she knew Sarah would be all right. If the pine was
nicked or worn smooth in any spot, it should be
mended quickly. And it wouldn't hurt to examine the
area carefully, just to understand what had happened.
Something bothered her, but she couldn't piece it to-

gether from the tidbits in her brain. Too many incidents, that's all.

"Samuel, ask the sisters not to clean the staircase and hallway of the Sisters' Shop until I've had a chance to look them over."

Samuel nodded and left immediately.

Josie pierced Sarah's skin with another stitch, and the injured sister moaned. As the needle entered her scalp yet again, Sarah cried out.

"One more, Sarah dear, just one more," Josie said.

The final stitch jerked Sarah to full consciousness. Her unfocused brown eyes wandered among the faces before her. As the pain reached her awareness, her face puckered.

"Cal," she said, and, "Nay, nay." Her eyes closed and she lost consciousness again.

Josie raised her round face and searched Rose's eyes. "What's that all about, Rose? Who is Cal?"

"I don't know, Josie. But, believe me, I'll do my best to find out."

THREE

"WHAT CAN BE HAPPENING?" ROSE ASKED THE
empty hallway. The hum of spinning wheels and low
murmuring voices drifted from the spinning room to
the bottom step of the Sisters' Shop staircase, where
Rose sat, chin in hands. With an irritated shake of her
head, she began her task again. She walked slowly
upstairs and back down again, her skirts held away
from the wood, her eyes trained on the steps. Again,
she saw nothing, nothing that could explain Sarah's
fall, nor even a hint that she had indeed fallen. Not a
drop of blood, except on the floor at the spot where
her head had lain.

At the spinning-room door, Rose caught the eye of
a young sister, who glanced up without pausing in her
work. Her eyebrows lifted to indicate attention, while
her deft fingers continued to guide and pull the clouds
of fluffy wool into long, thin strands.

"Isabel," Rose said, "are you certain no one has
cleaned here today?"

"Yea, certain," Isabel said. "We cleaned the
rooms, of course, but we left the hallway, as Samuel
said you wanted."

Rose nodded and turned to leave, ready to give up.

16

And there, on the lower doorframe and nearby on the floor, she saw the blood. Rose knelt and peered closely at the stains. They lightly smudged the area, as if someone had tried to rub them off but hadn't had time to finish the job. Not the sisters, Rose was sure. They would have left nothing but smooth, shiny wood, even if they'd had to sand it down and buff it. Nay, she was certain now. Someone from the world had been here, a hurried outsider who attacked Sarah and arranged the scene to look like an accident.

Unlike the large office in the Trustees' building, which was used for meetings with the world's people, the Ministry office was meant for spiritual study and private confession. Elder Wilhelm seemed to fill any room, no matter what its size, so in this small, cozy room, Rose felt overwhelmed by his presence. He paced in rapid strides, his broad shoulders drawn back in rigid tension. He ran his hand through his thick white hair and glared at Rose, seeming to dare her to contradict him.

"The world's people will kill us if they can," he said. "They have tried, again and again. From the beginning, they have imprisoned our leaders, burned our buildings, even sent their own so-called clergy to revile us. The world is carnal, violent, spiritually bereft. And these days they are at their most evil. They attack animals, Believers, it makes no difference to them; they are no more than animals themselves."

"We would be wise not to leap to conclusions," Rose said. "We don't yet understand—"

"Wisdom. Ha!" Wilhelm snorted in derision. "I leave wisdom to God. I listen to Mother Ann for understanding. And so should thee, if thy calling to be eldress is a true one.''

Rose closed her eyes briefly and breathed a prayer. Calm returned. When she opened her eyes, Wilhelm was watching her, a disturbing light in his eyes.

''Is thy position truly a calling, I wonder?'' he asked.

Rose steeled herself—not to engage in battle, but to avoid one, if she could. It was pointless to argue with Wilhelm. Rose believed that Shakers and the world could live in harmony. Wilhelm did not. He had barely tolerated her as the village's trustee, in charge of business relations with the world. So to him she could never be worthy of the position of eldress— spiritual co-leader of the North Homage Believers. His equal.

''The issue we must discuss,'' she said firmly, ''is whether we should call in the police to investigate what has been going on here.''

''The police are of the world.''

''Yea, of course, Wilhelm, but they have helped us before. Why not now? I could talk to that young deputy, Grady O'Neal. Maybe he could check around quietly. You said yourself that someone from the world let our animals go free.''

''The police will not bother with such a matter. They would be glad to see us lose our livelihood.''

''What about Sarah?''

''Sarah fell down the stairs, nothing more, that is what they will say. She was too tired and slipped. Never mind that she is a Believer and used to hard work and early hours.''

''I found no blood on the Sisters' Shop stairs, but

I clearly saw traces near the spinning-room door. Did Sarah fling herself against the doorjamb, then crumple herself at the base of the stairs to make it look like an accident? Nay, I think it more likely that she was attacked.''

Now she had Wilhelm's attention, but she wasn't sure she wanted it as she watched his calculating glint reappear. When his thin lips curved into a tight smirk, she wished she had kept her thoughts to herself.

''The police will not help thee,'' Wilhelm said, ''We are the Ministry, and we should work as a team, but I cannot stop thee from talking to them.''

Rose knew Wilhelm all too well. Her every nerve flashed a warning. While it was true that he could no longer issue her orders, now that she was eldress, it was most unlike him to admit it.

The United Society of Believers encouraged the practice of confession to cleanse the heart of impure thoughts and deeds and bind the Believer inextricably to the community. In the late-eighteenth century, the days of the Society's foundress Mother Ann, the confession might include mortification and exposure of the Believer's sins to the entire leadership.

In later Shaker villages, including North Homage, this painful practice had evolved into private confession, sister to eldress and brethren to elder. Now that she was eldress, Rose knew full well that some Believers avoided confession for much longer than their goodness could possibly last. Rose herself had confessed at least monthly to Eldress Agatha, and had always felt purer for it. She hoped that Agatha would soon regain enough strength to hear her confession.

Besides, she admitted to herself, she sorely needed Agatha's wise counsel on these disturbing recent incidents. Wilhelm certainly was no help.

Rose impatiently straightened a stack of papers on her office desk and drew out a ledger. She'd have to delay her visit with Agatha until later. In just twenty minutes, she had an appointment with Richard Worthington, perhaps the most prominent, and unpleasant, citizen of Languor, the county seat, eight miles of rutted road from North Homage. Worthington was president of the town's largest bank. Rose had sparred with him many times before, and she found herself anticipating a rematch. The result of an overwrought temper, she supposed, or that's what Agatha would have called it.

Until the Society could find a suitable replacement, Rose had to perform double duty as eldress and as trustee, the business director of the community. Having grown up with the Shakers, she had left at eighteen to spend a year in the world. She had even fallen in love and had planned to marry. But she'd felt a powerful call to return. She signed the covenant, pledging all that she owned and all that she was to the United Society of Believers in Christ's Second Appearing. Her talents and experiences soon brought her the job of trustee.

She had always loved being trustee, meeting with the world's businessmen, overseeing real estate transactions, directing the practical side of Shaker life. To be truthful, she was in no hurry to train a new trustee. The role gave her a break from the difficulties of learning to be eldress, and an excuse not to live in the Ministry House, where elders and eldresses traditionally lived. She knew that eventually, as part of the Ministry, she would have to share the house and most of her meals with Wilhelm, but she hoped to delay the move until she felt more sure of herself.

Twenty minutes passed quickly, and Rose glanced out her window to see Richard Worthington stride up the walk to the Trustees' Office, a familiar arrogant tilt to his head. She had a few moments to study him. He was tall and firmly built, with precisely trimmed black hair streaked with gray. His suit and vest hung with tailor-made precision on his lean body. He had driven to North Homage, she knew, in a late-model car of some sort, probably newer than whatever car she had last seen him drive.

Rose often saw Worthington in Languor when she was in town to perform some errand for the Society. From the giddy fluttering of the townswomen, she knew they thought him handsome and charming. To Rose, though, his thin lips, with their odd sneering curve, mirrored the coldness of his personality. Self-satisfied in his wife's inherited wealth and his own success, he lacked compassion for his less fortunate neighbors who struggled in a grinding Depression. Several of the children recently sent to live with the Shakers were there because Richard Worthington had foreclosed on their parents' farms. It was hard to believe that he himself had been brought up to the age of seventeen by the North Homage Shakers.

"I hear you've had more trouble out here," Worthington said, speculation in his ice-blue eyes.

They were settled in Rose's office on ladder-back chairs with firm, comfortable woven seats. Worthington carefully crossed one leg over the other so that the crease in his pants lay perfectly straight. Rose took in his highly polished black shoes and wondered if he even remembered how to muck out a barn or till the earth. *I'm thinking uncharitable thoughts again,* she scolded herself with a slight shake of her head. *This is becoming a reprehensible habit.*

"Just a broken fence," Rose responded with a forced smile. "Nothing serious. The sheep took advantage of the situation to nibble on a few tasty seedlings, but we rounded them up in no time. How did you hear about it?"

Worthington shrugged an elegant shoulder. "You are in rural Kentucky, remember? All of Languor knows. Probably all of Languor County will know by tomorrow morning." He narrowed his eyes. "I heard it was more than just a few sheep. I heard there was an injury, as well." He paused and raised his eyebrows. Rose merely tilted her head in a gesture of polite attention. When Richard Worthington dug for information, he had a purpose in mind—a purpose that would benefit only Richard Worthington.

"Rumor is it was deliberate," he continued. "All this could be a problem, you know. If you've been making your neighbors angry again, I'd need to think hard about whether to approve any more loan applications from you. In fact, if there's danger of property damage here, I might even need to call in a loan or two. To protect the bank's investment, you understand." He watched her face.

Rose took a deep breath. She'd known Richard Worthington since she was four years old and he was nine, though she'd come to know him better as an adult. She had grown used to his ways. He was just toying with her, trying to get the upper hand.

"There's nothing serious going on, I assure you," she said. Talking to the police might be unwise after all, she thought. Worthington would hear about it somehow. "Your investment is quite safe. In fact, Elder Wilhelm is eager to pay off our debts to your bank as quickly as possible."

This was true, Wilhelm yearned for the Society to be completely self-sufficient and debt-free. Unfortunately, Rose knew there was no money to finance his dream. She shifted subjects.

"Why did you wish to see me today, Richard? I know our loan payments have arrived on time; I've counted and delivered them myself. I can't imagine that—"

"I'm not here as a banker," Worthington interrupted, an edge to his normally smooth voice. "I've been asked to represent the Languor business community." He cleared his throat. "We—the Languor businessmen, that is—we believe that you Shakers are trying to drive us out of business."

"Good heavens, how? Why?"

Worthington's thin lips curved into a stern frown. "We think that's clear. You're undercutting our prices. When Floyd Foster sells carrots for six cents a bunch, his customers tell him they can come out here and get the same amount for four cents."

"We sell carrots to Floyd Foster for three cents! If he is so foolish as to double the price he paid, naturally he takes the risk that someone will sell for a lower price. It seems to me that this problem stops at Mr. Foster's door, not ours." Rose clenched her teeth to control her rising temper. It didn't work.

"Furthermore, we Believers are not driven by unbridled greed, as some are. We strive for perfection in our work for the glory of God, and you know that, Richard Worthington."

Worthington's thin, aristocratic face showed only the faintest pink, but Rose knew she had hit a nerve. "Unbridled greed?" he said, too quietly. "You accuse us of unbridled greed? Everyone knows how you are able to undercut our prices. Slave labor, that's how. You use your people like workhorses. You get them up in the middle of the night, you keep them working till they drop, and you don't pay them wages."

"Nonsense! All our needs are met. We are a community of Believers."

"A community of slaves, you mean. And don't forget, I was one of them. I know."

"I don't forget," Rose murmured.

"Oh, I know full well your reputation in business," Worthington said. "You Shakers are a shrewd lot. Everyone says how good Shaker products are. But they don't know you like I do. You don't give a damn about anyone but yourselves."

He composed his face and rose from his chair with elegant ease. His trouser legs fell perfectly into place. "However, I bear no personal grudge against you, Rose," he said. "Some of you Shakers were kind to me when I was a child, and I have no desire to see you hurt. I'm afraid, though, that this morning's episode is merely the beginning." He retrieved his black silk hat from a wall peg and turned back to Rose. "Your neighbors feel you've worn out your welcome here. There may come a time when you'll need to sell some or even all of your land, maybe move on to another state. The Languor Citizens' Bank will be delighted to work with you when that time comes.'' He inclined his head in a faint imitation of a bow. ''We'll talk about this again, I'm sure. In the meantime, just remember—if your situation becomes intolerable, there are ways I can help.''

As Worthington raised his eyes to the door, his features hardened. Rose turned and saw Brother Samuel Bickford pausing just inside the office doorway. Samuel stepped into the room and toward Worthington.

''Richard,'' he said, his hand outstretched. Worthington slammed his hat on his head and pushed past Samuel.

''What was that about?'' Rose asked.

Samuel shrugged. ''Can't imagine. Richard and I don't run into each other much anymore.''

''You were here when he left the Society, weren't you? Why did he leave?''

Samuel's body seemed to close in on itself. ''Those were dark days,'' he said. ''Many Believers lost their faith and left.''

''But why? What happened?''

''Nothing,'' Samuel said. ''Nothing.''

''But something must have caused so many to leave at once,'' Rose said.

After several moments of silence, Rose realized there was no point in pushing any harder just then. Samuel was elsewhere; his heart and his mind struggled with a memory that Rose could neither guess nor capture. She would ask again soon, though; she sensed the information would be helpful.

"I came to speak with you about Sarah," Samuel said. "I am concerned for her welfare." He shifted from one foot to the other. "She seemed badly injured when we brought her in, and I left before Josie had finished stitching her up."

"That is kind of you, Samuel," Rose said, in some confusion. "Have you spoken with Josie about Sarah?"

Samuel shifted position again and stared over Rose's head. "I wanted to speak with you."

"All right. Well, Josie called me an hour or so ago and said Sarah is fully alert and yearning to return to the sewing room. But she remembers nothing of the incident."

Samuel nodded slowly. "That is good news." He grew silent, and Rose wondered if he had slipped back into his reverie.

"Watch over her, won't you?" Samuel whispered, his eyes snapping back to the present. "The sins belong to others, not to her." He turned on his heel and left the Trustees' Office.

FOUR

LAURA HILL PAUSED ON THE BOTTOM BASEMENT step to watch her husband, Kentuck, slouched over the keys attached to his ancient printing press. She was a tall woman, taller than her husband, and straight-backed still, despite reaching her fiftieth year after a lifetime of unhappiness. For much of her marriage, her height had grieved her. It had given her husband yet one more reason to sneer at her. In recent years, though, she had found herself buying high heels and piling her thick, gray-streaked dark hair on top of her head. She found increasing pleasure in staring at the thinning spot in the center of her husband's own graying hair. She enjoyed watching him finger-comb his remaining curls over the bald spot, then grinned secretly as they slid inevitably downward again. Once she had worshiped those locks of hair; they had awakened her heart. But twenty-four years of marriage and almost as many betrayals had wrapped her heart in winter-weight wool.

Laura . . . She smiled at the pretty sound of the name. It wasn't hers, of course, any more than Kentuck was her husband's real name. They were using assumed names to keep their presence in town a secret—especially from the Shakers—and they'd sworn to use those names even with each other, so they wouldn't slip in public.

She didn't dare think about all that she had done and abandoned to be with him. Her bitterest regret was her failure to have children. Every day of her youth, she had longed for a pregnancy that never happened. Her own body had betrayed her, that much was clear. Her unfaithful husband had certainly fathered enough children with other women over the past few decades.

The stair creaked as she stepped off. Her husband's head jerked up, irritation on his florid features. He clucked in annoyance. His reactions no longer touched her.

"I can't be bothered now, Laura. I'm busy." He bent again over the press.

"I know. I hate to disturb you when you're working, but it's important." She spoke with a practiced deference that she no longer felt. "It's just that—"

"What? What? Hurry it up, can't you, woman? You're breaking my concentration."

She fixed her eyes on his bald spot and felt herself detach once again from his disdain for her. It didn't matter. He didn't matter; she wouldn't let him.

"There's been an accident at North Homage," she said in an even voice. "That girl fell down the stairs. That's what I hear, anyway."

Her husband stopped his work and tossed a look of disgust at her, which, for a reason she couldn't articulate, she enjoyed. "Can't you make sense for once? What girl? Why should I care?"

"Because it's that Sarah; she's the one who fell down the stairs."

That silenced him for a moment.

"Where did you hear this?" he asked finally.

"In town," she said. "People talk to me. Richard had heard about it, too. I wouldn't be surprised if Caleb told everybody. You know how he is about that girl, and his tongue runs wild when he's been drinking. I've said it before, you're wrong to trust those two."

"I don't trust them." For once, he looked directly at his wife. "But that girl is our important link. It's her being back with the Shakers that makes this whole plan possible. I've waited a long time to punish those murderers." He turned back to his task.

His wife shook her head, but not enough so that he could see her from the corner of his eye. She needed to tread carefully. Her husband's precious plan for revenge could ruin their own lives, but he didn't seem to know that. She cursed herself for not having left things as they were. If she had, her husband would still be dreaming of revenge, but maybe he would never have put his plan into action.

"You shouldn't be talking to anyone in town. We've been over and over that. You never understand anything, do you?" he said, not looking at her.

In the warm one-room Shaker schoolhouse, ten girls and seven boys gazed out the windows with half-closed eyes on pink magnolia blossoms and Kentucky bluegrass. The spring afternoon had turned warm and lazy. A blue jay chattered through a window cracked open for ventilation. The only human-made sound was the soft creak of a nearby door as it opened and closed.

Their young teacher, Sister Charlotte, had paused in the middle of explaining a story problem to shake her own groggy head. None of the children noticed that she'd stopped talking. Charlotte frowned at her students' slack, dreamy faces. She'd best liven things up, or they'd all be napping, and that wouldn't do. The year's schooling had another four weeks to go. Surely they could pay attention for one more hour.

She tried to catch the eye of one of her best, most alert students, Timmy, who sat on the boys' side of the room. He stared out the nearest window, chin in hand, lank blond hair skimming his nearly closed eyes.

With so few children these days, the North Homage Ministry had decided the boys and girls should be taught at the same time, instead of girls in the summer and boys in the winter, as was historical custom. A six-foot space filled with bookcases separated the girls from the boys. So awkward, Charlotte thought, and rather silly. She'd grown up in the world, sat right next to boys at school, and she'd still become a Shaker, hadn't she? A calling is a calling, and that's that.

Her best girl student, Nora, slumped in her seat near the front. Her eyes were shut.

"Nora!" Charlotte snapped more harshly than she meant to.

"Yea, Sister." The eight-year-old's eyes snapped open.

"We were discussing a story problem involving two trains going different speeds. Could you summarize the problem for the class, please?"

Nora widened her translucent eyes, sucked her bottom lip, and finally gave Charlotte a tiny, contrite smile.

"Nay, Sister, I can't. But I'd like to hear the story again."

Snickers erupted from both sides of the classroom. Charlotte just managed not to smile, though Nora had accomplished what she couldn't. The class was almost attentive again. For the moment, at least.

"All right, then, Timmy, can you—"

A child's scream, high and piercing, sliced through the air. Charlotte slewed her eyes back over the bookcases to the girls' side. A quick movement on the ground stopped her. Nay, it couldn't be a mouse, could it? The sisters cleaned daily, and no food was stored anywhere in the school building. How could they have a mouse? And here it was spring. The field mice should be back outdoors.

Charlotte squinted at the bottom edge of the bookcase, which stood a few inches off the floor. The thin end of a rodent's tail protruded from under the bottom shelf. It swished into a ray of sunshine.

A familiar chill traveled through Charlotte's body. The tail was too thick. Not a mouse. A rat.

Rats terrified Charlotte. Before coming to the Shakers, she'd lived with her mother in an abandoned cottage on the outskirts of Languor. The roof leaked, the wood floor was rotting, and one early morning she had awakened to find a rat sharing her bed.

Another little girl screamed. Within seconds, all the girls scrambled on top of their desks and shrieked. The boys, too, abandoned all pretense of manliness and jumped on their chairs.

Charlotte stood rooted to the floor, paralyzed by the pulsing rhythm of the screams. She squeezed her eyes shut against the nightmare memory of seeing those bright rodent eyes staring at her.

I'm responsible for these children, she reminded herself, and this is just a small, pesky animal. She had to calm the children down, get them out quickly so the brethren could come and eliminate the creature.

"Children! Children!" she croaked. "Stop screaming. Please stop screaming." The noise level lowered, but only a fraction. "Breathe deeply, children. One . . . two . . . three, come on." She sucked in a deep breath, as much for herself as for them. "That's it. It's only a—a small animal."

She threw more control into her voice than she felt. "Quiet down and leave by whatever door is nearest you. We'll meet again outside. Do you hear me? Children!"

Renewed shrieking swallowed the last of her plea. Paralyzed by helplessness and shock, Charlotte watched as more rats appeared, and more and more, spewing out from the back of the room. Amanda, a young girl seated toward the front, tried to jump from her chair to a spot beyond the swarming creatures. She twisted her foot as she landed, stumbled backward, and fell on top of several rats, which squirmed and squealed under her. The girl writhed to her feet, crying in convulsive bursts. She wailed as a panicked rat bit her on the ankle.

Seeing Amanda bitten, Charlotte clamped down on her own terror. She grabbed for the injured child. As the hiccup-sobbing girl leaped into her arms, Charlotte felt something scuttle across her foot. She held her breath and forced herself to look down.

Rats swarmed around the desks and bookcases, their sharp faces thrusting into every corner of the room as they sought escape.

Charlotte resisted nausea, felt her consciousness slip, fought against it. She couldn't faint, she just couldn't. She had a child in her arms . . . all these children. . . .

"Great God in Heaven!" Rose said, barely above a whisper.

She had heard the screams of terrified children from the Trustees' Office, across the central path, and had come running. Her light indoor cap had shaken loose and tufts of red hair floated around her flushed face. She had arrived at the schoolhouse door at the same time as Brother Samuel. They saw Charlotte clutching a sobbing child, stock-still before a room of screaming children and swarming rats.

Rose wasn't afraid of rodents, or most animals in small enough numbers. But rats were not her favorite, and these were far too many. Three scrawny gray rats scurried past her and fled outdoors, as panicked as the children they had terrified. What looked like at least a dozen more scrambled around the classroom. Their fur was matted and streaked with dirt, their eyes feverish with God knew what diseases. Rose shuddered. Some might already have escaped through the open windows. She dared not think where they'd come from, not yet anyway.

"Rebecca," Rose shouted to a young sister who was hurrying toward the shouting in the schoolhouse. "Run and get the brethren from the fields. Tell them to bring sticks and sacks. Quickly. We can't let these creatures roam the village.''

She turned to the schoolhouse door as Samuel plunged into the room, trampling a squealing rat that wasn't quick enough to get out of his way. He scooped up two boys around their middles, one under each muscular arm, and hauled them out.

Rose kicked a rat away from Charlotte's paralyzed feet and grabbed her elbow.

"Come on, Charlotte, don't look down, that's a girl . . .'' Rose dragged the young sister though the classroom door.

Once outside in the sunshine, Rose took a look at the sobbing child's ankle. The rat had pierced the skin and drawn blood.

"Take Amanda to the Infirmary,'' she told Charlotte. "Tell Josie just what happened. She will need to summon Doc Irwin.'' Rose did not mention the possibility of rabies. It would only panic the child even more.

As Charlotte left, Rose went back inside to help Samuel herd out the rest of the children. Exhaustion had quieted the screams, and the children fell gratefully into Rose's and Samuel's arms to be carried outside. Rats—dozens of them, it seemed, frightened and starving—were finding their way outdoors, too. The brethren had a job ahead of them.

As the children were bustled off to the Trustees' Office in Samuel's care, Rose closed the front door of the school building and all the windows to trap the few remaining rats indoors. She left by the closed door at the back of the classroom, which led into a storage room and then to an outside door.

She closed the storage-room entrance behind her. The door to the outside was shut, and only one small window allowed light into the room. Like most Shaker rooms, this one was neat and clean. Extra student desks lined one wall, their attached chairs side by side. Dust-free pine shelves held squared stacks of books, chalk, and other supplies. Wall pegs circling the small room held flat brooms and dustpans and two ladder-back chairs hung upside down.

A wrinkled and dirty burlap sack, which lay just inside the inner door, stood out like poison ivy in the medic's garden. The sack's open end faced toward the classroom. With her thumb and forefinger, Rose lifted one corner of the sack's opening and peered inside. The rough brown weave had snagged dozens of small gray hairs. So that's how the rats were transported to the building. She dropped the burlap and backed away as her stomach spasmed in revulsion.

Whoever had sneaked in here with a squealing, wriggling bag of rodents had taken a terrible chance on being seen or heard. Yet, to someone familiar with Shaker routine, this might have seemed the safest time. Planting season had just begun. On a good day, they had perhaps twenty able-bodied workers who could be spared for fieldwork, and that's where they would be at this time of the afternoon. There were fields near the schoolhouse, but they were always last to be planted in the spring. At that time of day, no one should be in the nearest buildings: the Children's Dwelling House and the currently unused Carpenters' Shop. Anyone arriving on the road from Languor could easily have veered behind the Carpenters' Shop to reach the back entrance of the schoolhouse. Though a few kitchen sisters would be across the street, cooking the evening meal in the Center Family Dwelling House, they would have seen nothing unless they left the building for some reason.

Could a stranger, someone from the world, possibly have sneaked into the village on such a horrible mission? Or was it a Believer? And most alarming to contemplate—why?

"We thought our children were attending a clean, well-run school, not some open sewer! Who knows what dreadful diseases they've been exposed to—and bringing home to the younger ones, too!" Mrs. Franklin Saunders, a plump and wealthy mother of four, stood with her arms crossed on her matronly bosom and glowered at Rose. Behind Mrs. Saunders crowded eight more angry parents, people of the world who had sent their children to the Shaker school because of its excellent reputation. The afternoon sun brightening the Trustees' Office seemed out of place in the midst of their fury.

Rose spread her hands, palms outward. "I understand your alarm, truly I do, but I assure you that this incident is a mystery to us as yet. We have never found so much as a field mouse in the schoolhouse. We've always kept it—all our buildings—spotless."

"Then how do you explain them rats, huh?" A thin farmer in dirty torn overalls poked his finger in the air toward Rose. The man's wife, her skin pulled tightly over her cheekbones in fear and hunger, held a young boy in front of her. The child's eyes were dark holes in his bony face.

Rose thought quickly. She couldn't leave the impression that the village harbored rats. Yet if she revealed finding the burlap sack and her suspicion that someone had planted the rats, she might start a panic among parents fearful for their children's safety. The Shaker school might be forced to close forever. Having their own school district meant income from the state. Since Sister Charlotte taught without a salary, all the money was used to buy supplies and up-to-date books. If the School Board closed their district, the Shaker children would have to attend a school in the world, where Believers could not watch over them.

"I can't explain the rodents," she said finally, "not yet. But I promise you that I will find out what happened. Please give me some time."

"And what about that girl who was bit, huh?" The thin farmer wasn't ready to give in so easily. "I heared she was bit real bad, might not make it. What about that, huh?"

Gasps and high-pitched chatter greeted the farmer's announcement. Rose shouted to be heard above the din.

"Amanda is fine. She has been seen by Doc Irwin and is doing well. She is heading home with her family right now. Please, I know how concerned you must be, and I assure you we will do everything in our power to protect the children."

"What about rabies? Have you even given a thought to that?" Mrs. Saunders asked. As a young woman, she had volunteered as a hospital aide during the Great War, and she could be counted on to trigger medical anxiety on any occasion.

"We will certainly take care that Amanda does not

contract rabies," Rose said in a voice calmer than she felt. "She will be given the best of care, and we will pay for it. Nothing will happen to her, and no one else has been injured. In the meantime, I will get to the bottom of this, you have my word." She looked into the eyes of the frightened parents and smiled. There were no answering smiles, but at least they were listening.

"Now I suggest that you all go home. I am closing our school for the time being. I'll alert the School Board myself." She certainly intended to capture the School Board president's ear before any of these furious parents did. She dreaded the Board's reaction and assumed she would have to deal with an inspector at some point. But she would tell the state officials about the burlap sack; perhaps she could convince them that the rats were brought into the village, not sharing room and board with them.

"I assure you I'll look into this incident carefully," Rose said. "I'll personally oversee the extermination and investigation. I will reopen the school only when I am certain it is safe."

The parents whispered among themselves for a few minutes. Mrs. Saunders, who assumed the role of spokesperson, gave their response.

"You may be sure we will not allow our precious children to set foot in your school until we are absolutely convinced of its safety," she said in a tone she might use with a servant on probation. "When the time comes, we will inspect this place from top to bottom ourselves." She gave a brisk, dismissive nod of her head and nudged the shoulder of a plump boy whose sulky face had brightened at hearing he'd have no school for a while. "Come along, Thomas," she said, loudly enough so all the children and parents could hear. "Be sure to watch your feet when we get outside. Heaven knows how many of those foul creatures are waiting for us."

FIVE

ROSE WATCHED FROM HER OFFICE WINDOW AS THE parents herded their youngsters in the direction of their cars and wagons. Sinking down at her desk, she allowed herself a moment of rest. But she couldn't sit still for long. She put through a call to the president of the School Board, who was out until the next day, and left a message with his secretary for him to call her immediately. She hung up and instantly the phone jangled.

"Eat in the Ministry dining room this evening. We must talk." Elder Wilhelm's terse command crackled over the wire. Even though she was now eldress, his female counterpart in the Ministry, Wilhelm still treated her as a subordinate. He could make her feel for a moment like a guilty schoolgirl.

"So you've heard about the incident in the schoolhouse?"

"It should be clear to thee by now that little escapes me," he said. "Though I had to hear it from Brother Samuel, instead of from thee, as I should have."

"It's unfortunate I was unable to call you immediately, but too much was happening at once." Rose sighed, but she tried to do so quietly.

"A child was bitten, I hear," Wilhelm continued. "How is she? Did anyone think to call Dr. Irwin?"

At least Wilhelm was showing concern for the child, and Rose liked him better for it.

"Yea, of course Josie called him in. Amanda is well for now, but the doctor says she'll need rabies shots, to be on the safe side, since we can't possibly know which rat bit her."

"Rabies?" Wilhelm's tone was outraged. Rose closed her eyes and imagined Wilhelm's craggy face hardening with fury. She knew all too well what a rabies scare would mean for the Society's reputation, but she supposed that Wilhelm would explain it to her anyway and blame either her or the world or both.

But Wilhelm surprised her again. "We'll talk this evening," he said.

Rose spent a grueling hour lending a hand in the Laundry before allowing herself her promised visit to Agatha's sickroom. The former eldress, Rose's friend and spiritual adviser, had survived her third stroke, just barely. Visiting her, watching her struggle to survive, was painful, but Rose was drawn by hope and by love.

"How is she today, Josie?" Rose poked her head into the Infirmary nurse's office. Josie sat behind her desk, her several chins in her palms as she peered through reading glasses at an open medical book. Her cherubic face, surrounded by wisps of white hair that had escaped her cap, looked more suited to a nursery than to this room filled with apothecary jars, tins, splints, and bandages. At hearing Rose's voice, she brightened.

"About the same, dear, about the same," Josie said with the gentle acceptance of one who has seen many deaths in her eighty years. "Have you come to sit with her awhile?" Rose nodded. "Good, that'll cheer her. Here, I'll go along with you." Rose followed as Josie bounced down a short hallway.

The room glowed with afternoon sunlight softened by thin white curtains. Unlike sickrooms Rose had visited in the world, this one smelled of lavender and roses and lemon balm. It was too early in the season for fresh sprigs of herbs, but Josie had placed bowls of crushed dried herbs on any surface she could find. A small bowl of rosewater sweetened the air next to Agatha.

The former eldress's frail body lay bundled in an adult-size cradle bed, so that she could be rocked to prevent bed sores and to help her sleep. The right half of her face hung loosely from the thin cheekbones. Agatha stared with cloudy eyes at her visitors before registering recognition and pleasure. She opened her mouth to greet them, but only the left side responded with a garbled syllable.

"I'll leave you now and go back to my studies," Josie said.

Rose pulled over a chair and reached into the cradle bed for Agatha's left hand.

"I've got a nerve coming here and pouring my troubles out to you every day, don't I? Well, all I can say in my own defense is that it was you who insisted I become eldress!" She laughed, which brought a slight, lopsided smile to Agatha's face. "Did you warn me how hard it would be? Not that I remember, but then I was so insistent I didn't want to be eldress, you probably thought it best to keep the difficult parts to yourself.

"Agatha, I really don't want to burden you. I know I should let you heal, but I also know how much you love the Society and would want to know . . . nay, I'm not fooling anyone, not even myself. I just miss talking out problems with you." Rose felt Agatha's fingers wind around two of her own and squeeze lightly. Rose squeezed back.

"Okay, you've talked me into it," she said. "I'll tell all. It started so mildly, you see, with just some stolen raspberry preserves. Then someone sneaked into the village early the other morning, opened the barn and smashed part of the fence, and let all the animals loose. Whoever it was actually sedated poor Freddie."

With surprising strength, Agatha gripped Rose's fingers. "Oh, I should have told you right away," Rose said. "Freddie has come out of it just fine. And so has Sarah. You remember Sister Sarah Baker, don't you?" Agatha's face showed confusion and she shook her head slightly. "She was here with us as a child, and then left to live with her mother. I barely remember Sarah; she was five or six years younger, and we had many more children then. She came back to us about two years ago."

Agatha's facial features softened, but her puzzled expression did not clear completely. Rose wondered if she should stop right then and leave out the details of the apparent assault on Sarah. But Agatha squeezed her fingers again and stared intently at her, as if to urge her to continue.

"Sarah had . . . an accident. At least, it could have

been an accident.'' Agatha's eyes widened. ''Nay, truly, Sarah is fine. She either fell down the Sisters' Shop stairs or was hit on the back of the head, but, aside from a nasty wound that Josie fixed right up, she didn't suffer serious damage. It's just that . . . you see, I checked in the shop, and I found blood near the spinning-room door, almost as if someone hit her as she turned away.''

Rose's thoughts had drifted to the Sisters' Shop, imagining the scene as it could have happened. A jerking on her fingers brought her back. Agatha writhed and tried to lift herself from the bed, but only her left side moved. In an anguished voice, she tried to form words. She could produce only short bits of nonsense.

''Agatha, please, don't upset yourself. I'm afraid for you. I'll go get Josie,'' Rose said, extricating her fingers from Agatha's grip. ''We'll give you something calming.''

Agatha's breathing was quick and shallow. Her head spun. She laid her head back on the pillow and closed her eyes. The spinning slowed to a stop, and she opened her eyes. Rose was gone. Something calming. Sleep. Nay, danger, *danger*. Flashes like old stories in her head, stories she had lived. Remember. Remember.

Agatha grimaced as she tried to bring order to her thoughts. She heard Rose's voice say, ''Josie, I think she's in pain.'' Rose's face over her again. Sweet face, warm eyes. Remember for Rose. She remembered the beginning of a prayer, or maybe it was a song. It floated through her mind like a summer brook, clear and full. *Mother and Father, be with me and help me. Bring me daylight in my heart. Push me, prod me, twist and bend me, till ... till ...* Stolen food. Broken fence. Tiny little girl. Everyone gone, all gone at once. Faith, faith is dead. Faithless faithful.

A warm hand caressed her cheek. "Agatha, I wish you could tell us what is wrong." Rose's voice.

The year that faith died. She tried to say it.

"Just take a sip now, dear." Josie lifted her head and pressed a glass to her lips, but Agatha wrenched her head to the side. She pushed out her mouth, the part that would listen to her. Liquid spilled down her chin, a sweet-bitter smell.

"She doesn't want the sedative," Josie said.

Agatha tried again, sputtering syllables to puzzled faces, rage at her impotence rising in her chest.

"I know Agatha." Rose's voice again. "Even with her body so weak, she has a powerful will, and she is using it now to reach us. It sounds as if she is trying to say the same thing over and over, until we understand it. She wants to tell us something."

Listen, Rose, listen.

"Don't try to talk just now. I know you can use this hand," she said, taking Agatha's left hand in her own. "I'll ask you questions. If your answer is 'yea,' squeeze my hand. Do you understand that?" Agatha squeezed her hand.

"Are you feeling ill in any way?" Agatha focused all her strength on the questions, and left her hand still.

"Are you trying to tell us something important?" Squeeze.

"Are you saying something about what I told you

earlier? The incidents in the village?'' Squeeze hard.

"About Sarah?''

Agatha squeezed, then wrenched her hand from Rose's grip and lifted her thin arm. She pointed straight ahead of her, beyond the foot of the cradle bed. Rose and Josie followed her shaking hand and stared at the wall across from her bed. Agatha's heart pounded dangerously as she willed them to understand.

In an effort to ease Agatha's confusion, Josie had brought to the sickroom a number of items from Agatha's retiring room and arranged them so that Agatha would see them each time she awakened. The room was small, the wall close enough that even Agatha's weak eyes could see the spines of her own journals filling a narrow bookshelf hanging from two wall pegs. These were the old ones; she could tell by the cracked bindings. They held the answer. Exhaustion swept through her body and her will dissolved; her arm dropped. Her eyes drifted shut.

"She pointed to the journals, I'm sure of it," Rose said.

"She's far too weak to write," Josie said. "Look at her, poor sweet dear, she'd never be able to hold a pen. That's all there is to it.''

"Nay, Josie, I don't think that's what she meant. She pointed to the old journals, not the newer ones.'' Another, larger shelf hung to the right and held the journals made since 1920, when North Homage started its small book-binding business.

"Ah, but would she know left from right? Rose, dear, you remember her as she was. That Agatha is gone.'' Josie laid a comforting hand on Rose's arm.

Rose studied her friend's sleeping face. Her translucent skin stretched so tightly across the fine bones that any wrinkles were smoothed away. How clear was the mind behind that fragile skull? Agatha couldn't speak, but did that mean she couldn't think or remember?

"I'm going to try something, Josie. I'll take those early journals with me to read in my retiring room. If Agatha notices they are gone, tell her what I've done. Watch her reaction. If she seems agitated or upset, I'll bring them back, but if she seems relieved, well, then we'll know something. In the meantime, it can't hurt to take a look at them,'' she said, pulling the thirteen volumes, dated 1908 to 1920, off the shelves. "Just in case.''

The small Ministry dining room, despite its simple beauty, felt empty to Rose without Eldress Agatha. She took her seat at the long trestle table, set for two with plain white china and worn utensils. Wilhelm hadn't arrived yet. Rose could smell fresh bread and hear clanking from the small kitchen separated from the dining room by a swinging door.

The dining room, like the building itself, served the Society's spiritual leaders, the Ministry. Once North Homage had contained two "families,'' each led by two elders and two eldresses. Discussions over meals must have been lively in those days, Rose thought. Especially a century earlier, when so much was happening, when converts—sometimes entire families— were eager to sign the covenant and live the ordered and celibate lives of Believers. Even then, women like

Agatha and Rose could serve the Society as spiritual leaders, as had their foundress, Mother Ann. Though, of course, Rose would never equate herself with Mother Ann, who was specially chosen, God's emissary, the embodiment of Christ's second appearing. Rose stifled a sigh. Now it was just Wilhelm and Rose, and their discussions usually ended in an angry impasse.

Wilhelm arrived, his broad shoulders filling the doorway as he entered. They nodded to each other, and he took his place at the trestle table. The Ministry's kitchen sister pushed through the swinging door, placed a platter of bread between them, and left. Wilhelm smoothed his white cotton napkin on his lap, and narrowed his eyes at Rose.

"Wilhelm, before you say anything, I'm sure the school will be all right. I'll handle the School Board, and—"

"We must discuss Sister Sarah," Wilhelm interrupted.

Caught off-guard, Rose stared at him. "Sarah?"

"Yea, Sarah. She has eluded thy control." His contemptuous tone implied that eluding Rose's control was neither difficult nor unexpected.

"What can you mean?"

"She has been slipping away from her work. For what purpose, I hardly dare contemplate. Not to pursue more work, though, I do assure thee. Ask thyself, why was she in the Sisters' Shop so early the morning she was injured? And was she alone?" He ripped off a hunk of bread and pointed it at her. "I believe the world was there with her. I suspect she welcomed it, and it turned on her."

The kitchen sister arrived with a tray holding a tureen of steaming tomato celery soup and a vegetable pie. Rose silently ladled the soup as she thought furiously. The sisters were her responsibility. It wounded her pride that Wilhelm knew more than she did about one of the sisters, but as a Believer she welcomed reminders of the dangers of pride. Or she tried to.

More to the point, where did he get his information? It had to be from Sister Elsa Pike, who had recently been assigned to work in the sewing room, after the laundry sisters found her impossible to tolerate. Elsa had always been Wilhelm's supporter. She was the only Believer willing to follow his example and adopt the old-fashioned speech of earlier Shakers, though she often confused "thee" with "y'all."

"And what in particular did Elsa tell you about Sarah's activities?" Rose asked as she handed Wilhelm his serving of vegetable pie. Only a flicker in his steely eyes showed that she had guessed right.

"It is thy duty to know what Sarah does," Wilhelm said. He took a large bite of pie and chewed slowly.

"And I shall see to it that I do know," Rose said.

Wilhelm nodded. "An eldress—a competent eldress—will strive to know always the spiritual health of those who are entrusted to her care." He paused for a sip of water. "She cannot perform two roles at once, particularly when she is inexperienced at one of them." He looked hard at Rose. "We need a new trustee," he said, "or a new eldress."

"Wilhelm, we've been over this already. It will take some time to find a new trustee. We have no appropriate brethren available except Samuel, and he has always refused a position of leadership. I'm getting to know the talents of the younger sisters. Sometime in the next year or so, I'm sure a likely candidate will emerge."

"I've been in touch with the lead Society," Wilhelm said. "One of their own younger brethren is right for trustee. They will send him from New York whenever we request him."

Rose leaned forward over her forgotten vegetable pie. "Wilhelm, I'm sure he is valuable to Mount Lebanon. Why send for someone new when we have several sisters who could—"

"Thy place is here, now. The Society needs an eldress who will focus wholly on her duty and not be lingering at her former position. North Homage needs thee in the Ministry House, not the Trustees' Office. If trustee is a more comfortable position for thee, then go back to it, and I'll bring in a new eldress. We must act now. We must stop the flood of Believers leaving the Society." Wilhelm pointed his fork at Rose. "Why, there are fewer Believers remaining here than cursed apostates gathered in Languor. These are dangerous times for us. We need strong leadership to preserve our faith and our ways. If the task is too great for thee, then step down and let others who are stronger take charge."

After a session of quiet prayer, Rose ended her long, unsettling day by sinking into the rocking chair in the outer chamber of her retiring room. She spread a soft wool blanket around her knees. Hugo, the Society's carpenter before he'd begun to go blind, had designed and built the chair to fit Rose's tall, lean body, and over the years it seemed to have molded itself to her bones. She relaxed against the slats and rocked gently.

This room always calmed her. Its south and east windows afforded her almost a complete view of the village, though she was rarely here during daylight hours. The furnishings were simple and spare, as befit a Believer's quarters. The room held a simple oak desk lined with her journals, a wooden desk chair, and the small table at her elbow. Small wooden doors hid storage spaces built into the wall. From the pegs circling the room hung an extra ladder-back chair, a flat broom, and her heavy wool Dorothy cloak.

Nothing in the room truly belonged to Rose. Since they contained some community records woven among her own observations, she considered even her journals to be community property. It felt right to her. She knew, too, that it was time for her to leave these rooms behind and move to the Ministry to be eldress in earnest. Wilhelm had tossed her a challenge she could not ignore. No matter how greatly—and how frequently—they disagreed, Wilhelm was strong and far more experienced than she. In calmer moments, she knew that when he fought with her it was out of his fierce love for the Society. She would find a way to work with him.

Rose glanced down at the journal spread open on her lap, one of the stack of thirteen she had removed from Agatha's sickroom. She had read through two volumes already and found nothing helpful. This one was dated 1910. Firm handwriting filled the page with clear, rounded letters. The gentle, earnest style triggered memories of Agatha as she had been before age and repeated strokes had sapped her strength.

Agatha had been eldress of North Homage for thirty-five years, and she had so many journals that most had been packed away in storage. Where on earth did she get the time and energy to write so much? Rose made a few notations a day in her own journal, but she was happier working than writing.

It was late and Rose could feel her heavy eyes protest that they wanted to close, but she picked up the book. Agatha had seemed insistent that the old volumes contained something related to recent incidents in the community. Unsure what to look for, Rose began to read. She came to a passage that intrigued her.

> *Obadiah tells me those boys are at it again. C. is a trial—sweet and pliable one moment, angry and excitable the next. Josie said she found him rummaging in her medicines this afternoon. And R.W.—What shall we do with that young man? He is after his mother to leave with him, since it serves his purposes. I fear the World has its claws in his heart. He worships money more than God.*

R.W.—Richard Worthington, perhaps? Agatha, knowing her journals would be seen by succeeding generations, had been careful to obscure identities by using initials in her entries when the information was sensitive.

In 1910, Worthington would have been about sixteen and living in North Homage. He despised the Shakers who had fed and clothed and educated him. Why? And why had he looked so—cold, was it, or

frightened maybe?—at the sight of Brother Samuel
Bickford? They would have known each other, of
course. Rose's interest quickened. Worthington could
pose a serious threat to the community if he called in
their debts. If he had suffered some injury at the Believers' hands, she wanted to know about it. Perhaps
she could heal the wounds.

Rose read on, but nothing that followed referred to
R.W. or his mother until she came across a passage
close to the end of the journal. She shivered underneath her warm blanket, though Agatha herself
seemed to have believed that the events she described
were no more than bothersome.

Someone has been in the storeroom to no good
purpose. Sister Martha reported this morning
that two dozen jars of plums are missing from
storage, just a day after she and the kitchen sis-
ters put them up, she says. Not two hours later
the brethren found them, smashed to pulp
against the barn. I looked at it myself and
prayed for the soul of the poor creature that
would do such a wasteful thing with people al-
ways going hungry. Well, what's done is done.
We'll watch the storeroom more carefully. We
don't mind a bite or two of food disappearing
now and again, it's not stealing if it fills an
empty belly, that I believe. But this is wanton.
Poor angry creature. Meanwhile, we have too
much work to do to worry about this. The breth-
ren are repairing the broken window in the
Meetinghouse and the damage to the east stone

fence that keeps the cattle from wandering amid the wheat. It's one thing or it's another, isn't it?

Rose smiled at this picture of Agatha, so accurately conveyed by her journal entries. Praying for the miscreant who had smashed their plum preserves against the barn would not have been Rose's first reaction. But her enjoyment faded as she read the end of the passage.

The worst, though, is the arrival of field mice in the schoolhouse, frightening the children and Sister Flora, who couldn't stop sobbing, poor thing, though she would have done better to think more of the children. As it was, the older children comforted the younger ones—and their teacher, as well!

Stolen jars of plums, a damaged fence, and mice in the schoolhouse. These incidents struck Rose as far too similar to recent events. Whatever had happened twenty-five years ago was happening again, here and now.

SIX

THE NEXT MORNING, ROSE AWAKENED AS USUAL AT five-thirty. She slipped into her work clothes and quickly brushed her hair before covering it with her white indoor cap. Agatha's journal passages still absorbed her thoughts. She pulled the wool coverlet tight over her bed, splashed her face with a handful of cold water from the chipped bowl on her washstand, and patted it dry with a white cotton towel. Shaking her head, she turned her mind to a morning prayer, asking Mother Ann for guidance during the day.

She lifted the broom from a wall peg and swept away any dirt that might have accumulated in the corners of her retiring room since the previous morning. After dusting the few pieces of furniture, she folded her nightclothes and stored them in dresser drawers built into the wall of her bedroom.

A quick look in the small mirror hanging from another wall peg reassured Rose that no strands of her curly red hair poked out of her cap. It wouldn't last, of course. By nightfall she would have pushed curls back under the thin cotton dozens of times, and there would still be a red halo surrounding her face. Worry pinched her thin features. The green irises that gazed back at her were surrounded by tiny red lines. If she lived in the world, she would soothe her eyes with cotton balls soaked in witch hazel, then apply rouge, powder, and lipstick. But she had chosen the life of a Shaker sister. On the whole, she was much happier being useful than being beautiful.

Rose tidied her way into the sitting room, opened the curtains, and stowed Agatha's journals inside a small recessed cupboard. She swept and dusted that room, as well. Every morning she followed the same routine, and every morning she drew contentment from it. Her life had a rhythm, as if the heartbeat of God paced her movements and gave them meaning beyond her selfish needs and desires. She took a last look around her plain, comfortable room as she closed the door behind her.

Her office was directly below her retiring rooms. She descended the well-swept wooden staircase, treasuring the cheerful sounds of arising Believers and the warm sunlight splashing through the front windows and across the bottom steps.

She headed toward the Trustees' Office kitchen, used only sporadically nowadays, to make her morning pot of rose hip and lemon balm tea. As she passed the door to her office, she noticed that it stood slightly ajar. She remembered closing it firmly the night before. It was always unlocked. Anyone could enter, but few would without her knowledge. And any Believer would be careful to close it again upon leaving, for the sake of courtesy and order.

With a prick of discomfort, Rose pushed the door fully open. The room looked normal in the dim light.

She threw open the shuttered windows to brighten the room with natural sunlight. As she did, warm rays spread across the golden orange of her pine double desk. She'd left the desk clear of papers or ledgers, as she always did. Now, though, what looked like a newspaper lay in a patch of sun.

She picked it up. It was folded in half like a newspaper but was only one sheet of high-quality newsprint. One long article, arranged in columns and without a byline, covered both sides of the sheet. There were no classified advertisements, no wedding announcements or reports of grown children back in town to visit their parents. Inch-high, ornately typeset letters across the top of the page announced: LANGUOR COUNTY WATCHER. Smaller, bold-face letters called it a free journal intended to warn the people of Languor County about dangers in their midst.

Rose shivered. She suspected what the topic would be, didn't want to read on, but knew she had to. It was her job. Her hand shook as she tilted the paper toward the light from the window.

The article began as an apparent news report about events in Europe. "Hitler is a shining beacon," the anonymous correspondent wrote in overblown prose, "lighting the way toward a purer mankind."

Like other Believers, Rose maintained her spiritual distance from the world, yet she believed deeply in pacifism and equality. God willing, there would be no more wars, but if one erupted, the Believers would refuse to fight, as they had refused to fight in the Great War. Hitler disturbed Rose. He inspired anger and hatred, which bred violence.

She skimmed the article, feeling sick at heart about

the world and glad to be in her own. Toward the middle of the piece, her eyes slid over and then snapped back to a passage that did more than sadden her. The message terrified her.

... We have dangerous foreigners in our very midst, a SCOURGE that calls themselves Americans. They are Americans second, if at all. These so-called Shakers are shrewd and canny, driving our local businesses into bankruptcy without sparing a thought to the lives they are ruining, the women and children they are driving to the streets. These frightening enemies living among us are known by their strange dress, stolen from our Puritan ancestors, which they dishonor by wearing. They pretend to purity of thought and deed. They claim to be far more holy than mere Christian mortals like you and I, my friends. You will never see them in Toby's buying a beer for a friend who is down on his luck. And you'll never find them sharing a harmless smoke out on a neighbor's porch. Oh, no, they are too good for such evil pursuits as you and I may enjoy and call it harmless pleasure.

These Shakers SCORN THE FAMILY as the EVIL OF ALL EVILS!!! That's right, according to these folks, if you marry your sweetheart and start a family, you'll burn in the fires of Hell. Yet these so-called sisters and brothers share food together and even join one another in the evenings! They live together, men and women both, in one building, sometimes five or six to a room, doing God only knows what behind those cold limestone walls!!!

This tumor must be sliced from our side. The surgery must be swift and precise. As Kentuckians, Citizens of Languor County, you can help. Watch this column to find out how! There will be more to come, very soon.

Rose crushed the thin sheet between her hands and threw it at the wall. The ball hit with a light tap and bounced back toward her. She clenched her fists and frowned down at it, breathing in short, fierce bursts until her temper drained away. Fear remained.

Believers had been objects of both respect and resentment, often at the same time, but nothing like this. At least not in Rose's memory, which went back more than thirty years to when she arrived in North Homage as an orphaned toddler. Who could write such things? And just as confusing, who had delivered it here and why? To warn them or to scare them?

Rose reached down and scooped up the wrinkled paper, grimacing in distaste. She slid into her desk chair and smoothed the page out under her lamp. Trying to ignore the blaring headline, she examined the top edge for any clues about the diatribe's origin. It was dated that morning. So someone had made sure she received it as it came off the press.

The paper announced itself to be Volume I, Number 1, attacking under the pretense of being a bona-fide newspaper. A cowardly attack, too, since the editors hid behind false names: Mr. and Mrs. Languor County. Mr. and Mrs.—could this mean the authors were a man and a woman, or was someone just calling attention to the Believers' celibate way of life?

The article itself looked expertly typeset. The prose was more menacing than the style favored by the *Languor Weekly Advocate*, which avoided the social issues of the larger world and advocated nothing stronger than barring horses from the main street.

The page spread out before Rose seemed the work of an experienced newspaperman—or woman. She had no illusions. If men and woman were equal in their potential for work and leadership, as the Shakers believed, they must then be equal in their capacity to make mischief.

"Rose?"

She swiveled in her chair to see Brother Hugo's round frame in her doorway. His old eyes squinted at her, then registered concern as he moved into the room far enough to make out her expression.

"Wilhelm sent me to find you," he said. "He's quite upset about something. And it seems that you are, as well."

"Why can't he just call me? We have phones, he needn't have sent you running all over the place. Oh, I'm sorry to be short with you, Hugo, you only delivered the message. It's just that I've had some . . . bad news."

Hugo's eyes followed hers to the wrinkled printed sheet on her desk.

"I think," he said, "that Wilhelm may have gotten the same bad news."

"So what do you make of this?"

Hugo glanced toward the offensive tract and shook his head. "I didn't examine it carefully."

Hugo had lived in North Homage for more than fifty years. He might remember something, connect it somehow with an element in Languor that resented the Shakers.

"Look through it," Rose said, pushing the paper

closer to him. Hugo took it between the tips of his thumb and forefinger. Without turning to the other side, he tossed it back on the desk.

"It's just the usual vileness," he said with a quiet snort. "You've seen this sort of abomination before; why worry about it?"

"Nay, Hugo, I don't believe this is the same nonsense we've seen in the past—or at least the recent past. These people know what they are doing. They may be connected somehow with a newspaper. They bring considerable skills to their task, which clearly is to drive us out of Languor County. I take them very, very seriously."

Without touching him, she gestured to Hugo to sit at the other half of her double desk. She knew he was slowly losing his sight and could not have read more than the headline. "Turn it over and read the entire piece," she urged. "You've been here longer than I have. I need your memory. Read it, just read it first, and tell me what you think."

Hugo settled his round body into the spare desk chair, which had once belonged to North Homage's second trustee. He fished a pair of wire-rimmed spectacles from his shirt pocket and settled them on his nose. With one finger, he pulled the paper toward him. Bending so that his eyes were inches from the print, he read both sides.

"There are details . . ." His voice trailed off as his gaze lifted to the neatly stuffed shelves and cubbyholes piled high on the desk.

"Indeed." Rose pointed to a paragraph on the second side. "The author knows how we live and how we eat and work, our living arrangements, even about our Union Meetings, though he makes it sound like much more than getting together to chat in the evening.''

Hugo slumped against the back of the chair. "Of course, we don't hide how we live. Anyone who wanted to could find out.''

"Yea, but this writer also knows about how we lived in the past, when we had more Believers. Five or six to a retiring room—we haven't slept like that for at least fifteen years, have we?''

"More like twenty,'' Hugo said.

The outside door clicked open and shut as the last resident of the Trustees' building left after a quick breakfast of fresh-baked bread and preserves. Probably heading to the fields to help with spring plowing and planting. Hugo frowned at the paper in front of him.

"Apostates,'' he said.

"Yea, those who have left the faith,'' Rose agreed. "Or someone who knows them well enough to have learned a great deal about us. Angry, spiteful apostates, not just folks who came to us as children for schooling.''

Though she didn't say so, Rose thought of Richard Worthington. Could he have begun a campaign to destroy them? If he had, though, why tip his hand by visiting with such obvious animosity, then turn coy and print an anonymous diatribe against them? A direct, out-in-the-open grab for power seemed more his style. Still, he could be involved.

"Hugo, can you think of anyone—especially anyone who left the Society fifteen or more years ago— who might do something like this? Anyone with newspaper experience, perhaps? Someone who hated us dreadfully?''

A shadow passed over Hugo's face. Rose became aware of the silence.

"There was one," Hugo said. "My memory isn't what it was. I don't recall his name, but he signed the covenant. He worked awhile for the *Cincinnati Enquirer* after he left us, or so I heard."

"When was this?"

"Must have been twenty, twenty-five years ago now. Yea, it would have been at least twenty-five because it was before I stopped traveling so much to gather souls and took over the Carpenters' Shop. So I didn't really know him, you see. I knew little about what went on then; I was away so much of the time. But Samuel would know about him. They were friends, good friends, as I remember." Hugo pulled a handkerchief from his jacket pocket and began to clean his spectacles. "But you'd best ask Samuel about all that."

SEVEN

"MIND TELLING ME WHERE YA GOT THE MONEY FOR this?" The beefy clerk behind the counter at Languor Liquors kept a firm grip on the neck of the bottle of Jack Daniels.

Caleb Cox shifted from one foot to the other and winced at the pain behind his eyes as he stared at the bottle. His threadbare jacket hung on his bony shoulders, and he was uncomfortably aware that neither he nor the jacket had bathed recently.

Caleb's confidence was low, but his need was great. He ran his tongue over his cracked lips. He couldn't figure out if he had to answer the guy's question to get his hands on that whiskey. He'd seen the clerk dozens of times, hell, maybe hundreds, he had better things to do than keep count. Did that give the guy the right to ask a question like that? It should be enough that he could pay for it, never mind how he got the money. None of the guy's business.

Did they know each other outside of this podunk little liquor store? Caleb's eyes drifted to the man's face. A closed, stern face. Nope, not a drinking buddy. Caleb didn't always remember his drinking buddies, but he was sure he wouldn't drink with someone so suspicious.

"I sold you a lot of bottles, Caleb," the clerk said, "but never nothing like this. This here's our best whiskey. Not many folks buy it excepting maybe Mr. Worthington, and he can afford it. So what I'm wondering is, how come you can afford it all of a sudden?"

Caleb breathed in deep and let the air whistle out through the gap where he'd lost a front tooth in a barroom brawl. Or maybe it was back in the war he'd lost that tooth. Yeah, that sounded better, lost his tooth in the Big One.

The clerk's eyes narrowed. It was no use. Caleb knew he'd have to concentrate, come up with some explanation for how he had this money in his hand, enough to buy really good whiskey for a change, stuff that maybe wouldn't rot his stomach out so fast. Truth was, he wasn't sure himself why he was buying Jack Daniels instead of his usual cheap brand. He'd just felt different ever since that day he'd met Sarah in town, while she was shopping for fabric. He'd told her how he'd been a Shaker, too. They'd got to talking. Something about Sarah made him want the best for a change. Prove he was worth her, maybe.

"Won it in a poker game," Caleb said, grinning with pride at his quickness of mind. Not so boozed up as everybody thought, was he? Could still think on his feet when he had to. And he had to get that bottle.

"You telling me you stayed sober long enough to win that much off somebody? You telling me somebody with that kind of money would even play poker with the likes of you?"

Caleb sagged. Two questions this time, and they were getting harder.

"Well, yeah, that's what I'm sayin'," he finally managed, not sure which question he might be answering, if either.

The clerk eyed him a few more moments, then shrugged. Caleb relaxed, knowing he'd won. It was closing time, and the man was tired.

"Hell, it don't make me no never mind," the clerk said. "Money's money." He slipped the bills out of Caleb's shaking hand and replaced them with the whiskey bottle.

Caleb clutched the bottle by the neck and headed for the door before the clerk could hand him his change.

"Keep it," Caleb tossed over his shoulder as he pulled the shop's screen door carefully toward him to demonstrate his dignity and stone-cold sobriety. The effect was spoiled somewhat when he let go of the door too soon and it whacked him on the rear. Caleb didn't mind too much. He had himself a bottle of real Jack Daniels, and he'd earned it. He was helping Sarah, too. It all made him feel good, like he really deserved a reward.

Caleb sat cross-legged on his army cot, winded from climbing the three floors to his boardinghouse room. Despite the whiskey bottle in his hand, his buoyant mood was fading. There was a time, before Sarah came into his life, when he'd have had that bottle half drunk by now. He took a swig, let it trickle down his throat, savored the burning sensation. He felt it reach his stomach and explode through his veins. Best stuff he'd ever tasted. He raised the bottle to his lips again, hesitated, and lowered it slowly.

Sarah. He would see her today, and he'd made her a solemn promise to cut back on the booze. She'd said her uncle had been a boozer, and it made her sad to watch.

Caleb leaned across the cot and plunked the bottle on the upended orange crate that served as his nightstand. Trouble was, life drunk was plain easier for Caleb. His nightmares struck as the alcohol wore off—the shelling that still blasted his brain every night, though the war had been over for nearly twenty years. Then there was his wasted life, filled only with empty bottles. Sarah was the only happiness he'd known in the past twenty years. Too bad she was a Shaker, but he'd change all that. He'd get her away from that place. He couldn't remember why exactly, but he knew it was their fault his life had gone so bad. Yeah, he'd save Sarah from those people, and then they'd be together, and he wouldn't have nightmares or need to drink anymore.

Content again, Caleb grabbed the bottle and took another swallow. He reached in his pocket and pulled out a sheet of paper. He settled on the cot with his thin legs crossed underneath him. He was to deliver the page to Sarah when he saw her next. He knew it was a page torn from a journal, and it held information Sarah wanted, stuff about her mother and who her father was. He knew, too, how she'd react—excited and scared at the same time. Steadying the whiskey bottle against his thigh, he unfolded the paper and read it through. It began in the middle of a sentence.

. . . my sister is Faithfull, and yet she is not, not to me, neither to her vows. But I cannot blame

her. My own heart betrayed me, and I have paid with my soul. Indeed, I gave all for a touch of her wheat-brown hair, not knowing that there would never be a second touch. Not after she turned her eyes back to him. I hate even his name and will not grant it substance by writing it. I know that he has been with her. I see every flick of her eyes, every tiny gesture. When she is out of my sight, I dream every movement and each sleeping breath she takes. Nay, I cannot blame her. I see the purity of her soul through her clear eyes, blue as a lake in the sun, and as deep. The fault is with him, Brother Satan, Satan himself. He seduced her innocent heart, and Mother Ann is a witness. There will be a reckoning. God grant that I may be His instrument.

EIGHT

ROSE WAS STILL LEARNING TO BE A SPIRITUAL leader for her people, but she knew that her way was not Wilhelm's, nor was it Agatha's. Wilhelm was a visionary, whose eyes saw only what had once been. He was a powerful force, though, as she'd found out more than once. Agatha was contemplative, closely linked to the realm of spirit, increasingly so as she grew older and more feeble.

Though drawn to spiritual concerns, Rose's practical nature fit perfectly with the world of business: herb sales, real estate purchases, new economic ventures. Once the nation's economy improved, and their own debts lightened, she hoped to dabble again in investments to provide monetary security for the Society. For now, she kept in daily contact with her people, eating with them when she could avoid Wilhelm's demands that she eat at the Ministry House, helping with the ironing on hot afternoons, watching for signs of unhappiness. She prayed, of course, and derived great comfort from that. But if she saw a problem, she wanted to solve it.

Now she had several problems. She extracted a sheet of paper and a pen from her desk drawer and began a list. A familiar relief settled in as she organized her thoughts and plans on paper. Under "episodes," she listed:

1. Stolen jars of raspberry preserves
2. Broken fence—and Freddie drugged
3. Sister Sarah injured (attacked?) in the Sisters' Shop
4. Rats released in the schoolroom—and Amanda bitten
5. Anti-Shaker literature left in the Trustees' Office and Ministry House, for me and for Wilhelm to find

Rose leaned against her chair back and studied the list. All the incidents had occurred in the space of a week, most within the last few days. Seen individually, they were disturbing, though surely no worse than Believers had experienced since Mother Ann suffered at the hands of an angry mob. Taken together, a pattern formed. The episodes had grown increasingly threatening, beginning with an ordinary theft and proceeding, so far, to attacks on Believers and children and a call for the eradication of the Society. What would be next?

Hugo had suggested she ask Samuel for his memories of apostates, but he was busy planting and would probably remain in the fields until late in the day. She would try to catch him after worship the next morning.

In the meantime, Wilhelm's accusation that she was not watching over Sister Sarah Baker stung, and she could not put it out of her mind. It was time to have a chat with Sarah, who was recovering well from her injury and had insisted on going back to work in the sewing room.

. The Sisters' Shop was a two-story white clapboard building set back from the path that cut through the village center. The shop ran so smoothly that Rose rarely visited, but she always enjoyed doing so. Though not herself skilled in the weaving arts, Rose loved to watch the patterns take shape on the looms. She paused on the first floor to chat with the sisters who were dyeing woolen yarns to earthy golds and browns, then made her way to the second floor sewing room. The plain wooden staircase was well swept and dusted, she was pleased to see.

As she approached the top of the stairs, she heard a subdued voice, undoubtedly Sarah's. The words were unclear, but the voice that responded to them was unmistakable. Rose recognized the familiar grating tone of Sister Elsa Pike. She had momentarily forgotten that she had reassigned Elsa to the sewing room.

Rose tried to be even-handed toward all Believers, but she had to admit that Elsa was not one of her favorite sisters. Elsa came from poor hill-country stock and had left her husband and grown sons less than two years earlier to join the Shakers. None of this disturbed Rose. The Society welcomed anyone who wished to become a Believer—whether rich or poor, learned or unschooled. Elsa, though, was inclined to hubris and unseemly ambition, and no amount of confession or correction seemed to cure her of these sins.

''Well, a person's gotta wonder, that's all. Leavin'

thy work like that, a person's gonna wonder,'' Elsa
said.

The softer voice rose in tone, but the words were
still indistinct.

''Nay, I ain't sayin' I spread rumors around, but
bein' a Believer and all, I know my duty.''

Rose decided to make her presence known, though
her enthusiasm for the visit had dimmed considerably.

Sarah and Elsa raised their heads and grew silent
as Rose entered the room. Each was hunched over her
own sewing desk at opposite corners of the large
room, as far away as they could get from one another.

''Good day, Sisters,'' Rose said. ''I knew many of
the sewing sisters would be helping with the planting
today, so I've come to help you, if I can.''

Elsa responded with a grunt and a nod of her head.

''So kind of you, Eldress,'' Sarah said. Her skin
was pallid, and she wore a bandage around her head.

Needles, a pin cushion, and embroidery floss lay on
Sarah's sewing desk. The warm patina of the desk's
aged pine surface glowed in the sunlight from the east
window. Sarah herself was plain, but an exquisite
seamstress, creating beauty with every stitch. When
she spoke, her lithe fingers barely slowed as they
guided her embroidery needle in and out of the fabric
with sureness.

Elsa's stitchery, on the other hand, was effective
but graceless. Her desk held messy piles of fabric
scraps and sewing implements. Her round, flat-
featured face registered boredom. She shot a malev-
olent glance over at Sarah before bending again to the
work dress she was mending.

The room was brightly lit by the large, clean windows lining the walls. Between the windows, pine strips studded with shiny maple pegs circled the entire room. Nearly every peg held some object, from chairs and a flatbroom to partially finished garments on hangers. Several empty sewing desks had been pushed against the walls until they were called for again, probably after planting season, when more sisters would be free. In the center of the room stood a large cutting table covered with a length of fine, dark blue wool. Tissue pattern pieces were pinned along the fabric, their edges touching so as not to waste any of the precious wool.

Since neither Sarah nor Elsa offered her a task to do, Rose wandered over to the table. She picked up a pair of shears that lay on the corner.

"Shall I cut this pattern for you, Sarah?" she asked.

Sarah's head bobbed up, her brown eyes protruding even more than usual. "Oh nay, that's all right, you needn't bother. You don't usually . . . I mean, I'll be getting to it just as soon as I've finished putting these initials in Brother Hugo's new shirt." She lowered her eyes again to her needlework.

Rose hesitated, the shears already open. "I don't mind at all," she said. "I know I haven't helped out in the sewing room as often as some other places, but you've only the two of you until planting is done, so I'd truly like to pitch in. If you'll let me." She knew it would be a mistake to sound as if she were challenging Sarah's oversight of the sewing. She closed the shears and waited.

Sarah looked up again, this time with a frown. Rose glanced over at Elsa just in time to see the last of a crooked grin directed at Sarah. Rose permitted herself a quiet sigh. This conversation would be tougher than she'd anticipated. The two women were clearly battling, an unfortunate consequence of having Elsa in a room with any other sister.

"All right, then, Eldress," Sarah said. "You can cut if you really want to. I appreciate the help." Her voice always sounded as if it should belong to a more delicate woman.

"Just call me Rose, please, Sarah," Rose said, laughing. "I'm not sure I'll ever get used to 'eldress,' it makes me feel as if I'll take off my cap and find nothing but wisps of white hair."

This drew a timid grin from Sarah and a snicker from Elsa.

Rose felt the sharp shears slice through the soft wool and let the silence grow in the room. She knew so little about Sarah. The sister was in her early thirties, but her painful history gave her an older look. She had lived among them as a child. Rose remembered her as a timid little girl with whom she had had little contact. As Rose recalled hearing from other Believers, Sarah's mother had sent for her, when she was still quite young, and raised her to adulthood. She had come back to North Homage about two years ago, reporting that her mother had died. Sarah had a sadness about her but kept the reasons to herself. Her confessions were earnest but along the lines of "gazing out the window instead of working," or "showing a hint of temper."

Rose glanced up to catch Elsa watching Sarah instead of mending. When Elsa realized she'd been caught, Rose said, "Elsa, you seem tired of mending.

The kitchen sisters are short-handed, so go ahead to the kitchen and help with the noon meal. They'll appreciate it. Go on, just leave the mending, it'll keep.''

Elsa's face moved swiftly from relief to suspicion. But she put down her mending.

"I thank thee," she said and clumped out on sturdy legs.

Rose went back to her pattern cutting until Elsa's footsteps receded down the staircase. She put down her shears and picked up Elsa's unfinished mending.

"I'll just finish this, shall I?" She took down a ladder-back chair from its wall peg, and placed it next to Sarah's sewing desk.

Sarah shifted in her own chair and chewed on her lower lip.

"You do enjoy fine needlework, don't you, Sarah?"

This earned a shy nod.

"Your work is excellent, you know, and well appreciated, I assure you."

A quick, tiny smile.

"Did you learn it here in the village as a child, or did your mother teach you?"

Sarah's needle hesitated. "Here, at first," she said. "I learned from Sister Ariel. I loved to watch her stitch, and she gave me special lessons, even though I was so young. I kept it up afterwards. Sewing gave me comfort."

"Of course, Sister Ariel. She was a wonderful seamstress, and such a kind person."

"I loved her," Sarah said. "I was so sad to hear that she died while I was with my . . . while I was away."

"We were all sad to lose her, but I'm sure she is happy to be where she is, Sarah. You will see her again, you know."

Sarah's head bobbed in a quick nod as she made a finishing knot in her embroidery floss and snipped the end with a small pair of scissors. Placing the garment in a nearly full basket next to her chair, she reached for another from a second basket.

"Tell me, are you happy with us, Sarah?"

The needle paused in mid-stitch. "Yea, of course, Eldress, I've said so many times."

"I know you have, but I just wondered: Do you ever miss your own mother, your family?"

Sarah cut and separated a length of yellow embroidery floss. She picked up the garment, a deep-brown work dress, and began embroidering initials inside the collar.

"The Society is my family," she said, without lifting her eyes. "In a way, I guess they always have been. My mother is here." She flashed an unreadable glance at Rose. "Sister Ariel was as much my mother as anybody, and Sister Josie, and Eldress Agatha. I am happy here and I never want to leave."

"Tell me about your mother."

Sarah's head jerked up. "What . . . what do you mean?"

"Well, what was she like?"

"Beautiful," she said. "She was beautiful. I don't look like her."

"As I remember, you went to live with her as a youngster," Rose prodded. "What would you have been, seven or eight years old?"

"Six." Sarah kept her eyes on her work as she spoke.

"What did she enjoy doing? Did she sew, like you?"

"Nay."

Rose felt as if she were trying to pry information from the fieldstone fence outside the Sisters' Shop.

"Sarah," she said, switching from gentleness to a firmer tone, "I have been told something that disturbs me, something about you."

This time the needle stopped completely.

"There are reports that you have left the Sisters' Shop for as much as an hour on mysterious errands, and even that you've been out past bedtime. I can't help but notice that you have avoided confession for weeks." She halted at the look of anguish and fury on Sarah's face.

"*She* told you, didn't she. Elsa has been telling tales about me."

"No sister has told me anything." It was the truth, since only Wilhelm had told her, but Rose felt as uncomfortable as if she were lying. She wanted to discuss Sarah's behavior, not who told what to whom.

"Sarah, if you are in any kind of trouble, I urge you to confide in me. I can't help you if I don't know what's going on, and I do want to help you."

Sarah secured her needle by weaving it through the fabric in her lap. "Truly, Eldress, I have nothing to tell you. She's been lying about me. She's just jealous, that's all, she's jealous of me and everyone." She looked at Rose again, her mouth set in a hard line. "If you really want to help me, send Elsa to work somewhere else. You don't even have to send anyone else to help me. I usually have to redo her work, anyway, so I'd be ahead if I was working on my own.''

Rose sighed as the bell rang for the noon meal. ''I'll see what I can do. In the meantime, come along and eat at my table. On the way, we will set a time for your next confession.''

''I'll be there shortly, Eldress. I just want to finish up a stitch or two. Samuel needs this new work shirt right away.''

Caleb Cox thrust his hands in the pockets of his worn jacket and fastened his eyes on the trees Sarah would come through on her way from the Sisters' Shop to him. He was sober—always as sober as possible for Sarah. Lately it had gotten tougher, though.

Dry leaves crackled. Caleb stiffened, alert. It might not be Sarah; could be any Shaker out on an errand. But it was Sarah, and he watched fondly as she walked through the budding apple trees. She wasn't what a lot of men would call pretty. Wisps of light brown hair escaped her heavy woven bonnet. Her brown eyes protruded maybe a bit too much, her shoulders were too narrow, and her hips too wide. But Caleb's war-battered, booze-deadened heart quickened at the sight of her hopeful smile as she spotted him. He held open his arms and Sarah ran to them. He held her tightly, afraid to loosen his grip even to kiss her.

''Cal, I'm getting really scared,'' Sarah said, putting her hands on his chest and pushing away from him. ''You haven't told me everything, have you? What's really going on?''

Caleb sighed and pulled her close again. To tell the

truth, that was one reason he always made sure to be sober around Sarah. Not just because he loved her and didn't want to lose her, but because if he got drunk and opened his stupid big mouth, he'd tell her everything, and that would be the end.

"Nothin's going on, Sarah. I'd tell you if there was, honest. It's just what I told you before."

Sarah frowned at him. "Then explain how those rats got in the schoolhouse. And that awful newspaper; who wrote that?"

Caleb started to back away from her, but she caught his arm.

"And why did someone hit me?"

"What? I thought it was an accident."

"I didn't tell any of the brethren, but I know I didn't fall down the stairs. Someone hit me, twice."

Caleb stared at her. "That wasn't supposed to happen," he mumbled. "Damn it, that wasn't supposed to happen."

"Caleb!"

"Sorry, Sarah. Sorry. Look, I'll take care of things and make sure you're never hurt again, okay? I'll never let anyone hurt you again."

Sarah's trusting expression almost warmed the chill taking hold of his heart. Seemed like there was more going on than even he knew, and, damn it, he'd find out what. He'd stay sober as long as it took. Yet even as he made the vow, he thought of Jack Daniels waiting on the orange crate in his room, and more where that came from. He pushed the enticing image from his mind.

"Look what I brought for you," he said, slipping the journal page out of his jacket pocket. "My friend found another one for me. He said we're gettin' closer to who might've killed your mother.''

Sarah drew in her breath with hopeful excitement, as he'd known she would. She slowly opened the folded sheet, as if she didn't want to know its contents but couldn't keep herself from looking. Her eyes widened as she read it through.

"Does your friend really think he can figure out who this man is—this man who took advantage of her?"

"Yeah, pretty sure."

"It says here that her soul was pure, that she was innocent. She was, wasn't she?"

Caleb nodded, feeling a little sick to his stomach. He knew different, but he could never tell Sarah. It would kill her.

"Whoever wrote this loved her very much."

"Yes."

"Caleb?" She looked shyly up at him. "Is my hair the same color as hers was? I can only remember her with her hair covered up, and I can't ask anyone around here because then they'd know who she was."

Caleb pulled a strand from beneath her cap and wound it around his index finger. "Yes," he said. "It sure is."

Sarah wrapped her arms around his neck and kissed him.

NINE

SARAH DID NOT APPEAR FOR THE NOON MEAL. ROSE would have noticed her absence, even if she hadn't been saving a place for her. With only twenty-nine Believers, ten of whom were men who ate at the opposite end of the large dining room, it was easy to spot a missing sister. Rose wanted to tell Sarah that Elsa would be transferred to kitchen rotation following the noon meal, though Sister Gertrude, the new kitchen deaconess, was none too happy about it. Rose had promised that Elsa would do only washing up and chopping, not baking, as she used to do. She turned up her nose at herbs and spices of any sort, so even her apple pies were bland.

Fifteen minutes into the simple meal, Rose spread her white linen napkin over her spring-vegetable soup and slipped away from the table. Josie glanced up at her with a question, but Rose tossed her a reassuring look. Her expression tightened as soon as she cleared the women's entrance to the dining room. Something was wrong, she could sense it. Sarah shouldn't have taken so long to finish embroidering an initial. She might have taken ill on the way over, a dizzy spell perhaps, as a result of her head injury. If so, she may have gone directly up to her retiring room, which was on the second floor, just above the dining room. Rose knocked on the door and called her name. When no one answered, she eased open the door. Though Sarah lived alone in the room, it still contained three narrow beds, all neatly made as if waiting for the arrival of new Believers. Bright sunlight warmed the simple pine table and drawers built into the clean white walls. A few dust motes caught the light, but otherwise the room sparkled with cleanliness. There was no sign of Sarah.

Each floor of the dwelling house was equipped with one telephone, located in the hallway. Always open to labor-saving inventions, the Shakers had been the first in Languor County to install a phone system to connect them both with the world and with each other. Rose felt the skin prickle on the back of her neck as she waited for her connection to the sewing room and listened to the hollow, unanswered ring.

Rose picked up her long skirts and ran toward the Sisters' Shop. She told herself it was always possible that Sarah had decided to work through the noon meal. Believers worked hard; it wasn't unheard of to skip a meal. But the work wasn't so pressing that Sarah needed to stay, and she hadn't answered the phone. She was alone in the Sisters' Shop, as she had been the morning of her so-called accident. Rose ran faster. If that had been no accident, her attacker could have come back to finish the job.

Rose's heart was pounding nearly as loudly as her thick-soled work shoes, which thudded against the steps as she hurried upstairs to the sewing room.

"Sarah?" she called, as she pushed open the door.

Soft stacks of fabric absorbed her voice. She paused to catch her breath and called more loudly. No one answered.

Rose rushed across the empty room to Sarah's sewing desk, on which lay the embroidery she'd interrupted for the noon meal. It was still unfinished.

The window next to Sarah's desk looked out toward the Society's orchard, now studded with apple blossoms about to burst. Rose's eyesight was excellent, and the severely pruned branches allowed her a clear view of two people embracing among the trees. One of them wore the stiff bonnet and loose, long dress of a Shaker sister.

Rose turned on her heel and flew down the Sisters' Shop staircase. She'd be very surprised if that was anyone but Sarah. No wonder she wanted to work alone. The better to break her vow of chastity. Rose was furious not just at Sarah's deception but that she had allowed herself to be duped.

Her angry strides brought her to the orchard in minutes. She heard their voices just before she saw them, arms intertwined, strolling away from her toward the older, abandoned portion of the orchard. Sarah's pear-shaped body moved with surprising grace as she matched her stride to that of her companion. Rose didn't recognize the man's slight figure and shaggy brown hair. His clothes were of the world and much patched. He gently unlinked their elbows and slid his arm around Sarah's waist.

Rose hesitated. Unlike some of the other sisters, she knew what Sarah was feeling as she leaned into the man's protective embrace. But as eldress she had a duty to watch over the sisters and help them with just such temptations as the feel of a man's arm. Suddenly embarrassed, as if she were peeping in a private window, Rose purposely crunched a branch with her foot.

"Sarah," she called out in her sternest voice.

The couple leaped apart and whirled around to face her.

Now the man looked familiar to Rose. He might have been anywhere from his thirties to his sixties. A hard life—probably on the streets, judging from his shabby clothes—had etched deep lines in his thin face, and his pale blue eyes were haunted and red-rimmed. A drunk, or getting there, Rose thought. He looked sober now, though, and alarmed.

"Sarah, I am deeply disappointed in you," Rose said.

Sarah's round, pleasant face reddened, and her eyes filled with tears. She hung her head until Rose could see only the top of her white cap.

"Mr.——?"

"Caleb Cox, Eldress, ma'am," he answered, dipping his head in a gesture of conciliation. "We meant no harm, Eldress. Sarah, she's innocent, it's all my doing. Please don't blame her. I just never met a woman like Sarah before, so kind and gentle. I guess I pushed where I shouldn't't've."

"You understand our ways, then. You know that Sarah has taken a vow of celibacy, that she may not associate with men?"

"Yeah, I know your ways real well." With that, he flashed a glance at Sarah, turned on his heel, and trudged off through the apple trees toward the fields just south of the village. Apparently he knew how to get back to the town of Languor without following the unpaved road through the center of North Homage. Rose wondered if he'd walked all the way to the village in the first place, since Languor was eight miles away. He didn't look the sort to own a car or even a horse. Never mind, he wasn't her responsibility. Sarah was.

Tears streamed down Sarah's cheeks as she watched Caleb's retreating back.

Rose couldn't help but feel saddened. In her ten years as trustee, she had watched too many sisters stumble over the rule of celibacy. Some longed for their own children; others fell in love. Most of them lost their faith and left the Society, becoming apostates. Only a few, like Rose herself, ever returned.

As trustee, Rose had helped many apostates find a job and a place to live in the world. She would give the young ones money to start out. Those who had contributed goods or property to the community when they signed the covenant would receive some recompense, though the land remained with the Society.

Now Rose was eldress. Her responsibility to Sarah was more spiritual than practical.

"Come along, Sarah," Rose said, taking the sister by the elbow. "We'll have a private talk in the sewing room." She avoided the word "confession," which was what she knew Sarah would need to do, both for her own peace and forgiveness and to remain in the community.

After a backward glance at Caleb's back disappearing through the trees, Sarah bit her lip and followed Rose docilely.

*   *   *

"I know it was wrong to meet alone with a man from the world, and I'll accept any punishment you say," Sarah whispered. She and Rose sat close together, back at her sewing desk. Sarah sniffled, and her blotched, tear-stained face hung as though her neck had lost the strength to hold it upright. In her lap she crumpled a soggy handkerchief.

Rose was exhausted from the storm, a burst of inconsolable weeping and self-recrimination. She felt more competent to handle real estate negotiations than emotional floods. She thought about how Agatha would have dealt with Sarah. She'd have been firm, no doubt, yet always compassionate. True to the principles of the Society, and forever ready to convey God's forgiveness. She placed her hand over Sarah's convulsive ones, wet handkerchief and all.

"Sarah, it isn't so much a matter of punishment, you know that. You must confess to me, and you must mend your behavior, but just now I'm more concerned with what your actions mean. Answer me truthfully: Do you wish to leave us and go to the world?" She squeezed Sarah's hands. "Have you lost your faith?"

Sarah gasped and her head snapped up. "Nay," she cried. "Oh, nay. Eldress, please don't make me leave." She grabbed Rose's hand in a fierce grip. Rose winced as her fingers were smashed together and surrounded by a clammy handkerchief. She gently extricated her hand.

"I know how it must look to you," Sarah said, gulping hard. "I know I should not have allowed Caleb to speak to me privately or to touch me, but he is just an old friend, I promise you. He didn't mean anything wrong, he wouldn't do that. He is kind. He just wanted to help me.''

"How do you need help?'' Rose sensed a lie. Sarah's speech was too rushed, too earnest, and she was avoiding Rose's eyes.

"Well, not exactly help. He just . . . he just wanted to pass along some news about my family. Caleb's an old family friend, you see. He knew my mother.'' Sarah's voice hushed as she spoke of her mother. "He came to tell me about a family death, that's all. He was just comforting me.''

Rose frowned. "You never mentioned any other family.''

Sarah shrugged.

"Why didn't Mr. Cox come to my office first?''

"He didn't know. He just walked into the village and looked for me, that's all, just looked until he found me.''

"But he did know, Sarah. He said he knew our ways. When he spoke of you, he sounded like a man who felt more than friendship. And I saw the two of you embracing.''

Sarah hung her head and looked as if she might cry again, but this time Rose hardened her heart. There were lies in the air between them, and she meant to run them to ground.

"I'm waiting to hear the truth,'' she said. "I do not believe that a mere 'family friend,' and one who knows Shaker ways, would ask you to risk meeting him in private and even go so far as to touch you, which he would know is expressly forbidden. Sarah, who is Mr. Cox to you?''

Sarah raised her head and sat up straight, her round

face and murky eyes swept clear of emotion.

"Caleb is just a friend," she said. "He touched me only to offer me comfort."

"And what else did he come for?" Rose asked, her voice clipped.

"Nothing. I can't say."

"So there is more, after all. Why can't you say? Are you frightened?"

"It is . . . a private matter."

"A private matter? Sarah, you are a Believer. You have vowed to live a communal life, and a chaste one." Rose shook her head. "I can't let this incident go without confession, you must know that."

"I understand." Sarah's lip trembled, yet this time she met Rose's gaze. "But I cannot tell you more than I have."

"I am deeply disappointed in you, Sarah." Rose regarded her for a long moment. "I'll give you some time to think this through. Your future in the Society depends on your willingness to open your heart to confession. We'll meet again day after tomorrow, after breakfast, in the Trustees' Office." She leaned forward and touched Sarah's wrist. "Please think about your confession carefully, Sarah. I want to help you, but I can't unless I know the whole truth."

Sarah's voice shook as she answered, "I can't. Even if you make me leave, I can't tell you."

"Ah, she had a bad night, I'm afraid," Josie said, when Rose paid her daily visit to the Infirmary and asked about Agatha's condition. "But I do have an interesting tidbit to report, my dear. I did as you asked—when Agatha noticed the absence of her older journals, I told her you'd taken them to read. She smiled, my dear, as big a smile as she could manage, just like the old days!'' Josie's cheeks bunched up in her own show of delight.

''That is very good news,'' Rose said. She made a mental note to stay up all night, if necessary, to read more of the journals. Agatha clearly wanted to tell her something important.

''Is she too tired for a visit, do you think?''

''Nay, run along to her room. I'll let you go alone this time. I'm up to my ears in tonic mixing, what with these spring coughs and colds going around.'' With a wave at Rose, Josie turned back to her desk, littered with opened tins and apothecary jars containing syrups and ground dried roots.

Agatha was awake but pale and groggy. ''Don't tax yourself, my friend,'' Rose said. ''Josie tells me you slept poorly, so you rest and I'll do all the talking. As if that weren't always the way!'' She was glad to see a feeble smile, though it faded quickly. She began to stroke Agatha's forehead, hoping she might drift into sleep.

Agatha opened her eyes wide and stared at the empty shelves where her old journals had been. She pushed her forehead up against Rose's hand.

''What is it, Agatha? Are you concerned about your journals? I took them, remember? I thought you wanted me to.''

Agatha fell back against the pillow. With her left hand, she fumbled for Rose's hand, still hovering above her head. She grabbed it and squeezed. Despite her tiredness, her grip was firm. Rose was elated. She could see a change in Agatha, more clarity.

"Agatha, are you feeling well enough for me to tell you what else has been happening lately?" Agatha squeezed and gave a slight nod.

"Well, I'm in a pickle, I don't mind telling you. Sarah is in the middle of something. I found her walking through the orchard with a man, who was being much too familiar with her. Not one of the brethren, I'm thankful to say. She seemed genuinely contrite and begged to stay with us, but when I told her she would have to confess everything to me, she balked. Now I don't know what to do. She doesn't speak much of her life away from North Homage, but clearly she suffered deeply at some point. I'm not sure when or how, though. When she speaks of her mother, she seems to feel genuine affection, almost worship."

Agatha's brow furrowed, but she remained quiet.

"Sarah has seemed so at peace here," Rose continued, "and a very good Shaker as well. How can I ask her to leave? And yet how can I let her stay if she refuses purification through confession?"

Agatha's eyes closed briefly.

"But I shouldn't bother you with these problems," Rose said. "They are my job now, so I must solve them." She rocked the cradle gently. "I'll keep reading your journals, will that help?"

Agatha opened her eyes and gazed at Rose. She seemed to be tiring after her show of strength.

"There may be another way out of this mess," Rose said, patting Agatha's hand. "Perhaps I can find the man Sarah was with, talk with him, find out more about what is going on between them. It may be more innocent than it looked, after all. He looked familiar to me, so perhaps he lives in Languor. Yea, that is what I'll do, I'll speak with this Caleb Cox, and I needn't bother you about it anymore.''

Rose bent to kiss Agatha's forehead but halted halfway when she saw that her old friend's faded blue eyes had widened in what looked like alarm.

"What is it, Agatha? Do you know this Mr. Cox? Shouldn't I try to speak to him? Is that what concerns you?''

Agatha nodded her head repeatedly. Her thin chest rose and fell quickly with the effort. She made a strangled sound that conveyed fear.

Rose was puzzled. How would Agatha know this stranger? And why would she be alarmed by him? She longed to ask, but Agatha's breathing had become labored, and pink spots appeared in her cheeks. She'd had too many strokes, and Rose had no intention of causing yet another. She lifted Agatha's frail hand and held it lightly in her own.

"Quiet now, be at peace, it's all right. If you think it isn't a good idea, I'm sure there are others I could talk to instead of Mr. Cox." Rose stroked Agatha's hand and waited until she fell into an exhausted sleep. She tiptoed to the door and pulled it shut behind her. On her way out, she stopped to warn Josie that the visit had agitated Agatha.

Back out in the spring sunshine, Rose shook off Agatha's fear. She knew what to do. More than ever, she knew that she must find Caleb Cox and have a long talk with him. She hadn't exactly promised Agatha that she wouldn't seek him out. She just wouldn't tell her about it. It would only worry her.

*   *   *

Agatha's eyes snapped open as Rose closed the door to her room. She'd fallen asleep. Shouldn't have. But why? Why? She squirmed and her cradle began rocking. She cried out in confusion and fear. She froze, the rocking stopped. Cradle bed. She was ill, in bed in the Infirmary. Another stroke. She remembered now; Josie had told her.

Rose. Agatha relaxed as she thought of her young friend. Rose came to talk to her every day. Had she been here yet today? Agatha glanced at the wall, saw the empty shelf that had held her journals, and felt her mind disentangle and clear.

Rose, Caleb, Sarah, the Society. All in danger. Warn them, warn them. She tried to sit up, but her useless right side wouldn't budge. She forced herself to be still and concentrate. The journals. Rose has the journals, she'll see. She'll understand.

A wave of panic shot through her. *Nay, nay,* she thought, and heard the meaningless sounds that escaped her lips. *I kept the secret. Even from my journal. They all left. It was over, no proof. Nay, Evil will always come again. Should have known. Too late.*

She picked at her blanket and rolled her aching head from side to side on the feather pillow. The fog was moving into her mind again. She was losing something. What had she been thinking about? She screwed her eyes tightly shut and tried to concentrate.

She had to warn them. Warn Rose.

The words floated by and were gone, and Agatha fell into an exhausted sleep.

TEN

THE CRISP AIR OF SUNDAY MORNING AND PREPARA-
tions for the Sabbath celebration distracted Rose from
her plans to talk with Caleb Cox and with Samuel.
For now, her questions could wait. Worship came
first.

In quieter times, the worship service had been open
to the public. Many Believers had begun their journey
to faith with a visit to the Sabbathday service, where
they intended to jeer and mock but instead found
themselves entranced by the joy of the singing and
dancing. Today, however, recent events had convinced Rose and Wilhelm to close the service. Small
groups from neighboring Languor arrived by car or
wagon, hoping to slip through the Meetinghouse
doors, but brethren and sisters, stationed at the separate entrances for men and women, turned them away.

Rose settled onto her bench on the west side of the
large meeting room. She sat with the other sisters,
dressed in their blue-and-white striped Sabbathday
gowns, facing the dwindling group of brethren across
a large expanse of shiny pine floor. Rose felt the re-
lentless decline of their membership most acutely on
these mornings when the community of twenty-nine

adults and nine children gathered in a room that used to hold two hundred Believers, in addition to dozens of children and countless guests from the world.

At the sound of knocking on glass, she glanced toward one of the tall windows lining the two-story room. Bright eyes in a small round face stared at her with the rude curiosity of a child. The child wore a little boy's sailor hat perched on a wealth of dark curls. A well-dressed, well-fed, well-tended little boy of perhaps six or seven. Rose realized that she, too, had been staring when the boy covered his mouth with a small fist and his shoulders shook with laughter. Rose felt her own lips curve. Her smile froze as Richard Worthington's stern, patrician face appeared beside the boy. He must have been holding his son in the air to look in the window. The child disappeared, and Worthington continued to stare directly at Rose.

Rose averted her gaze, then scanned all the windows lining three sides of the meeting room. All were filled with staring faces. Now the bright, spacious room felt small and cramped, as if the world had wrapped it round in a tightening noose.

Rose exchanged a concerned glance with Josie, who sat next to her. Across the room, Wilhelm seemed impervious to the tense atmosphere. He stood to begin the service. His powerful voice began the lyrics to an old Shaker song well-known to all in the room. Three sisters and three brethren rose from their seats and joined their voices in a song welcoming everyone to worship.

Come to Zion, come to Zion, sin-sick souls in sorrow bound.

> *Lay your care before the altar where true*
> *healing may be found.*
> *Shout Halleluia! Halleluia! Praise resounds*
> *o'er land and sea.*
> *All who will may come and share the glories*
> *of this Jubilee.*

After singing the verse through twice, the six sing-ers joined together, keeping to one side of the room to provide plenty of space for dancing. Following Wilhelm's lead, the brethren removed their blue sur-coats and filed into the center of the room. Rose stood and led the sisters to stand across from the men, still separated from them by several yards of smooth floor.

The singers began again, stepping up the pace with a dance song.

> *Living souls, let's be marching on our journey*
> *to heaven*
> *With our lamps trimmed and burning with the*
> *oil of truth.*
> *Let us join the heav'nly chorus and unite with*
> *our parents.*
> *They will lead us on to heaven in the path of*
> *righteousness.*

The Believers began to dance, slowly at first, every step choreographed and executed so that the men and women formed flowing mirror images of each other. Rose concentrated on her movements, watching her own feet, even the brethren's feet, but still she felt the faces at the windows staring in on them.

After two more gentle dances the worshipers took

their seats, while Wilhelm slipped back into his sur-
coat and walked to a podium that stood between the
men and the women. He drew his spectacles from an
inner pocket in his coat and settled them on his nose,
then peered over the rims at the silent gathering. He
looked down at the empty podium as if reading notes,
letting the anticipation build.

"Cast thy minds back, brethren, and remember,"
he began quietly. Several of the older Believers leaned
forward to hear him better.

"What was thy first thought upon awakening this
morning?" He let his eyes slowly scan the room. As
always, he spoke most directly to the men, as though
only they were capable of understanding a spiritual
message.

"Was thy first unbidden thought of God? Of
Mother Ann and her joy in the face of suffering?"
Wilhelm's voice was still restrained but gathering
power like a rain-swollen river. "Was it a prayer of
thanks for the faith that binds us one to the other?
Nay," he said, with an audible sigh and a shake of
his head, "nay, I think not." He leaned over the podium, one thick hand grasping each side as if disappointment weakened him. With a deep breath, he
drew himself straight and squared his shoulders.

Rose realized that she was holding her own breath.
She forced herself to exhale. No matter how many
times she heard Wilhelm's homilies, she found herself
captured by their power. She knew his techniques,
resented them, yet fell under their spell. The reason,
she knew, was Wilhelm himself. What he believed,
he believed with such fervor that his strength, his pas-
sion, the whole force of his personality converged to

create a compelling performance. Rose always wished she could agree with him.

"Nay, brethren! I say to thee, thy thoughts are the playthings of sin!" Wilhelm's voice blasted through the tense room. Though she had expected the explosion, Rose jumped in her seat.

"We have been seduced by the world, by its comforts and pleasures, those sins as soft and tempting as a kitten's fur, yet slippery as a serpent's skin." With narrowed eyes, Wilhelm scanned the chilled faces of his people.

"In our thoughts, we are as carnal as the vilest worldly sinner ever to draw breath. We strive to perfect ourselves in our deeds, our work, and our worship, and all the while our thoughts trip freely down the path to Hell." His voice reached a rumbled shout. As he drew in his breath and raised his arm for his next blast, the crash of broken glass shattered the silence. A second crash followed, then a third.

Rose twisted in her seat to scan the room. The curious faces had disappeared from the windows. Inside the meeting room, no one moved. Even Wilhelm froze and stared, mesmerized, at one west window. A dark red liquid oozed in rivulets down the outside of the glass.

Rose shook her head slightly to break the spell. Keeping her movements slow and calm, she edged past Josie. The other Believers watched with such frightened faces that she felt like a sister in the Children's Dwelling House, chasing monsters out of dark corners. Cautiously, she peered out the window. She saw no one about on the lawn or path. On the grass under the window lay three piles of smashed glass with dark clumps clinging to their jagged edges.

Rose groaned in relief. Vandalism was always un-pleasant, but this didn't seem too threatening. As she turned to reassure the other worshipers, more smash-ing sounds startled the group into turning toward the east side of the meeting room. The sixth and final missile shattered a window and landed with a splat at Brother Hugo's feet.

Hugo stared for a moment, then lowered his bulky form on to one knee and stuck an index finger into the red mess on the floor. He raised the finger to his nose and sniffed. Then he lightly touched his tongue to his finger.

"Ha!" He grunted as he pulled his body upright. "Raspberry preserves," he announced. The silence in the room exploded into gasps and mumbling. While Wilhelm slapped his hand on the podium to bring or-der, Rose rushed across the room to Hugo. She knelt and tasted the red pulp herself, avoiding the chunks of broken glass mixed in.

"Our very own raspberry preserves, if my tongue does not deceive me," Hugo murmured, so only Rose could hear.

"I'd say someone has returned our stolen preserves in an unneighborly way," she said.

The click of the east door, near Hugo's chair, dis-tracted both of them. They looked up in time to see Brother Samuel's strong, straight back disappear. Rose ran to the nearest window. She saw Samuel sprint toward a brown car parked in the central path in front of the Meetinghouse. Two people sat in the front seat, but Rose couldn't see who they were. With-out stopping to think, she rushed toward the east door.

"Eldress Rose!" Wilhelm's booming voice stopped her with her hand on the doorknob. "Leave the world to wallow in its own filth. Our worship is not yet finished." She clenched her teeth in frustration. Wilhelm had taken her to task in front of the Society. And yet he was right. If she ran through the door, she'd be allowing the world to control them, to stop their worship whenever it wished. She wouldn't do that. With a show of calm dignity, she returned to her place and nodded to the sisters to take their seats. *Samuel will find out who they are*, she thought, as Wilhelm resumed the service. She would talk to him as soon as worship ended.

Along with the other sisters, Rose exited the west door of the Meetinghouse, steeling herself for what might be waiting. The grounds were quiet and empty. The world had withdrawn, but it had left a mess behind. The Believers spread out along the front wall of the Meetinghouse to inspect the damage. One window was shattered, and five shiny red-purple splotches dotted the white paint, chipped by the impact. The sticky substance dribbled to the ground. Rose counted five piles of broken glass, the remains of quart canning jars.

Like the others, Rose bowed her head for a few moments in silent prayer. One by one, the Believers scattered to attend to the practical problems of repair. The Meetinghouse was the spiritual core of their village and must always be clean and well maintained. The brethren, under Wilhelm's charge, went in search of white paint and brushes, while the sisters gathered cleaning equipment and scooped up the sticky broken glass.

Rose's immediate concern was of a different sort. She was puzzled by the incident. It seemed tame compared to rats in the schoolhouse and the attack on Sarah, but maybe the point was to keep up the pressure on the Shakers. If Hugo was right—and everyone agreed that Hugo's sense of taste was phenomenal—then their own raspberry preserves had been stolen with vandalism in mind. Apparently a fair amount of advance planning had gone into these ongoing incidents.

Rose wanted to know who had done this and why. She remembered reading an excerpt from Agatha's journal. Hadn't there been an incident much like this mentioned in passing? She made straight for the Trustees' Office, leaving the sisters to guide themselves in the clean-up effort.

As she passed her office, she noticed Sister Charlotte, along with all nine of the children being raised by the Shakers, camped out in a circle on the floor. Of course, the children had been at worship. They'd be terrified. She hated to delay her mission, but she poked her head in the open door. They seemed to be playing a game, led by Charlotte. Far from terrified, they were giggling and clapping their hands. Bless Charlotte, what a godsend.

Rose began to withdraw, but Charlotte saw her and signaled her to wait. Turning the children over to Hannah, one of the older girls, Charlotte hurried to the door.

"I took the children out the back door after worship, and we all ran over here. Is it safe to take them out? Is all well?''

"Under control, at least," Rose said. "Tell me, Charlotte, when you all ran here, did you see anyone?''

"Yea, indeed. We saw a car speeding out of the village toward Languor, going so fast it was stirring up a dust storm. I remember because it was the only car on the path. Everyone else must have left as soon as the trouble began.''

"Do you remember anything about the car? The color, who was in it?''

Charlotte frowned. "Brown, I'm sure, but that's all I can tell you about the car itself. I'm just dreadful about cars. They still scare me. Oh, I do remember it was quite dirty, and it looked old, not like ours. There were two people in it, but I couldn't see them well, what with all the dust they were kicking up. The passenger did look like a woman, though.''

"A woman!''

"Yea, at least that was my impression. I thought I saw piles of hair, like one of those old-fashioned hairstyles.'' Charlotte was still young enough to show a curiosity about the changing fashions of the world.

"Do you need my help with the children at the moment?'' Rose asked. "You seem to have them calm and happy. I doubt there's any danger to them now.''

Charlotte glanced back to see the children concentrating on their game, and she seemed to relax. "All right, Rose, if you say so. I'll just hope that their resilience rubs off on me. We'll be fine.''

Rose picked up her skirts and sprinted up the stairs

to her retiring room. She grabbed Agatha's 1910 journal from her small built-in cubbyhole and thumbed the pages impatiently. There it was, just as she'd remembered: *Sister Martha reported this morning that two dozen jars of plums are missing from storage . . . Not two hours later the brethren found them, smashed to pulp against the barn.* Rose knew just what Wilhelm would say if she showed him this passage— merely a coincidence. But her tingling skin told her it was more.

Samuel was lugging two cans of white paint to the Meetinghouse when Rose located him.

"I need to speak with you," she said.

"Could it wait an hour or two?" Samuel indicated the pails of paint.

"Nay, I'm afraid your memory may fade. Go ahead and deliver the paint, but the brethren can do the job without you. Then come to the Herb House. I'll be waiting in the drying room, and we can talk without prying ears nearby." She didn't dare direct him to the Trustees' Office, for fear the children were still in her office.

In no hurry now, Rose strolled alone to the Herb House, breathing in the freshness of the spring air. With its sudden explosion of new buds and sweet smells, spring always astonished and delighted her. She regretted any tension that spoiled her pleasure. Spring, she'd always thought, reflected God in an expansive mood, and she was grateful.

The Herb House—a two-story white clapboard building—stood well back from the path cutting through the center of the village. As Rose climbed to the second-floor drying room, she almost regretted her choice of a meeting place. Memories flooded her mind, memories of Gennie Malone, who had been like a daughter to her and had left the Society to live in the world. They'd spent many happy days in this room, Gennie's favorite, hanging herbs to dry from rafters and drying racks, spreading the smaller herbs on screens, and stuffing the dried products into small tins for sale to the world.

Rose shook her head at herself. Regrets were pointless, and one never knew the future. Gennie might come back someday. In the meantime, it wouldn't hurt to visit her at the Languor flower shop where she now worked. She might have overheard bits of gossip that could point Rose toward whoever was behind these incessant attacks on the Society. Rose had mixed feelings about Gennie's friendship with Languor's deputy sheriff, Grady O'Neal, but perhaps the two of them could be helpful.

The drying room was nearly bare of herbs now. Over the winter, everything had been packed and sold. To Rose's surprise, no one had yet tidied up. Bits of twine and broken dried herb sprigs littered the floor. Not enough hands to do the work, Rose thought with sadness. She lifted a flatbroom from one of the pegs lining the walls.

She had nearly finished sweeping the litter into a pile when she heard slow, heavy steps on the stairs. Samuel peered into the room, reluctance showing on his thin, weathered face.

''Ah, Samuel, come in and sit down.'' Rose beckoned him to the worktable under the east window.

Samuel hesitated, then seated himself across the

long table from her. Leaning forward, he interlaced his strong, knobby knuckles on the table. He stared at them, avoiding Rose's eyes.

Rose laughed aloud, and he glanced up, startled.

"Samuel, please do relax. You look so solemn. I'm not about to pronounce sentence, I promise you."

"Sorry, Rose," he said. But his expression remained grim.

"I saw you leave the service," Rose said. "I want to know who has been doing all this to us, and why. Tell me what you saw when you ran outside. Who was in the car?"

Samuel clenched his fingers. "I couldn't see them clearly."

"Samuel, do you know who is responsible for these incidents?"

"Nay," he said, shaking his head, "not for certain."

"But you have a suspicion."

"Rose, I wouldn't want to accuse—"

"No one is asking you to accuse. We've known one another for many years. Trust me that this is important. Tell me your suspicions. Please, Samuel. The safety of our village may depend on it."

To her surprise, when Samuel raised his eyes again, they glistened with tears. He slouched back in his chair and stared out the window.

"There is so much more I need to tell," he said, his voice low and husky. "So much that I've never told." With a deep sigh, he sat up straight and faced Rose.

"I was asked to be elder before Wilhelm was chosen. Did you know that?"

Rose nodded. Agatha had told her that Samuel had refused the invitation without explanation. More than once, both Agatha and Rose had regretted the second choice made by the Lead Society in Mount Lebanon— Wilhelm Lundel—and had longed for Samuel in his place.

"Was there something in your past that stopped you from accepting?" Rose asked. Despite her compassion for Samuel's obvious pain, she felt excited as she anticipated finally hearing the answers to questions that went back many years.

"Yea, my past," Samuel admitted. "I never confessed, you see. I could not accept a position of spiritual leadership, hear the confessions of others, knowing my own sins festered inside me."

"If there is something you need to confess, now is your chance to redeem yourself, Samuel. To free yourself."

Samuel nodded slowly. "Yea, it is time." With a deep breath, he began. "I believe that what is happening to us now began more than thirty years ago. It was 1904, and I was a young brother. I'd found my way to the Society just a few months earlier, and I thought nothing could shake my faith. Life is so simple at that age. You make up your mind, and you think, *That's that.* You believe completely in your own strength of will."

For the first time, Samuel smiled, a wistful half-smile. "Innocent hubris," he said, "yet hubris all the same. You see, that autumn a young woman arrived in North Homage, a widow with a young son. Her name was Faithfull."

He seemed to have drifted decades into the past and become lost in his memories.

"Faithfull," Rose mused. "Why does that name sound familiar to me?"

"Her full name was Faithfull Worthington."

"Worthington! Richard's mother?"

"Yea, though they had little contact. You would only have been a child when Faithfull arrived, and she did little with the children. It pained her, she said, because of giving up her own child." Samuel ran his hand over the notched surface of the worktable. "She was such a tender soul, you see. But strong in body and will."

"Samuel, did you . . . love her?"

He nodded slowly. "Yea, I loved her. We loved each other. She was gentle, giving, some said weak, but I believe she only gave more than most." Samuel's face crumpled in pain. "It was my fault, my weakness. And I compounded my own sin by never confessing. I stayed, lived as one of the brethren all these years, but I'm not worthy. I never had the strength to confess."

"Samuel, you are confessing now."

He raised his eyes, red and hollow. "There is more," he said.

"Tell me."

"We were together. We fell into the flesh. More than once, to my eternal shame."

Rose schooled her face to show no reaction. She felt little shock—it was a familiar story to her—but great sympathy. She had known love in the world, and she understood its power.

The creak of a floorboard startled them. They had

been so absorbed that they'd failed to hear footsteps ascending the stairs.

"What is this? What is going on here?" Elder Wilhelm's deep voice cut across the room from the landing just outside the drying-room door.

During the summer and fall, when herb bouquets hung upside down from every available hook and board, Wilhelm could not have seen them across the room. But now, they sat exposed. And exposed was just how Rose felt. She told herself sternly that she was eldress now and engaging in the work of an eldress.

"Well?" Wilhelm demanded, as he entered the room. "I'll ask thee again, what is this secret meeting? What has happened between thee?"

"Wilhelm!" Rose allowed shock to show this time. "You are imagining things. I assure you, there is nothing going on here that shouldn't. I have asked Samuel if he has any insights into these recent attacks on the Society."

"Attacks, hah! They are nothing but the feeble efforts of a feeble world to sap our strength. If they have an importance, they are a subject for the Ministry only. Nay, there is more here, and I demand to know it!"

Rose glared at Wilhelm in stony silence, while Samuel watched his whitening knuckles. The elder's hard eyes glittered with the power of righteous indignation.

"There is only one other reason for a secret meeting between a brother and an eldress," he said, turning to Rose. "Samuel has confessed to thee, has he not?"

Rose squared her shoulders. "You have interrupted his confession. If you will excuse us, he needs to continue."

"He should confess to me, his elder."

"Perhaps so, but he felt comfortable enough to do so with me."

"This is unacceptable." Wilhelm's voice approached sermon strength.

"A precedent has already been set," Rose pointed out, "and you are the one who set it."

Wilhelm's face reddened. Rose had silenced him by reminding him that Sister Elsa made a habit of confessing to him, rather than to her eldress. But Wilhelm was never quelled for long.

"Samuel, come with me," he commanded. "The brethren need thy help. We'll discuss thy confession later."

For a moment, Rose thought that Samuel would defy him. She willed him to do so. He lifted his face to her and sat still. But as she watched, his eyes flooded with pain and pleading, and she knew she had lost him. He stood and followed Wilhelm out of the room.

ELEVEN

"DADDY, YOU PROMISED YOU'D PLAY WITH ME TO-night. You *promised*." Rickie Worthington pouted like the spoiled six-year-old he was.

His father forgave the pout and the tiny lie—Worthington had not promised to play that evening—as he forgave his child everything. Instead, he noted with complacency the boy's aggressive stance, chubby legs planted apart, fists on hips. The effect was enhanced by the surroundings, Richard Worthington's study, decorated as a man's smoking room. Worthington sat in one of two leather chairs, which glowed in the light of a fire stoked up to ward off the damp evening chill. His cigar smoldered in a glass dish on a carved cherry-wood table between the chairs. He inhaled the pungent smoke, the aroma of power.

"Daddy's a very busy man, Rickie. I have an important meeting tonight." Worthington spoke in the gentle tone he used only with his son.

"Can I come? Please, Daddy?"

"No, Rickie, but soon. I promise."

Rickie distorted his face into an angry frown. "I don't want to wait. I want to go tonight."

"I said 'soon,' Rickie." A stern edge crept into

Worthington's voice, though his son's childish command pleased him as much as it irritated him.

The family's fat, orange tabby sauntered into the room, distracting the boy. He grabbed the cat around the middle and squeezed it to his chest. Used to such treatment, the tabby went limp, biding his time, then squirmed free and fled the room when Rickie momentarily loosened his grip. The boy giggled and raced after it.

Worthington watched his son's retreating figure. The boy would do well. He had the drive to conquer, you could see that just by the way he went after that cat. Worthington turned to his mirror to give his tie a final tug.

"You're meeting with *them* again, aren't you?" Frances Worthington watched her husband from the same stance her son had recently struck, hands on hips. Unlike Rickie, though, she remained in the open doorway, knowing she wasn't welcome in this male sanctum.

Worthington eyed his wife critically. The pose that had looked so admirable on Rickie made her look like a nagging fishwife, if an ineffective one with her slight figure and small-featured face.

"You know how much I hate it when you've been with those people. You come home all riled up, and sometimes I think you're going to kill somebody. It scares me, and it isn't good for Rickie to see you like that."

Worthington shrugged into his custom-tailored coat and gathered up some papers from his desk, ignoring his wife.

"Well, I don't want you upsetting Rickie anymore,'' Frances said, her voice traveling up the scale to peevish. "Last time he couldn't get back to sleep for hours after you came home slamming doors. If you must go, I want you to promise to come home quietly—Richard, are you listening to me? Quietly! And I heard you promise to take him along soon. I want you to stop that. I don't ever want him near those people.''

Worthington whirled around, his eyes glittering with cold anger.

"*Never* tell me where I may take my son, do you understand? Never.''

"He's my son, too.'' But the life had left her voice and she backed into the hallway.

Sensing victory, Worthington relaxed. He strode past Frances, barely bending to toss a kiss somewhere near her cheek.

He felt her eyes on him as he followed the long hallway to the foyer. He squared his shoulders as he passed under a portrait of his grandfather, one of several hanging in prominent spots throughout the twenty-room mansion. Other portraits of ancestors dating back to well before 1860, when the house was built, graced the remaining walls.

But there were no pictures of Worthington's mother, his grandfather's only child. Worthington's jaw tightened as the thought of his mother flitted through his mind. He'd loved her, in his own way, though he couldn't imagine that she had loved him back—not as fiercely as he loved Rickie. He could never willingly have given up his son to be raised by strangers.

And Frances was his wife, the mother of his child—

even if they weren't in love the way he'd once thought they were. He wanted her to understand. Pulling his hand back from the front-door handle, he turned to face her.

"Do you really think I'd do violence to anyone, Fanny? Is that what you think of me?" Frances lowered her eyes. "I only want to right the wrong that was done to me, to my family—for Rickie and you as much as me." He sighed and swiveled back to the front door. "Fanny, we've been over and over this. It's got to be done. I've got to set things right."

By the time Richard Worthington knocked on the front door of the run-down brick colonial, he'd run through all the arguments again in his head, and he'd reached the same conclusion as always. He was right to do this. There was some risk. If he got caught, it would mean the end of his banking career, maybe even worse. It wasn't worth doing for hatred alone, though his hatred fueled his determination. No, it was for Rickie. Securing Rickie's future was worth any amount of risk.

The old house had once been a speakeasy and still had a tiny peephole in the door. Worthington heard the hinged cover squeak twice as it was moved aside and then swung back into place. Caleb Cox opened the door enough for Worthington to squeeze past him into the dark hallway. He didn't greet Caleb. The man was a pathetic drunk, a weak link.

Worthington made directly for the kitchen, also dark. He knew the house well. He'd foreclosed on it, and it had stood empty until recently. As far as the bank was concerned, it was still uninhabited.

Worthington entered the dark kitchen and ignored the light switch. The electricity was off, anyway. Instead he followed the dim outline of an old wood cooking stove to a door leading to the basement. All the light and activity in the house were downstairs. Black curtains covered the small, high basement windows, and dozens of candles supplemented the oil lamps. A large printing press dominated one side of the room. Fresh flowers always sweetened the air in Worthington's own home, and he wrinkled his nose at the harsh odors of cheap candle wax, printer's ink, and underground mustiness.

Across the room, three men and one woman sat in a circle. He took his place in one of the two empty chairs. Moments later, Caleb Cox slipped into the other one. Worthington knew three of the gathering from his youth, when they had all lived at North Homage. The other two, Floyd Foster and Ned Bergson, were not former Shakers but merely businessmen hoping to eliminate Shaker competition. The Shaker apostate who ran the group didn't want Floyd and Ned to be able to identify him. He and his wife went by the names of Kentuck and Laura Hill. Worthington thought the subterfuge doomed, but the fool had his reasons. If some of the older Shakers knew the two of them were in town, they'd suspect immediately who was behind the persistent attacks on North Homage. Since it was in Worthington's best interests, he had agreed to call them only by their assumed names, even to himself.

The man everyone had been instructed to call ''Kentuck'' leaned into the circle, his fists planted on his knees. His round belly rolled forward and rested on his thighs. Flickering candlelight reflected off the balding spot on the top of his head. Worthington barely hid his distaste.

"We'll have the reports first," Kentuck said, as if he were running a business meeting. "Caleb?"

Caleb straightened from his habitual slouch and cleared his throat. *Half drunk,* Worthington thought.

"Fine, everything's just fine," Caleb said. "Sarah's been a real trooper, did just what I said, even though it—" Caleb twitched and shot a nervous glance at the group leader.

The woman called Laura leaned forward and her angular face sharpened. "What? What do you mean, Caleb? Has something gone wrong?" Her high, squeaking voice grated on Worthington's ears. To him, she looked more like a spinster schoolteacher, and he couldn't understand why she didn't make more effort to sound like one. It would help her stand up to that husband of hers.

"Shut up, Laura," her husband snapped. "Everything has gone exactly as I—as we—planned. We've got those Shakers confused and scared now. When they see what's in store for them next, they'll crack."

"Just so long as it isn't Sarah who cracks first," she said, her voice growing shrill. "I told you not to use her. I warned you not to give her that journal page. Now she knows too much."

"That's enough. One more word and you are excused from this meeting. We don't need you, anyway."

They locked eyes like old enemies. A candle wick sputtered and dissolved into a spiral of smoke. No one stirred. Finally, her gaze fell to her lap. He smirked in triumph and nodded to Caleb to continue.

"As I said, Sarah's been true blue, and she's set to do her part," Caleb said. His eyes darted nervously around the group. "I gotta say something, though. There ain't no call for no one to go hurting Sarah. She done what she was supposed to the other morning, took care of the dog and all. It ain't fair to her. She's all upset because she didn't know the meat she gave to the dog was fixed up to knock him out. And then she gets knocked out, too. She coulda got killed."

"Whatever happened to Sarah had nothing to do with us, Caleb," Kentuck said. "As I hear it, she tripped and fell down the stairs. An accident, surely."

Worthington, too, wondered how the "accident" happened. It hadn't been part of the original plan. Did someone besides himself have a separate, secret plan? He studied the faces around him. Caleb glared defiantly at Kentuck, who frowned back. Laura stared stonily at the floor. The others looked confused and embarrassed.

"I also heard that Sarah has recovered well, right?" Kentuck asked.

"Well as could be expected," Caleb said.

"Good. Then we'll carry on. Just one question, though. That eldress, Sister Rose, somehow she got hold of a copy of our first *Watcher*. You know anything about that, Caleb?"

"No, sir, not me. Not a chance. I ain't that dumb."

Worthington hid the arrogant smile he felt. Caleb may have been a moderately bright kid once, but the war and years of drink had wiped that out. He wondered, as he had before, why the older apostate used

Caleb as a go-between. Sure, they had been friends of a sort back when they had all lived in North Homage—at least, they had seemed to confer a lot in those days. Didn't Kentuck remember how unpredictable Caleb could be? Of course, he'd also make a perfect patsy should anything go wrong.

He felt the leader's eyes on him. "What's the news from your end, Richard?"

Worthington crossed his legs and watched the candlelight catch the high shine of his expensive shoes.

"I've made all the necessary preparations," he said. He had no intention of revealing to this mangy group the details of his late nights of careful calculations, and changes in bank records that would give them the upper hand with those Shakers.

"If it comes to that, we can foreclose quickly and easily. I'm assuming, of course, that actual foreclosure will be unnecessary, if the rest of you succeed in your plans." Worthington wanted to distance himself from their scheme as much as possible.

"We will succeed," Kentuck said. "But we need to be prepared for anything. Floyd and Ned, are you set for the gathering tomorrow evening?"

The two men nodded. "I've got my lines learned real good," Floyd said. He looked ready to leap up and demonstrate, but Kentuck only nodded and riffled through a few pages of notes.

"All right," he said, "The next issue of the *Watcher* goes to press tonight. We've got people riled up enough about those Shakers so we'll get a good showing tomorrow night." He raised his head and narrowed his eyes at the circle of listeners. "But it's important the Shakers not cotton on to what's happening in Languor. Everybody understand?'' Heads nodded, except for Worthington, who raised an eyebrow. The apostate leader's folksy style amused him. It wasn't real, just another role developed for this setting and audience. Even back in North Homage, Worthington had found him puzzling. He had seemed a devout Shaker, then he had left so suddenly, right around the time Worthington himself had finally gotten free, shortly after his mother died.

''Those Shakers are clever, especially that new eldress. If she catches on and starts contradicting us, folks'll get confused. They won't know who to believe,'' Kentuck said. Heads nodded again.

''Now, that *Watcher* will be ready by three A.M. Caleb will pick them up for distribution—''

If he can sober up by then, Worthington thought.

''—and you'll all give copies to the parties we've listed in your assigned parts of town. We have to work fast but real quiet. Don't leave any copies out for the wrong folks to see. Warn people not to talk about the contents to anyone who is real friendly with the Shakers. Most folks won't get involved, but there's a few might take the trouble to call over to North Homage if they got wind of our meeting.''

Worthington couldn't contain himself any longer. ''Do you really think the Shakers won't find out about this? They seemed to know about the first *Watcher* almost as soon as it came off the presses. Obviously, they have efficient sources of information. They probably have spies all over. All they care about is their own survival.'' Worthington made himself pause. He had his own plans for survival. No need to give too much away.

Kentuck rolled back in his chair and laced his fingers over his skin-tight vest. "We all agree with you, of course, Richard," he said. "They've likely got spies all over. Getting rid of the whole lot is the best thing we could do for this town, and I'm betting most folks will agree with us when they hear what we have to say. So, I'm thinking it's worth the risk of them finding out."

"I agree with Richard," Laura said, rushing to get the words out before her husband quelled her. "All we want is to get rid of the Shakers, right? So why don't we just foreclose, if Richard thinks he can do it? Harassing them, getting people all riled up against them, it's plain dangerous, has been since we pulled in that girl, Sarah."

The men stared at her. Even Kentuck was speechless. His wife usually said a few words only, or nothing. Worthington began to calculate. In fact, he agreed with her, but he didn't want to be pushed into foreclosure too early. If he had enough time, he could get what he wanted without actually foreclosing and making a significant number of townspeople angry with his bank.

"Let's go on with the original plan," Worthington said. "We need the townspeople on our side. If we foreclose too soon, it might turn the town against us, create sympathy for the Shakers."

Kentuck threw a triumphant glance at Laura and cleared his throat.

"Just to be on the safe side, no reflection on anyone here, but I'll keep the contents of the *Watcher* to myself for now." He scanned the group with narrowed eyes. "Now, we have one more problem. No need to panic, but we'll need to tread carefully. I'm sure we all remember Samuel Bickford—Brother Samuel to some of us.''

Worthington felt his chest tighten. Laura stiffened, and the others nodded.

''I reckon he saw more than he should have last Sunday. He knows us all, including me and Laura. I warned Laura not to go along on Sunday, but she did anyway. Always wants to be part of the action, thinks we menfolk won't do things right. Anyway, maybe she thought she had a reason, but never mind now, the damage is done. Samuel saw her and recognized her—called her by name, I heard him. That means he suspected I was there, too. No need to hide from him anymore, I figured; might as well take the situation in hand. So I called over to North Homage this morning and talked to Samuel.'' Laura emitted a high-pitched squawk, which her husband ignored. ''Told him we had enough dirt on him to get him booted out of the Shakers so fast there'd be nothing left but a swirl of dust to mark his place.''

''Was this wise?'' Worthington asked. ''Even if you know something about his past, how do you know he hasn't already confessed?''

Kentuck shrugged. ''Unlikely. I know Samuel. We were friends once, remember. He plays it safe, never could admit his own failings. If he'd confessed, he'd be elder by now, or trustee, or something better than plain Brother Samuel. He'll keep quiet about us.''

Still Worthington had his doubts, but he kept them to himself.

TWELVE

Sticky Kentucky nights would arrive soon enough, but for now Rose felt more comfortable in her long-sleeved winter nightgown. She slipped the worn garment over her head and settled in bed with all of Agatha's old journals stacked on her nightstand. After Samuel's interrupted confession about his relationship with a Shaker sister decades earlier, Rose was deeply curious. The affair might have been mentioned during the thirteen-year period reported in the journals that Agatha seemed to want her to read. She'd already finished the volumes for 1908 through 1910, so she picked up 1911, squirmed closer to her headboard, and began to read.

The rough binding cracked as she opened the volume, and a few bits of dry glue fell onto her coverlet. The handmade paper had yellowed and smelled faintly of mildew. The reading was slow-going and required alertness, because of Agatha's habit of using initials often, instead of names.

Rose's eyes had begun to blur when she finally found anything of interest, nestled between cheerful crop reports. It was late summer 1911.

I worry about C.C., such a troubled boy, so nervous and unsure these days. K.H. has been tak-

ing a guiding hand to him—working him long days in the fields and the Broom-makers Shop, teaching him to read and write in the free evenings—but it doesn't seem to do much good. The child always looks so forlorn and gloomy, as if his life stretched before him as a long sadness. I shall pray for him.

The incidents continue. There was a terrible screaming yesterday morning, I heard it from my retiring room as I prayed before breakfast. I ran outside and saw all the kitchen sisters scurry from the Center Family House, hysterical every one of them. They'd all arrived in the kitchen to fix breakfast only to find a dead rat hung by its tail from a wall peg. Horrible, cruel joke. We have an evil with us.

Rose felt chilled and pulled her coverlet up over her chest. Rats, again. Recent episodes in the village were not identical to Agatha's reports, but they were eerily similar. She remembered something that Agatha used to say to her: "If evil is not vanquished, it will think it has won." Had the same evil returned to fight again?

Rose ran a hand through her tangled hair, free of its daytime cap. She still wore it long, even now in her mid-thirties and as eldress, to provide warmth during the damp Kentucky winters. Or so she told herself. Her hair was her sole point of beauty and the one conceit she had been unable to release. When it fell around her shoulders at night, she could, for a moment, feel like a young girl again, instead of a woman with too many worries.

She skimmed through to the end of the journal in her hands. Aside from a small fire in the Broom-makers Shop—blamed on the hot, dry weather and piles of broom straw—nothing suspicious caught her eye.

She put the 1911 volume aside and picked up the next in the pile. Her bedside clock said midnight. Breakfast at 6 A.M. during planting season, and she had promised to help in the herb fields afterward. She would be starting the new week with too little sleep, but that was nothing new. She stretched and settled down with Agatha's observations of North Homage in 1912. Her efforts were rewarded quickly.

The new year has barely begun, and already the signs are bad. I found F. and S. in private conversation behind the Herb House. Never mind how cold it was, there were the two of them, their heads shamelessly close together, their shoulders nearly touching. I stopped them, of course, and made no bones about my displeasure and disappointment. They stammered and said they had merely run into one another. I cannot believe them, and that saddens me. I am not so old nor so unworldly that I could not see the brightness in their eyes. I have given them a warning, and I'll be watching them from now on. I pray they have not fallen into the flesh! They have been good Shakers, hard-working and kind. I told F. to meet me at the Ministry tomorrow for a thorough confession.

F. and S. could refer to Faithfull and Samuel. Her heart racing, Rose skipped through Agatha's four-page summary of how many tins of rosemary and basil and other herbs the sisters in the Herb House had prepared for sale to the world. She came to the section she sought, but she sighed in frustration. All Agatha had written the next day was:

F. was here to confess this morning. It is even worse than I feared, and still I may not know it all. There are more involved. Must talk to S. soon.

Rose flipped through page after page of everything from homily ideas to a variation on a recipe for rose-water cookies before Agatha reported meeting with S. in the office of the Ministry House.

S. has refused to confess to me, or to Obadiah, but I have been watching carefully, and I believe my worst fears are confirmed. And more. The anger runs deep. There is great danger to all of us if this is not handled quickly and well. Must pray for guidance.

The clock said 1 A.M. Rose tried to read on, but her eyelids dragged despite her curiosity. The open journal dropped against her chest, and she fell asleep.

"Eldress! Eldress, wake up! It's Samuel, you've got to get up and come to the kitchen right now, Josie said so."

At first Rose thought she must be dreaming, as if

she had fallen into Agatha's journal and was writing her own details to the skimpy story about Samuel and Faithfull. Then she recognized Sarah's voice and opened her eyes to find herself still slouched against her headboard. She winced at the crick in her neck as she reached for her clock. Five-thirty A.M. Rose noticed that the room was lit. Usually she awakened as soon as a light came on. She must have been deeply asleep.

"What is it?"

Sarah stood over her, holding Agatha's journal against her chest, her eyes wide with an unreadable emotion, grief or fear. "The kitchen sisters found him when they arrived to cook breakfast. He was just . . . just sitting there at the table, as if he'd gotten hungry and gone for a snack. The cookies were still sitting in front of him. He never even got to enjoy them." Her voice sounded faint and far away. "Samuel is dead," she said.

"What?!" Rose tossed aside her covers and jumped out of bed. "But I spoke with him only yesterday. How can this be?" She noticed Sarah begin to sway. Waving her hand toward the bed, Rose said, "Sarah, sit down, catch your breath and get warm. Why didn't you wear your cloak, for goodness' sake? I'll be ready in a few moments and you can tell me the rest on the way to the kitchen. You don't have to go in again if it upsets you." She turned to pull her work clothes out of drawers and off wall pegs. Hurriedly she dressed and stuffed her unpinned hair into her cap, where it bulged to one side. Never mind, she'd fix it later, or, more likely, forget about it.

"Come along, Sarah, let's . . ." Rose turned to find

Sarah staring down at the open journal in her lap. She was shivering. "Sarah!"

Sarah's head jerked up and she closed the book. Rose lifted the journal from her loose grasp, placed it with the other volumes, and carried the pile into her sitting room. Sarah followed obediently.

"Let's find something to keep you warmer," she said, pulling a small coverlet off the back of her rocking chair and folding it into a shawl. As Sarah wrapped the soft wool around her shoulders, Rose piled the journals into the small cupboard in the wall of her sitting room and led Sarah into the hallway.

"Has Wilhelm been called?" Rose asked as they approached the Center Family dining room. She suspected that Josie, who was no supporter of Wilhelm, would bypass him.

"Nay, I don't think so."

"Then call over to the Ministry from the hall phone, please." Rose had learned her lesson from the rat episode in the schoolhouse—no matter how difficult Wilhelm could be in a crisis, it was best not to leave bad news for him to find out from others.

Brother Samuel Bickford slumped sideways in a large rocking chair pulled up to the kitchen worktable. One arm hung over the chair arm and touched the floor. Samuel's eyes were closed, his face expressionless, as if he had slipped away peacefully during a nap. In front of him, piled on the notched wood of the table, sat three rosewater cookies. One cookie was partially eaten.

Samuel's rocking chair looked low to the ground because of the unusual height of the table, which was designed for sisters to stand and slice bread or mix ingredients. Rose thought the arrangement an uncomfortable way to have a snack.

"I left him just as he was when Gertrude found him," Josie said. She and Rose were alone with Samuel. The kitchen sisters were in the dining room, praying for him.

"There was nothing to be done for him, anyway, I'm afraid. It looks very much like a heart attack to me, but . . ."

Rose brushed her hand against Samuel's cheek. It felt slack and cool. "He has been gone awhile," she said. "Josie, did something seem odd to you? Is that why you left him here instead of having the brethren carry him back to the Infirmary?"

"Yea, though I could be wrong. Samuel was fifty-five, I know, but he was so lean and strong, no hint of heart weakness. Why, he rarely came to the Infirmary for more than peppermint tea to soothe a cold."

"Yet heart attacks do not always announce themselves, do they?" Rose asked.

"Nay, you are right, of course." Josie frowned and pursed her lips.

"Something is bothering you, isn't it? Do tell me now. I asked Sarah to call Wilhelm, so we won't be alone for long."

"It's the cookies. I've never known Samuel to eat sweets of any kind," Josie said with a rueful smile. Her own fondness for sweets was apparent from her rotund form. "For years I thought he didn't like them, and I used to tease him about it, but one day he looked very sad and told me it was penance for his sins, that he'd never touch anything sweet again. You knew

Samuel, he was so serious about keeping his vows. I can't believe he would sneak into the kitchen at night to eat cookies; I just can't.''

Rose thought of the vow that Samuel had broken many years ago. His guilt had been so strong that she could understand his spending the rest of his life making pointless vows and following them to the letter in an endless effort to atone. It saddened her that he had died without the relief that full confession and true atonement would have brought.

Without touching Samuel again, Rose studied his position and the area around him. He looked almost too peaceful, leaning sideways in the chair. Had he experienced any pain at all? Surely he would have writhed and fallen forward, or tried to get to the door to call for help from the sleeping Believers upstairs. Instead, he looked all too much as if he had sat down for a snack, eaten one bite, and died instantly. The cookies were arranged too precisely, the bite a large, perfect semicircle. No crumbs on the table or floor. The effect was unreal, like a stage set for a scene in a play.

''Let's call Doc Irwin and ask him to take a look at Samuel,'' Rose said.

The swinging door from the dining room slammed open against the kitchen wall. ''What is going on?'' Wilhelm glowered at Rose as if she must be responsible for whatever had happened. Rose stepped aside to reveal Samuel's lifeless form. Wilhelm's stern face crumpled. ''Samuel,'' he said. ''Nay, not thee.'' He bent over the body and began to lift.

''Nay, wait,'' Rose said.

Wilhelm turned in surprise. ''Sarah said he had a

heart attack. We must prepare him for burial. He shouldn't just sit here."

"I think Doc Irwin should see him."

Wilhelm's expression hardened. "Nay, no more outsiders. Josie's diagnosis is enough. There is nothing here but a heart attack. Surely we can handle our own natural deaths."

"Josie is troubled by this death, too," Rose said. "What if it isn't a natural one?"

"Nonsense. And to suggest such a thing to anyone from the world would be more than foolish; it would be dangerous. Outsiders are prone to mindless persecution and would accuse the first Believer to cross their path."

Rose exchanged a glance with Josie, who raised her eyebrows. "Wilhelm," Rose said, "did Samuel confess to you?"

Wilhelm shook his head and looked down with sadness on Samuel. "Nay, we hadn't time. He had agreed to confess, though. We were to meet this morning after breakfast."

Samuel was a good man. If he was killed, as Rose believed, he deserved better than this—to hang over the side of a chair in a cold, empty kitchen, with half-eaten cookies, the evidence of a broken personal vow lying out for all to see. That Wilhelm felt his death softened Rose's heart toward him.

"Who else knew of Samuel's intention to confess?" she asked.

"No one that I know of."

"I suspect someone did. Wilhelm, you yourself have said that these recent incidents—the broken fence, the rats in the schoolhouse, the smashed preserves—are the world trying to strike at us. Suppose Samuel's death and what happened to Sarah are somehow related to the other incidents? Suppose the world means us very serious harm? Shouldn't we do everything we can to protect ourselves, to find out what is going on?''

Wilhelm stared at the kitchen walls, where shiny copper-bottom pans, hanging from pegs, sparkled with the first light of the morning sun. When he turned again to Rose, the fatigue in his eyes made him look all of his sixty-one years.

''All right,'' he said. ''Call Doc Irwin. But I must be here when he examines Samuel.''

THIRTEEN

"NOTHING BUT A HEART ATTACK, PLAIN AND SIM-ple," Doc Irwin announced to Rose and Wilhelm. "No doubt in my mind. I'll be glad to sign the death certificate. Don't see why we need to bother Sheriff Brock over this. Remember, he's none too fond of y'all. Wouldn't do to go stirring him up over nothing." Doc snapped shut his battered brown medical case and slipped his spectacles into his vest pocket.

"I'm confused about why Samuel would eat rosewater cookies when he had vowed to avoid sweets," Rose said as the three of them moved into the dining room, away from Samuel's still body.

"Because it was a foolish vow, and he got hungry," Wilhelm said.

Doc Irwin laughed. "That would be a mighty tough vow to keep," he said, patting his own round stomach. "Anyway, Miss Callahan, I just can't find any evidence of foul play. Best to let things be."

Wilhelm fidgeted, clearly longing to do something active. He was a man whose limbs always sought motion. "I'll begin preparations for the burial," he said, pushing the end of a bench to make it line up with a long dining table. "Eat at the Ministry this evening, Rose. We have much to discuss."

130

"Did Samuel ever show signs of heart problems?" Rose asked Doc Irwin after Wilhelm had left.

"No, but those pesky things can sneak up on a man. Samuel didn't complain much, far as I could tell, so he might have had pains no one knew about. Sometimes a man doesn't want to know what his own body is telling him.

"I knew Samuel for years, you know," he said, touching Samuel's shoulder lightly. "He used to stop by the office back when he delivered herbs around to the hotels in town, twenty-five or thirty years ago now. He liked to talk about medicine and what herbs might be good for this or that. Used to leave some samples with me, trying to get me to broaden my horizons, he used to say. I'm mighty sad he's gone. We had some good talks, me and him and that other fellow he used to travel with a lot."

"What other fellow?"

Doc Irwin frowned and the furrows spread up to his bald head. "Can't quite recall, it's been so long now. I do remember he was real interested in my medicines and how they worked. He was a young fellow about Samuel's age, as I recall. But we were all young then. Is it important?"

"Probably not. Thank you for your time, Doc." But she vowed to herself to have a private chat with Deputy O'Neal soon. Perhaps he would be more open to hearing her suspicions.

Rose had not expected pangs of guilt to be part of learning to be eldress, but here she was, feeling guilty as she ascended the sisters' staircase to the second floor of the Center Family Dwelling House, then slipped across to the east side of the building, where the men's retiring rooms were located. Her heart hammered noisily, or so it seemed to Rose, but she told herself she had no reason for either guilt or fear. She was on a legitimate errand. Besides, she had waited impatiently through the noon meal and made sure that all of the brethren, as well as the hired men, had headed back to the fields for an afternoon of planting before attempting her visit to the men's living quarters.

She had been in the rooms many times before, of course, especially when she was a young sister. After the brethren left for work in the morning, sisters came through to clean and mend. But this time she was alone and trying hard not to be seen as she eased open the door of Samuel's retiring room and slipped inside.

Brilliant sunshine struggled to penetrate the white curtains still drawn across Samuel's window. Unlike Rose, who had been a trustee and needed more space, Samuel had spent his sleeping hours in a small, one-person retiring room at the far east end of the hallway. He could have had a much larger room. So few brethren remained that each could almost have had a floor to himself, though most chose to live closer together than that. Samuel had chosen the smallest room. More atonement for his sins, Rose supposed.

She took a moment to let her eyes roam around the room, not sure what she was looking for. Like other retiring rooms, this one was plain and sparsely furnished, much like her own. Contrasting with the white walls, a pine furring strip circled the room and held evenly spaced wall pegs, most of them empty. A flat-broom hung from one peg, and a clothes hanger holding Samuel's blue Sabbathday suit hung from another.

Rose opened the door of the cast-iron wood-burning stove and found it thoroughly cleaned. She was not surprised; the nights were growing warmer. A built-in maple chest of drawers reached nearly to the ceiling. Taking care to be quiet, she pulled open the drawers one by one. Her heart began to pound again. She was certainly familiar with men's clothing, having mended her share, in addition to spending time in the world. But she would have difficulty explaining to a passing brethren why she was going through a dead man's dresser. She paused and breathed deeply until the silence of the building calmed her.

Samuel had organized his belongings with a neatness that seemed excessive, even for a Believer, who was expected to strive for perfection. He owned few pieces of clothing, but he had spaced them out among the drawers so that nothing overlapped and no article was piled on top of another. Rose saw quickly that nothing unusual hid in those drawers.

She turned to the recessed storage cupboard, identical to her own. She opened the cupboard door to find a stack of four books, arranged precisely, with the largest on the bottom and the smallest on top. She picked up the top one, Benjamin Youngs' *The Testimony of Christ's Second Appearing Containing a General Statement of All Things Pertaining to the Faith and Practice of the Church of God in this Latter-day*, a well-thumbed volume published more than one hundred years earlier. Samuel's spiritual path should have led to the role of elder had it not been for his one mistake—not his sin of the flesh; that could have been forgiven and forgotten. Nay, it was his weakness of pride that had kept him alone in this tiny room and unfulfilled as a Believer. He could not bear for anyone to hear his sin.

A floorboard creaked outside the retiring-room door. Rose placed the book back as she had found it but did not dare close the cupboard door for fear a hinge would squeak. She caught her breath and waited. The sounds stopped. Was someone listening outside the door? Down the hall, a door opened and closed. Rose slowly exhaled. Merely a brethren getting something from his room. She eased the cupboard door shut and waited again. Soon she heard a door open and close once more, and footsteps creaked past and tapped down the staircase.

Rose told herself to contemplate the sadness of Samuel's life later, in prayer. Now she moved toward his bed, a thin mattress and small wooden frame on wheels for easy movement during cleaning. The coverlet had been turned down for bedtime, and a nightshirt lay across the sheet, but the bed looked as if no one had slept in it. Rose had left instructions that no one clean the room, so Samuel must have begun to prepare for bed before leaving his room the previous evening.

Finally, Rose turned to Samuel's desk, the most elaborate piece of furniture in the room. Samuel had been known for his devotion to the Shaker tradition of keeping a daily journal. According to the brethren, he often sat up writing an hour or more before bedtime. Many years earlier, Hugo, the Society's carpenter, had designed and crafted Samuel's desk especially to make his writing hours more comfortable after a day spent tilling or planting or harvesting. The basic design was called a "workstand," the same one used for all the sewing tables, with drawers that pulled out the sides rather than forward into the knees. Hugo had made an extra-large writing surface that extended out from the desk at a proper height for Samuel's long legs to move freely underneath. The writing surface swung upward to reveal a recessed area, as in a child's school desk, for storing papers and pens and books.

Rose lifted the desktop, and this time her heart pounded with excitement. Samuel would never have left the storage area in this condition. Papers were strewn chaotically, some bent and crumpled. Most of the pages contained calculations, lists, and production figures. Spare pens, pencils, and a ruler lay scattered in no order. An ink bottle with a loose lid rested on its side, and a splotch of india ink stained the paper underneath. Someone besides Samuel had been in this room. Rose pulled open all the desk drawers and found the same mess whenever the drawer held papers. A small drawer holding stationery and postal supplies was jostled but still neat.

The journals. All this—the special desk, writing materials, notes—everything existed so that Samuel could write his journals. But there were no journals. Rose reexamined every drawer and cupboard in the room, and she found not a single journal, including the one in which Samuel probably had written just hours before his death.

FOURTEEN

ROSE TORE INTO THE EMPTY TRUSTEES' OFFICE, closed the door, and paced across the room three times. She grabbed the phone, hung it up again without speaking, and returned to her pacing. Tendrils of hair escaped from her thin cap and gathered like puffs of pale red cotton around her face.

That evening she was to dine with Elder Wilhelm in the Ministry. When she'd left Samuel's room, after finding his journals missing, she had fully intended to use her own authority to insist the police investigate Samuel's death as a murder. Now she found herself in a dilemma. As Doc Irwin had pointed out, Sheriff Brock was no friend to the Shakers. If Samuel had indeed been murdered, Brock would not be inclined to look beyond the boundaries of North Homage for his killer. He could be more of a hindrance than a help in finding the truth. She could not imagine convincing him to consider any links between Samuel's death and the recent attacks on the Society, let alone incidents that happened decades ago.

Wilhelm, on the other hand, was convinced that whenever anything went wrong, the world was at fault. If she convinced him that Samuel was murdered, he would use the information as an opportunity to grandstand against the world. Rather than seek the killer through conventional means, he would shout the evils of the world from the Meetinghouse floor. She wouldn't put it past him to go out among the world's people and fault them to their faces. In the end, he might tighten the bonds among Believers, but at the expense of peace with their neighbors.

Rose suspected what Wilhelm would refuse to consider—that Samuel was probably killed because he knew something damaging. The killer might know that Samuel was a devoted journal-keeper. It would be like Samuel, who could not bring himself to confess in person, to write his sins as a way of salving his guilt. Suppose those sins, if they came to light, could damage another person—or persons?

Who else but a Shaker, one of their own, would even know where Samuel's room was located, let alone be able to sneak into it and remove his journals? Was there any other possibility?

An apostate. An apostate might have known Samuel well enough to be aware of his journals, but could he convince Samuel to meet in the kitchen, kill him, find his room, remove all the many journal volumes, and escape without being seen? Surely not. If an apostate was involved, and Rose believed it probable, it looked as if a Believer might be assisting him.

The name she had resisted thinking forced itself into her mind. Sister Sarah Baker. She had caught Sarah meeting with Caleb Cox, an apostate. Perhaps it was a coincidence. Perhaps Caleb was just a sad drunk for whom Sarah felt pity, not a dangerous man with a secret. Rose hoped so, but would not count on hope alone. Certainly Agatha, in her journal, had noted Caleb's unpredictability—assuming that C.C. meant Caleb Cox.

Rose placed a call to the Ministry House and left a message for Wilhelm with the kitchen sister. She would be unable to be there for the evening meal because neglected trustee's work called her to town. She said nothing about trying to meet with him later. She would put that off as long as possible.

In the Trustees' Office kitchen, Rose greeted the two young kitchen sisters and brewed herself a pot of rose hip and lemon balm tea. She carried a tea tray upstairs to one of the unoccupied retiring rooms on the second floor. Years earlier she had converted the room to storage for years of trustees' records that were cluttering her office downstairs. Trustees were generally meticulous about record keeping when it came to the Society's finances, businesses, and real estate. If anyone had recorded with whom Samuel traveled and worked, besides Samuel himself, it would have been a trustee.

The room had a musty, closed-in smell. Rose slid aside the plain white curtain and cracked open the window. Dust motes swirled in the sunlight. She'd ask one of the sisters to clean soon. They were always short-handed these days, and the room was often forgotten. Hugo had built the tall, simple bookcases that lined one entire wall. Otherwise, the room held only a small writing desk and a ladder-back chair. The strip of pegs lining the remaining three walls was empty. Even the broom had been pressed into service elsewhere.

She ran her fingers along the filmy spines of her

predecessors' journals until she came to 1910. Though she had started with Agatha's 1908 journal, she had found nothing pertinent until 1910, so this seemed a good choice. She also pulled 1911 and 1912, settled at the desk, and opened the first volume. She crinkled her nose at the fetid odor of mildew, the legacy of decades of steamy Kentucky summers, and pulled her sweet-smelling tea closer.

Sister Fiona had written the volume. Rose had worked beside Fee until her death several years earlier, when the Society decided that one trustee was enough for the shrinking community. Fee was a small, bright Irishwoman, with quick eyes that missed little. Ever frugal, her longhand was tiny, and she crammed as many words as she could onto each page.

Rose had drunk half a pot of cooling tea and squinted at the difficult writing for nearly an hour before she began to find what she sought. Thank goodness Fiona had not felt compelled to identify people only by their initials, as Agatha had.

Samuel checked in this morning to report on his very successful journey to Cincinnati and back. He did the trip in a circle, visiting as well all the hotels and restaurants in Languor, Lexington, Frankfort, Louisville, and Covington—avoiding, of course, the less reputable establishments known to be scattered about. He took young Klaus along and kept a close eye on him, but no problems arose. They were greeted warmly by most, if not all, but that's to be expected. They report the following sales:

Rosemary, sage, oregano, thyme, and dill: 72 dozen tins
Candied angelica root: 138 boxes
Applesauce: 254 jars
Raspberry, sour cherry, and peach preserves: 311 jars

All in all, a most productive trip. Samuel said that Klaus will do well enough as a traveling companion, but I had the feeling he was holding something in. All did not go well between them, I fear. I'm wondering if it was not so easy for Samuel to keep the lad from straying. Perhaps I'll keep him home next time and send another companion with Samuel.

Rose rubbed her eyes. She poured another cup of tea, now cold, and opened Fee's 1911 journal. This time she skimmed through the early section to the spring, when Fee returned to the issue of Samuel and his traveling companion.

Sometimes the brethren disappoint me no end. My word, do we sisters act this way? I shouldn't say these things, I know it well, but may the Lord forgive me, I'm losing my patience! Klaus is complaining of Samuel—he isn't working hard enough, he isn't where he is supposed to be, he is secretive. And Samuel—well, he is indeed secretive. He will say nothing. Poor old Elder Obadiah, his heart is with the spirits, he never could handle squabbles among the breth-

ren. But it's clear as clear I'll need to be sending someone besides Klaus along with Samuel this spring! Those two would kill each other, never mind their vows of pacifism. There are so few brethren and all have their special tasks, I've none to spare. I'm thinking of young Caleb, perhaps. He has had some troubles, poor lad. Agatha warns me against giving him too much responsibility, says he has two faces, and one of them can be turned too easily to evil. But perhaps it would do him good to learn a new task, and Samuel would be kind to him. I worry that Klaus has taken Caleb under his wing, so sending him with Samuel might worsen the situation. Oh, I've no patience at all with this nonsense! I'll send Caleb, and that's the end to it.

Rose read through to the end of the volume, her eyes blurring from the cramped handwriting. Nothing struck her until the last page.

Must remember to speak with Agatha about Evangeline and Faithfull. Can't get those two to stop squabbling long enough to keep decent records of the tonics they give out at the Infirmary. I certainly hope Josie returns soon from her nursing course in Cincinnati. Why she thought she needed more training, I can't imagine, when we need her so much here, and I can't get a thorough list of the herbs and medicines the Infirmary is using so we can keep up with needs.

Klaus? Was he perhaps the companion of Samuel's that Hugo had mentioned? The one who left to work on the *Cincinnati Enquirer*?

Samuel, Klaus, Caleb, Evangeline, and Faithfull. Rose tucked the third volume, for 1912, under her arm, picked up her tea tray, and hurried down to the kitchen. She might just have time to track down the full names of all these Believers and still make it into Languor before everyone in town had settled down to the evening meal.

To become a part of the Society, each Believer signed the covenant, a document outlining the religious beliefs and communal rules of the Society. Each village had its own copy, sometimes altered slightly. North Homage kept its covenant safe in the small library of the Ministry House, where few visited. Visiting was not forbidden to Believers, only unnecessary. Most were far too busy with their daily tasks to take time for spiritual reading and contemplation. They relied on their Ministry to provide them with spiritual insight and direction.

Wilhelm himself spent little time reading spiritual literature. His beliefs never wavered, and he preferred work and action to contemplation. Rose entered the library confident she would not encounter him there, nor elsewhere in the Ministry House. At this time of day, he would be in the fields, planting with the rest of the brethren and many of the sisters. But just to be private, she closed the door and left the curtains drawn.

The covenant and the signatures of those who had signed it since North Homage opened in 1817 were kept in a small drawer in a maple desk. Rose extracted the document, as well as a pen and paper, and settled at the desk. She began at the signatures for 1910 and worked backward, hoping that the Believers she sought had all joined the Shakers at North Homage. If they had joined at another Shaker village and simply moved here, their signatures might be missing.

This time her aching eyes had to contend with a variety of handwriting styles, ranging from Xs, followed by an elder or eldress's printing of the name, to fancy curlycues. With only nine years to examine, though, the task didn't take long. She found all the names except Samuel, who, she knew, had come to North Homage in 1904, as Pleasant Hill, Kentucky, declined. The apostates' names were Caleb Cox, Klaus Holker, Evangeline Frankell, and Faithfull Worthington. She folded her list and stuffed it in the pocket of her work dress.

The afternoon was well advanced by the time Rose drove the Society's black Plymouth the eight miles to Languor. She wanted to have her long-delayed chat with Mr. Caleb Cox. She didn't know where he lived, and had no wish to ask and call attention to herself. If Caleb didn't live on the streets, which was possible, he would most likely live in the town's one boardinghouse, located on the east side of town, close to the perimeter and away from the wealthier homes.

She drove quickly through the poor outskirts of town, where the still shiny automobile attracted curious stares from thin, dirty children and their equally thin, weary parents. Arriving in another section of town, less ramshackle but still seedy, she parked under the arching branches of an elm tree and rang the boardinghouse doorbell.

"I have an appointment to meet with Mr. Caleb Cox," she said in her deepest, most commanding voice, as if she already knew he lived there.

The matronly, middle-aged woman who answered the bell looked her up and down as if she didn't allow Rose's sort to cross her threshold. The warm spring weather had convinced Rose to leave her distinctive blue wool Dorothy cloak in her retiring room, but she knew she stood out in her long, loose cotton work dress with the white lawn kerchief crisscrossed over her bodice. As always, she wore her woven palm sugar-scoop bonnet over the white cap that covered her hair.

Rose swallowed her self-consciousness and repeated her request. The woman blinked slowly and drew back into the dark entryway. Rose stepped inside. She noticed the smell first, a dankness from years of too much sweat and too little air, overlaid by the sharp odor of ammonia. She followed the woman through a long corridor lit by a dingy chandelier in which only a few bulbs still shone. The peeling wallpaper was a rich burgundy with a raised design that, Rose suddenly realized, represented naked young men and women gamboling through hills and valleys. Rose did not shock easily, but she felt her cheeks grow warm and shifted her eyes to the staircase. Now she remembered. This building had been a bordello until around 1914, when its customers went off to war. The new owners had never bothered to redecorate.

The silent woman led Rose up the ornately carved staircase, which was lovely but in need of a good sanding and staining. They reached a room on the third floor. She knocked loudly.

"Caleb. Company," she said, and left without another glance at Rose. After several moments of scraping sounds, Caleb Cox opened the door and squinted at her with red-rimmed, unfocused eyes. Slowly he took in her garb. As comprehension dawned, he straightened his hunched back and his eyes widened.

"Eldreth, ma'am," he slurred. His pretension of sobriety was further doomed as soon as he opened his mouth and released waves of whiskey fumes.

"I wish to speak with you briefly, Mr. Cox. May I come in?"

"Uh, sure."

Caleb tottered backward and allowed Rose to enter. She cleared the doorway and put some distance between herself and Caleb, both for propriety and to avoid his sour breath. She glanced around her. No brothel furniture had found its way into the small room. Dim light from one small, grimy window revealed an army cot covered with a rumpled, moth-eaten wool blanket; a rickety wood chair over which was tossed the patched jacket he had been wearing when he met Sarah; and a scratched pine table with a broken leg supported by a scrap of wood. An upturned orange crate next to the cot held two bottles of Jack Daniels, one nearly empty.

Rose remained standing. With luck, this visit would be over quickly. She longed to return to the clean, bright rooms of North Homage.

"Mr. Cox, I'm afraid I must be blunt. How well do you know Sister Sarah Baker?"

Caleb wilted onto the cot and grabbed the nearly

empty Jack Daniels. He took a long swallow. "Jus' what she told you," he mumbled, staring at the bottle. "Whatever she told you."

"What did she tell me, Mr. Cox?"

Caleb directed his bloodshot stare in Rose's direction. "Am I supposed to know that?" He looked again at the bottle as if it were involved in the conversation. "How'm I supposed to know that?" he asked with more certainty.

"Mr. Cox, if you and Sarah are both telling the truth, your stories will be the same, will they not? Just tell me the truth."

"Tryin' to confuse me."

"If you would put away the bottle, you would not be so easily confused. How much of that have you drunk?"

Belligerence seeped into Caleb's drunken stare. For the first time since meeting him, Rose felt a spark of fear. What did she really know of him?

"None of your business," Caleb said. "Just need a sip now and then." He squinted at the low level of whiskey left in the bottle, and his face fell as if his mother had abandoned him.

"Don't put as much in a bottle as they used to," he said. His eyelids dropped in a lazy blink. Rose suspected he wouldn't be conscious much longer.

"Never drink when I'm with Sarah. No ma'am, not around Sarah." Caleb sniffed, and his lower lip quivered.

"Nay, of course you wouldn't drink around Sarah," Rose said, hoping to keep him on track. "Because you don't want to hurt her in any way, do you?"

"No, ma'am. No, sirree. Never hurt Sarah." He took an awkward swig from the bottle.

"Because you care for her, don't you? You love her."

Sudden tears spilled down his cheeks and dropped off his stubbly chin. "Sarah, she's an angel. A pure angel. In my whole life, no one ever understood me like her." He upturned the whiskey bottle and gulped until he'd drained it.

Rose knew her time was short now. "Mr. Cox, Sarah and I need your help."

Caleb narrowed his eyes at her and swayed sideways. "Wha—? Sarah needs me?"

"Yea, Sarah and all her Shaker sisters and brothers. We need you to tell us what you know about the apostates, the other people like you who have left our faith and are living here in Languor. We have reason to believe that some of them are trying to hurt us, maybe even to hurt Sarah. Please, if you know what is—"

Rose barely had time to plunge sideways and curl up in a ball on the floor as Caleb, with a sudden surge of energy, waved his empty Jack Daniels bottle and flung it against the wall in back of where she had been standing. The bottle smashed on impact with the wood doorframe, and knife-sharp shards flew back into the room. Rose felt slight pricks as a few pierced the sleeves of her cotton dress.

"Shakers! Them damn Shakers, it's all their fault!" Caleb shouted.

The room reeked of whiskey, and no doubt her clothing would, too, but right now Rose was more concerned with learning what she could from Caleb, then getting as far away from him as possible. Cautiously, she straightened. Caleb was struggling to open the fresh bottle of Jack Daniels.

"Just tell me one thing, Mr. Cox, and then I'll be glad to leave you alone." She edged backward toward the door. Caleb stopped his fumbling and frowned at her.

"Tell me why you are angry with the Shakers."

"Ruined my life," he mumbled. "Damn Shakers ruined my life."

"But how? How did we Believers ruin your life?"

"Just did, that's all. Always keeping after me, like I couldn't do a damn thing right. Now ruining Sarah's life. My sweet Sarah." Again instant tears appeared and tumbled downward. "Keeping her a prisoner so's we can't be together. But I'm gettin' her away from them. I got a way to do it." He glared at Rose. "I got a way, and I got friends." He got the bottle open and took another long gulp. Pale golden liquid dribbled from the corners of his mouth. His eyelids shut, and he fell backward on the cot, the nearly full bottle pouring whiskey on his stomach and down onto the blanket.

Rose pried the bottle from his hand and placed it on the orange cart. She hated to leave it for him to drink again when he awakened, but she would never be able to explain walking out of the house with an open bottle of Jack Daniels. She must leave Caleb to wrestle his demons without her interference.

She turned to leave. As she passed the table, she saw a pile of papers. The top sheet appeared to be a notice of some sort, and the typeface looked familiar. She picked it up. It read:

To our Languor Neighbors and Friends:
Are you worried about enemies among us?
Are your businesses being ruined by unjust practices?
Are you frightened for your children,
that they might be spirited away from your loving arms
and forced to live an Unnatural life?
Do you want to keep this great land of ours
free from the icy fingers of evil?
Then join us tonight, 7 P.M.,
at St. Christopher's Episcopal Church on Beech Street.
There is a way to keep Languor safe!
Come and find out how!

Rose now recognized both the writing style and the typeface. The author of this notice was the creator of the *Languor County Watcher*. She folded the paper and stuffed it in her pocket. She riffled through the pages to see if they were all the same. Wedged underneath the bottom page was a smaller, yellowed piece of paper, handwritten, with one ragged edge, as if it had been ripped from a pamphlet or book of some sort. She skimmed through it.

Sweet Faithfull died in her sleep last night. The Infirmary sisters attended her at the end, and Evangeline said it was a gentle death, that her heart simply gave out, but she said that only to soothe my pain. There was no need. My pain is soothed by anger, for I know the truth, that she did not die gently. She was taken from her body while it was still strong and beautiful. My own heart is spent, but I will live on anger the rest of my days. And though it may take the rest of my days, I will bring to justice the man who did this.

Richard is only a boy, but I can tell he suspects something, too. I can see it in the way he holds back and watches everyone. He must know his mother was strong and full of health and would never have slipped away in her sleep. When the time comes, he will be an ally. And the time will come.

Rose pushed the small paper back under the leaflets. No matter how drunk Caleb might be now, he would surely miss that intriguing page. Never mind, she would remember those words. Clearly they came from an old Shaker journal. Was this why Samuel's journals were stolen—because they pointed to Faithfull's murderer? Rose was unable to tell if this was Samuel's handwriting, but the anguished and literate style could easily have been his.

Caleb groaned and began to cough. Rose left the room as quickly as she could without crunching on broken glass.

"Rose! How lovely to see you, but what on earth have you been into?" Gennie Malone's expression was caught between shock and amusement. "There aren't enough flowers in the whole store to cover that . . . fragrance."

Rose had grown accustomed to the whiskey smell embedded in her clothing and was no longer aware of it. "I'll tell you the whole sad story soon enough," she said. "But let me look at you first." She hugged Gennie and then held her at arm's length. Gennie was eighteen now, and developing an air of confidence and serenity, despite her concern for Rose. Her auburn hair was fashionably bobbed and a riot of curls.

"Come along to the back room," Gennie said. "Customers can shout if they need me."

She led the way through a curtained doorway to a littered workroom. Rose paused to breathe in the heavy sweetness of fresh flowers. She saw white roses scattered on the table, but their delicate fragrance was overwhelmed by the heady perfume of a vase of white lilies. Everywhere she looked, she saw white flowers.

"Gennie, don't you use colors anymore?"

Gennie laughed, a throatier sound than the giggle Rose remembered and missed. "Of course we do. But these flowers are for a wedding."

"Ah, of course." Rose reached out and brushed her finger along a rose petal. She knew all about weddings in the world, had almost had one herself at eighteen. But it was a long time since she had thought about that.

"Let me show you my herb project," Gennie said, taking Rose's arm, "and then I want to hear why your dress smells like a distillery." She led the way to a sunny window. A long table held rows of small pots, each containing a lanky herb plant reaching toward the light. Many of the plants were in bloom, with long sprigs of tiny flowers—lavender, pale purple oregano, and faint blue rosemary.

"These are the seedlings we ordered from North Homage months ago. I know they look a bit scraggly just now," Gennie said. "But I'm trying to get people used to the idea of herb flowers in bouquets. They are healthful, inexpensive, and not nearly so likely to make people sneeze in the middle of a wedding ceremony.'' She gently fluffed the rosemary stems to release their pine-like fragrance. ''I know that you would never use flowers for such a frivolous purpose, but you must admit, it makes business sense.''

''Indeed it does,'' Rose said, regretting, as she often had, that Gennie would not be following her as North Homage's trustee. ''And you would be surprised—from what I'm hearing of other Shaker villages, if it weren't for Wilhelm, we would all be hanging pictures on our walls and gathering bouquets for our rooms. Maybe it wouldn't be so bad for us, after all. God created such beauty. Perhaps He means for us to enjoy it.''

''I won't tell Wilhelm you said that.''

''Thank you.''

''Now, tell me your story.''

Without comment, Rose drew the lurid announcement from her pocket and handed it to Gennie, who read it through with a deepening frown.

''Where did you come by this? I haven't seen it.''

''I suspect it was written by a group of apostates, and they must be limiting their efforts to people they identify as unfriendly to North Homage.'' She told Gennie about her encounter with Caleb Cox.

''Rose, I grew up under your wing, and I know you. You are planning to attend this . . . this meeting, aren't you? You mustn't, truly.''

''Gennie, dear, I must find out everything I can about these threats to our survival. Who else can—or will?''

''Please talk to Grady first—please.''

Rose winced as Gennie clutched her arms where

the shards of broken whiskey-bottle glass had pricked her.

"What is wrong? Have you been injured?" Gennie put her hands on her hips and frowned at Rose, who felt the sternness, despite her five-inch height advantage. "Rose, I insist you talk to Grady."

A bell tinkled in the outer room. "Oh, that's a customer. Look, Grady is expecting me to call about now, so I know he's in his office." She picked up the telephone receiver and spoke to the operator. "Here, he's coming on the line. Tell him what you've told me." She handed the phone to Rose and slid between the curtains to the salesroom.

"Tell me the address slowly," Grady said, after Rose had repeated her story to him. "And, for heaven's sake, Rose, don't go there alone. Just stay home. I'll take care of this."

"Will Sheriff Brock let you?"

"Harry's gone up to Ohio to fish with a buddy."

"This seems an odd time to leave, while we're in the midst of these frightening incidents."

"Between you and me, I think that's why he left. He's used to the sheriff's job being easy, like it usually is around here. He just doesn't want to deal with y'all anymore."

Grady's candor intrigued Rose. She wondered how long it would be before he tried to unseat Harry Brock as county sheriff. Not long, she hoped.

"Anyway, you stay put, Rose, do you hear me? You're not listening, I can tell. Look, I'll get to that meeting myself, God willin' and the crick don't rise, and I'll find out what's going on."

FIFTEEN

THE LITTLE-USED STAIRCASE TO THE TOP FLOOR OF the Trustees' building creaked as if it objected to un-expected feet upon it. The sisters and brethren were all at the midday meal, or Rose hoped they were. But just in case one had stayed behind, she climbed the steps on the balls of her feet to keep her heels from clanking against the wood. She wasn't doing some-thing wrong, she told herself, only difficult to explain.

She reached a large attic room warmly lit in the center by a skylight. With its usual economy, the So-ciety hadn't bothered to run electricity to this floor. It was so rarely used anymore.

An entire wall was lined with built-in drawers and closets, each with a number plate just above the han-dle. Until the last decade, inhabitants of the Trustees' Office had stored their off-season clothing in this attic. Now, since only a few sisters lived in the building, they simply used empty rooms for storage. The attic held only clothing of the world worn by Believers when they first arrived in North Homage.

Rose went directly to a closet near the middle of the west wall. She swung the door open and began sorting through the dresses inside, sliding the hangers aside as she searched. She worked quickly. If anyone mounted the stairs now and caught her riffling through these particular clothes, there'd be questions for sure. Rumors, too, she supposed. Everyone would wonder why their eldress had taken a sudden interest in clothing from the world.

Most of the dresses had been neither stylish nor new when they'd been worn by women who became sisters after living some years in the world. Several probably should have been turned into rags. In fact, all the dresses should have been given to charity, but Rose had thought they might be useful to the sewing-room sisters. But then she'd forgotten about them. There was no excuse for such an oversight, of course, but it certainly had turned out lucky in the end. She only hoped her mission would turn out as lucky.

Her evening visit to Languor would be riskier than she'd hoped. Grady wouldn't be there. Just as Rose had returned from visiting Caleb and Gennie, Grady had called her to tell her he and the only other officer in the small Sheriff's Department had been called to deal with a suspected child kidnapping in a far-flung corner of Languor County. He'd begged Rose, ordered her, to stay home. She had listened politely and promised nothing. In fact, she preferred to go alone. She suspected that the appearance of a sheriff's deputy at the meeting would surely put the apostates on their guard, and she would be less likely to learn their plans.

"Ah, here's one that might work," Rose whispered. She extracted a brown gabardine shift with a straight cut. She remembered Sarah Baker arriving in this dress two years earlier. It looked like a 1920s style, so it might have belonged originally to Sarah's mother. Well, never mind, Rose thought, it's made for a tall woman, so it might do the trick. Sarah was plumper than Rose, but wearing a belt around the middle would hide the extra fabric and update the style, too. Most important, the dress was dark and plain. Perfect for what Rose had in mind.

The small Episcopal church filled with whispering men and a few women. Rose slipped inside and settled in a corner of a back pew. She bowed her head to pray. This wasn't her church, but she still felt it to be holy space, and she needed strength and guidance. She also needed to calm herself. Her nerves had been ready to spasm at the slightest sound since she'd left North Homage. Rather than lie, she had taken the Society's Plymouth without comment while everyone ate a late evening meal after a long day of planting. If they missed her, they'd assume she was dining with Wilhelm in the Ministry dining room. Wilhelm would assume, from her note, that she was doing trustee's work in town.

She had pulled on the loose brown dress in her room, smashed her hair under a scarf covered by a bonnet, then wrapped herself in her long wool cloak. She chose a quiet moment to slip from her room and around to the west side of the Trustees' Office, where the car was kept. After arriving in town, she had left the telltale Shaker bonnet and cloak in the car.

Getting back would be a different matter. She would have to wait until very late and hope that no one had tried to find her after the evening meal. She counted on general physical exhaustion to send everyone to bed quickly and with closed windows, since the evening had turned windy. Rain would probably arrive before Rose had to trek the five blocks she had put, just to be sure, between the church and the Society's distinctive black, almost-new car.

The Episcopal population in Languor County was tiny compared to the Baptists. The county supported only one Episcopal church, and this was it. Rose wondered why such a meeting would be held here instead of in one of the many Baptist churches. Then she remembered. Most of the wealthier farmers and businessmen were Episcopalian. Richard Worthington was a deacon in this very church. He might be here tonight. Every nerve alert, she thought about the danger of being recognized and about how she had taken care to be alone. She glanced behind her at the open front door. She could still leave. It would be wise to leave. But there was no other way to discover what the Society was up against.

People filled in the pews clear back to where she sat. Could all these people truly hate the Shakers and want to drive them from the county? The crowds closed around Rose without showing curiosity in her. She was glad she'd thought to wrap her curly red hair in the brown silk scarf. The dimness of the church helped, too.

The whispering quieted as three people entered the chancel from the sacristy door. Rose recognized the man leading the small group as the church's rector, the Reverend Geoffrey Sim, though he wore street clothes rather than his usual cassock and stole. She had spoken with him on several occasions about ideas for providing food and clothing for the Depression-battered poor of Languor, and she had found him a kind and sympathetic man. She would not have expected him to be involved in a meeting like this. He crossed to the center of the chancel, bowed to the altar, and turned to face the audience.

He was followed by a tall woman, then a man, both strangers to Rose. With a brisk step and ramrod-straight back, the woman crossed in front of the altar without glancing at it and sat in a chair facing the pews. She had long gray hair piled on top of her head and surrounded by tight pincurls. Her body was all sharp angles in a severe navy-blue suit. As her cold eyes skimmed over the heads of the audience, her mouth tightened in a thin, down-curved line, as if she were about to discipline a group of unruly school-children.

The man who completed the trio took a chair to the priest's right. His eyes flickered toward the woman and then scanned the crowd, face by face.

Rose ducked her head behind a woman with a large hat. Though she didn't recognize the man, he might know her. Someone could have pointed her out to him at some time, especially if she was considered a leader of the enemy.

When the hat in front of her dipped to one side, Rose studied the man briefly. He was no taller than the woman, but while she seemed designed to use space efficiently, he took more than his share. He had the look of a muscular man gone to fat. A month in a Shaker village would do him no end of good, Rose thought. His arms showed evidence of some remaining strength, but most of his chest muscles had slid into a pool of fat at his belly. Still, there was nothing jolly or slothful about the man. His eyes narrowed in a way that tightened the knot in Rose's stomach.

The stream of arrivals finally thinned and the heavy double doors clanged shut. The chattering died away as the priest stepped forward and raised a hand in benediction.

"Let us pray . . ."

A sea of heads bobbed forward. Rose bowed her head, too, but she intended to say her own prayer for her own reasons.

"Lord," began the priest, "bless your followers in the endeavor they are about to undertake. Be with them as they struggle against any forces of evil in our midst. Help them to know Thy will and to do Thy will in all things. Amen."

Rose found little to object to in this prayer and added only that she hoped God's will included the immediate survival of the North Homage Shakers. She felt sure that God recognized evil when He saw it and that somehow He would convince these people that the evil in their midst came not from the Believers, but from their own hearts. She relaxed slightly, ready to leave the problem in God's hands.

What followed shattered any hope Rose had that the situation would dissolve into peace and goodwill.

The priest turned on his heel and disappeared through the sacristy door, as if to distance himself quickly from what was about to occur. The man in front heaved himself to his feet and planted himself in the space the priest had vacated. He took his time, surveying the crowd, giving quick nods to faces he recognized.

"Evenin', friends," he said with a smug grin.

"Y'all are a welcome sight, I don't mind telling you." The crowd murmured their greetings.

"Ned, good to see you. How's the wife and kids? The baby over that croup? Good, good."

He's enjoying this, Rose thought. He's feeding on it. Despite the folksy language, Rose heard an educated, cultured voice, with a bland northern accent putting on the trappings of a hill-country drawl. He may have grown up in Kentucky, but he'd clearly spent many years elsewhere. And there was something familiar about his choice of words.

Rose glanced behind him to the woman. She sat as if she had a fence post for a spine, but her grim expression had been replaced by a moue of distaste. Whether for the situation or for the man in front of her, Rose couldn't tell.

"Y'all know why you've been invited here, I reckon."

Nods and murmurs of assent rippled through the crowd.

"The wife and me"—he jerked his head toward the woman behind him—"we grew up here in Languor County, same as most of you. The name's Kentuck, Kentuck Hill. Named after this great state, I was. The wife's name's Laura."

The names aroused Rose's suspicions. Kentuck Hill was too convenient a combination, and Laura sounded like the wishful thinking of a plain but secretly romantic woman. Rose guessed these two were "Mr. and Mrs. Languor County," editors of the anti-Shaker *Languor County Watcher*, who also exhibited a penchant for geographical identities. It also explained the familiar ring of Mr. Hill's speech. Could this be Klaus

Holker as well? Rose noticed that, in common with the anonymous editorialist, Mr. Hill referred to everyone as "my friends." Everyone, presumably, except the Shakers.

"Laura and me," Mr. Hill continued, "we know what it's like trying to scrabble out a living from the dirt when the weather's too hot and dry and everybody's too poor to buy what you're selling anyways."

His friendly grin transformed to a scowl. "You got kids to feed, and it hurts to watch 'em go to bed hungry, don't it?"

The responses were louder this time. A man two rows in front of Rose jumped to his feet.

"Damn right it's hard," he shouted, poking his hat in the air. "I got my ma living with us, too, and I can't feed her neither."

Kentuck Hill nodded slowly. "Yes, my friends, we can see what you've endured. We know what you've been suffering." Like a puppeteer of emotions, he raised the crowd's anger, then soothed it by softening the tone of his voice.

"And do you know why you've had all this suffering here in Languor County when the rest of the country doesn't have it as bad?" He spoke now barely above a whisper, but his voice penetrated every corner of the room.

"Because you, my friends, have Shakers for neighbors. The wife and me, we've traveled a lot in the last few years, and we observed something real interesting. There's other Shakers, you know, besides these you got here. And you know what? Every place there's Shakers, we saw poverty much worse than in the places that kept 'em out. Now, why do you suppose that is?'' He beamed at the crowd as if they were all bright children who would puzzle out the right answer soon. Rose cringed as his lies went unchallenged.

"It's them Shakers, that's why!" shouted a man in front, right on cue. "They're undercutting me right and left. I'm about to lose my business 'cause of them."

When the man stood, Rose recognized the bald head and small frame of Floyd Foster, the town's greengrocer. He overcharged outrageously, often refused credit to the town's poorer folks, and was in no danger of bankruptcy as far as Rose could tell. She seethed. How could she keep quiet and listen to these vile, vicious lies about her people? But why was this "Mr. Hill" making up such falsehoods? What good would it do him and "the wife"? Rose had to listen to find out, no matter how much the lies enraged her. She clutched the edge of her pew to keep herself from leaping up and denouncing the crowd.

Her patience was to be tried even further. At a glance from her husband, Laura Hill left her chair to stand primly beside him, her fingers interlaced at waist level.

"My wife, Laura, has a few things to tell you. These are facts you may not know and . . . well, friends, I don't mean to alarm y'all, but your families' lives could be at stake here. We just wouldn't feel right if we kept this to ourselves." With a saintly nod, he stepped back a pace to give Laura the floor.

The woman trembled visibly and darted nervous glances into the crowd, then down at her feet.

"I want . . . I want you to understand about the

children," Laura stammered. "The children are so important. Many of you are parents, and you love your own children deeply. I myself was never blessed with the children I so longed for, but I know in my heart what it is to love a child. You would do anything for your children. You would rather die than let anything happen to them. And, oh, how it hurts when you cannot even give them food enough to fill their little stomachs."

Laura's high-pitched voice sounded childlike, yet there was an intensity about the woman that Rose recognized from her years as a Believer. Some Shakers were practical about their faith, preferring to demonstrate it mostly through their deeds and thoughts. Rose considered herself one such.

For some, though, their faith burned through their hearts and demanded fervent expression. Such were the early Believers, who endured beatings and the dangers of an uncivilized territory to spread their faith. Laura's eyes held that light. But she was talking about saving children rather than souls.

"These Shakers," Laura continued, "do we really know what they do with the children we so trustingly let them raise? Some of you have sent your own children to their school, and now you know what can happen to them. Filthy, vicious rats! Attacking your own innocent little children!"

Laura's voice broke as her breath caught in a sob. The tears were genuine. This woman lived for children, yet had none of her own. *What must that do to a woman?* Rose thought. Kentuck jumped up and put his arm around his wife's shoulders. With an air of tenderness, he whispered a few words in her ear. She sniffed and nodded. He led her to her seat on the stage and turned back to the crowd held spellbound by the drama.

"I know you folks will understand. My wife is a sweet soul, and she just gets all upset at the thought of those Shakers and what they might be doing to Languor's children, not to mention the innocents who must live under the Shakers' control. I know y'all feel just the same."

Heads nodded and voices murmured in assent.

"Then it's time we did something about it, isn't it? It's not just for our businesses, that put food on the table for our children, but for our children's very lives!"

A man across the aisle from Rose jumped out of his pew. "Darn right, it's time to do something!" he shouted. Rose slid down in her seat as she recognized the thin farmer who had challenged her during her meeting with parents after the rat incident.

"It was one of my kids in that schoolhouse with them rats. He coulda been bit to death—one little girl was bit, you know—and them Shakers just let it happen. I'm a poor man, but I protect my own. I'd shoot any rat that come near my kids. I'd never let 'em breed like that right on my land where they could hurt my family. That Shaker place is nothing but a filthy hellhole, and we oughta clean it up, get rid of those people forever."

"Yeah, he's right," said the man right next to Rose. Others jumped up, exclaiming and shaking fists in the air. People began to spill into the aisles. Rose stood, too, and began to edge out of the pew, keeping her head down to avoid being recognized. Moving slowly, she eased backward through the growing crowd and reached the narthex, inside the entrance to the church. Just before leaving the building, she turned and glanced back at the people shouting and pushing toward the man standing in front of the altar. Kentuck's arms extended outward in a calming gesture, as if he had more to say. Rose longed to listen, but she knew this was her chance to leave. She began to turn again toward the front door. Out of the corner of her eye, she saw someone standing still, facing her. Without thinking, she looked at him. Richard Worthington watched her, his thin lips curved into a mirthless grin.

SIXTEEN

ROSE SPED HOME FROM LANGUOR, BARELY AWARE OF the car bouncing over the rutted road. Disturbing questions flashed through her mind. Richard Worthington had recognized her—why hadn't he stopped her or called attention to her presence? Why had he merely smiled? Was it a smile of triumph, or something else? Whatever it meant, she could not seem to make her heart stop pounding. She wished above all that she had been able to remain and hear more about what Kentuck and Laura Hill had in store for the Shakers. Now she could only imagine, and she imagined the worst.

She went right to bed, but her fears refused to subside. Each time she drifted to sleep, nightmares jerked her awake. At 5 A.M., she finally gave up and tossed off her twisted bedclothes. She slipped into her brown cotton work dress, pinned her hair against her head, and tied her cap over it. The worldly clothes she had worn the night before were hanging from wall pegs. She might as well return them now, before everyone got up for breakfast. She gathered them in her arms and eased quietly out of her room.

Rose paused on the top step of the attic staircase,

her feet refusing to move forward. The strain of the last few days was catching up with her, and suddenly the plain Shaker storage room sent a chill of alarm through her. Dawn's light filtered weakly through the attic skylight, leaving the corners dark. Her exhausted, overstimulated imagination saw moving shapes in the shadows. She closed her eyes and shook her head in irritation. *Some eldress I'm turning out to be*, she thought. *I can't even face a dim room without cowering*. She opened her eyes and headed straight for the built-in cupboards without another glance toward the shadows. The other sisters in the house would be rising very soon. She hurriedly stashed away the clothing, annoyed that her hands were shaking.

Once everything was back in its place, she hurried down the stairs to the main floor. She found herself running the last few steps. Closing her office door behind her, she leaned back against it, catching her breath. The curtains were drawn, the room dark. She reached for the light, then drew her hand back and yelped as, this time, a shape did move in the shadows. She flipped on a light, and Elder Wilhelm faced her, his mouth set in a grim line.

"Wilhelm, for heaven's sake, you startled me. What are you doing here at this hour, and sitting in the dark?"

"The Lead Society Ministry will be as interested as I in thy explanation of this," Wilhelm said, waving a sheet of paper at her.

Rose took the paper and stifled a groan as she recognized the typeface. A "special edition" of the *Languor County Watcher*. They must have begun printing it as soon as they returned from their public meeting. She sank into her desk chair and began to read.

SPECIAL EDITION

LANGUOR COUNTY WATCHER

Citizens of Languor County, this is to alert you to IMMEDIATE DANGER!! We have shocking information about the Shakers, our close neighbors and our enemies, who threaten our peaceful way of life. We have told you before of their odd dress and their pretense of virtue, while all the while they live corrupt and wanton lives, free of marriage vows.

"Wilhelm, 'corrupt and wanton lives, free of marriage vows'? How can you even read this nonsense? It's all lies, and we can easily refute them, if we care to do so. Our friends will not believe any of this."

"Read on," Wilhelm said. He stood in front of her, hands crossed over his barrel chest, and watched her.

Last evening, a number of good citizens held a meeting—in a true Christian church, not one of those Shaker meetinghouses where men and women fly into babbling trances and worse. We wanted only to discuss, like reasonable people, how to preserve the safety and tranquillity of our great county. But a spy was in our midst! The Shakers sent one of their minions sneaking into our church to listen and report back, so that they can destroy all our hopes and plans.

Yes, friends, the danger is real. And why? Because the Shakers are running scared! You've no doubt heard about the strange death which came recently to one of the so-called Believers, a man named Samuel Bickford. Some of you may have known him, even done business with him, thinking him a gentle, honest soul. But he was no such paragon. His crimes go back decades and include the most heinous of all—murder of an innocent. He never confessed his wretched sins, nor paid the price. The others protected him, of course. They pretend they are so much against violence that they will not defend their country against an invader, but when one of their own kills, they cover it up.

The Shaker named Samuel Bickford did not die a natural death. We believe that he died by his own hand, after years of keeping his crimes to himself. His death is a confession of guilt, the confession he had not the courage to make in life. And the other Shakers would protect this secret as well, if we gave them the chance. They could not survive and continue to do business with us honest folks if this and other secrets were to see the light of day. That is why they sent their own eldress, dressed as a true citizen of Languor, to spy on our meeting!

Samuel Bickford's burial is to be this very afternoon, in the Shaker graveyard. We urge you all to attend! Bring your children and tell them all about the sinful doings of those people. Let them know we will not tolerate their kind among us!

Rose sank back in her chair. So this is what they had in mind—a mob at Samuel's funeral. But why? Did they truly wish to drive the Society out of the county?

"We can't hold the funeral, of course," she said. "We certainly can't have hordes of the world's people trampling our graves and shouting at us."

Wilhelm snorted in derision. "Nay, thy behavior has certainly put a halt to any hope we have of a respectful burial for Samuel. I've already made arrangements for a small, private ceremony late this evening, after we are sure that no one from the world is about.

"Samuel's name will be dragged through the filthy streets of the world for years to come, and he did not deserve such treatment. Believe me, the Lead Ministry will be hearing about thy behavior, sneaking into a worldly meeting at night, disguised as a slut, no doubt. I've already put a call in to the elder at Mount Lebanon, and we shall see how long they allow thee to continue as eldress."

"*My* behavior? Wilhelm, I did what seemed necessary, and I am certainly not responsible for this disgusting drivel. Mount Lebanon will not be bothered in the least by my doing my job. Yea, I went to the meeting, and I wore a castaway dress from storage. And before you ask why I didn't inform you, it is because I do not need to do so. I am not your servant, to be told to go or stay at your will. You should be much more concerned about what these people have in store for us, instead of leaving me to handle them on my own. That is all I have to say." She snatched up the copy of the *Watcher* and walked around Wilhelm and out the door of the office, leaving him standing alone, silent for once.

*   *   *

"Oh, Caleb, you shouldn't be here, and you've been drinking. I can smell it. You promised you wouldn't anymore; you promised you wouldn't—for me." Sarah's soft brown eyes filled with tears. Her nerves were overwrought anyway, what with creeping out into the orchard during the workday, once again, to meet Caleb. It was just too much that he'd been drinking again. He was a good man at heart, she knew that, and she had been so hopeful that he'd stop drinking for her. But lately she'd begun to despair. Maybe her love just wasn't strong enough. It had been the same with her uncle. She had loved him dearly, tried and tried to help him stop drinking. But the alcohol had killed him, and she'd been unable to stop it.

"I haven't had more than just the one drink, Sarah, just a little pick-me-up, is all."

"Cal, I'm really worried about what's going on here in the village. You never let on these awful things would happen. I'm scared you've been lying to me. I'm just not sure we should see each other for a while." She tried to sound sure of herself, but she knew her voice betrayed her. Despite her growing doubts, it hurt to think about losing him.

"Sarah, we gotta stick together, we belong together. I need you. Without you, there's just no point to anything."

"But what have you been doing? I sneaked you those brethren's work clothes the other day—just so you could get some of your old journals back, you said—and the next thing I know, the schoolchildren are being attacked by rats. I can't bear to think that you might have done that, Cal. And who attacked me in the Sisters' Shop? It wasn't you, was it, Cal? Please, please tell me it wasn't you.''

"As God is my witness, I never hit you, Sarah. Never. That could've just been some hobo sleeping in your building, and you surprised him." Caleb's face brightened as he warmed to his story. "Yeah, that's gotta be what happened.''

"What about all those other attacks? If you didn't do any of it, who did?''

"Look, Sarah, I've always told you whatever I knew. I got you those newspapers, didn't I? Those are the folks at the bottom of everything, not me. You can see that, can't you?''

Sarah lifted her chin defiantly. "I made sure Eldress Rose got those horrible papers," she said. "I gave one to Elder Wilhelm, too.''

"Dammit, Sarah, why'd you do that? You was supposed to keep those papers secret—I told you.'' His bloodshot eyes grew wild, and Sarah jumped back.

"You know who those people are, don't you? Don't you?'' Sarah's fear and anger and disappointment all dissolved into tears.

"Sarah, no, you gotta trust me. I'm gonna find that out, you just trust me. Whoever they are, I'll track them down.''

He reached into his pocket. "Look what I brought you," he said. He handed Sarah a wrinkled journal page.

She opened it with trembling fingers and read it through twice. Her anguish changed to hope. "I don't understand, Cal. This says . . . Does this mean that I have a brother?''

*   *   *

Richard Worthington glanced at the copy of the *Languor County Watcher* on the desk in his study. He'd tried to keep Frances from seeing it. He didn't have time for an argument; he needed to think. This diatribe wasn't exactly what he'd planned when he told the apostates about Rose's presence at the meeting the night before, but maybe he could still get things to work out his way. He had waited for her to get safely away—it wouldn't do to have some of those unpredictable creatures in the audience get rough with her. He wanted this done cleanly and quietly.

"Daddy, Daddy, look at me!" Rickie ran into the room, his arms flying out from his sides as if he were about to catch an air current and swoop into flight. Instead, he crashed into Worthington's smoking table, knocking it, himself, and a lit cigar to the rug. Rickie began to sob noisily.

"Rickie, what the—" Worthington quashed the expletive that hovered on his lips, as well as the look of irritation on his face. Rickie might be hurt; that was far more important than his Chippendale table and Partagas Corona. He scooped the boy off the floor and looked him over for signs of injury. His knees, showing below his short pants, were as plump and pink as ever. His pride was hurt, that was all.

"There, you're not hurt anywhere, are you?"

Rickie shook his head, his lower lip still quivering.

"Then there's nothing for a big boy like you to cry about, is there?" The boy had to learn not to look weak, and the sooner the better.

The cigar was still smoldering, so Worthington

gathered it and what ashes he could and threw the whole mess in the fireplace.

"I heard Rickie crying all the way upstairs." Frances Worthington ran into the room, her arms extended toward her son. "Rickie, darling, are you all right?" Kneeling in front of him, she stroked his cheeks and murmured soothing sounds. At the attention, Rickie began to sniffle again.

"That's enough, Frances. Leave the boy alone. Don't make a baby out of him." He took Rickie's arm and pulled him out of his mother's embrace. Yanked off balance, Frances stood too quickly and fell backward against Worthington's desk. As she steadied herself, she saw the *Watcher*. She snatched it up and began to read.

"That isn't important, Frances, give it to me."

Frances jumped away from him and continued to read. "Those people wrote this, didn't they? Didn't they, Richard?"

"Rickie, go play in your room now," Worthington said. With an uncertain glance that went from his father to his mother, who were staring angrily at each other, Rickie backed out of the room.

"Well, Richard?"

"It's none of your concern."

"It is very much my concern. You're involved with some frightening people who have plans to destroy the Shakers, and I don't like to think what those plans include. I want to know what your part in this is."

"There are no plans, Frances, you're imagining things again. That paper is no more than an expression of how everyone around here feels about those Shakers.'' Worthington held his hand out. ''Now give it here.''

''Why, Richard? Why do you want to destroy those people? They brought you up, gave you an education. They've always been good neighbors, and they make their loan payments on time, you've always said that. I've never understood why you hate them so.''

''You weren't there. You didn't live with them. If it weren't for them, my youth would have been completely different. If they hadn't enticed my weak mother into joining them when Father died, we could have lived so much better. Instead they took everything we owned. I've had to fight, work day and night, to provide you and Rickie with the kind of life we should have had all along.''

''That's nonsense, Richard. We had plenty of money from my family. We don't even need the bank.''

Richard's face darkened, and his eyes flashed. ''How dare you. I would never live off my wife's money. I won't rest until Rickie has every penny he would have had if those Shakers hadn't stolen it.''

He wiped the emotion from his face and busied himself stoking the fire, all the while feeling Frances's eyes on his back. He did not wish to discuss his life in North Homage with Frances. How could he explain any of it to her? Yes, they had fed and clothed and educated him, even shown him affection, and, yes, he should have been grateful. But he wasn't. A part of him—the part that was his gentle mother's son—knew it was selfish to feel as he did. Hadn't they all tried to teach the dominance of worship and charity and striving for perfection over the mere accumulation of wealth and possessions? But a stronger part of him could not release his intense resentment. They preached those ideas, but what did they do? They convinced his gullible mother to sign over all the land inherited from her well-to-do husband's family—rich farmland that should have come to Richard, and after him, to his son, Rickie. He could not forgive the Shakers for their hypocrisy.

He turned his back to the fire to find that Frances had left the room. *Just as well*, he thought. *She'll never understand what I have to do.*

SEVENTEEN

"WE'VE LOST THE BETTER PART OF AN AFTERNOON of planting," Rose complained. "People from the world trampled through all afternoon. You'd think they'd have better things to do than try to invade Shaker funerals." She handed Josie the bags of dried chamomile, thyme, basil, spearmint, and peppermint she'd requested from the Herb House. Rose felt tired and cross, a sure sign she needed to skip fewer meals and get more sleep. She sank wearily onto a ladder-back chair, its woven seat frayed by decades of ill Believers, and watched Josie refill her empty tins and put them back in the Infirmary medicine cabinet.

"Yea, my dear," Josie said, "but it had to be. We could hardly tell the world when the funeral would be held and take the risk of having poor Samuel put to rest with strangers shouting all those terrible lies at him. Gentle as he was, such a ruckus would surely have brought him back to have his say, and we'd have been all night getting him buried."

Rose managed a light laugh, and Josie eyed her with professional concern. "Rose, I was more amusing than that, surely. Would a tonic be in order, perhaps? Did you get any sleep at all last night?"

"So you've heard, have you?"

"Hasn't everyone?"

Rose groaned. "Of course everyone has. Nay, I slept very little, and this morning Wilhelm took me to task for my adventure last evening."

"I hope you told him to tend to his own business and leave the adventuring to you!"

"Less colorfully, but yea, I told him I needed to find out everything I could about what's happening here." She sighed. "Being eldress is far more exhausting than I'd expected. Agatha seemed to handle her burdens so lightly."

Josie's face bunched up into a grin. "You're doing fine, my dear. Agatha herself would have been just as troubled by recent events, I assure you."

"I find that hard to believe."

"Nay, it's true. When Agatha began as eldress, she was a bit older than you, but just as uncertain." Josie chuckled to herself as she stuffed crumbly dried chamomile flowers into a tin. "I remember an incident—I shouldn't tell this, but it'll do you good to hear it. Her first year as eldress, Agatha was faced with two pregnant sisters! She was beside herself, had no idea what to do. Elder Obadiah, who was not unlike our Wilhelm, wanted them thrown out, but then he'd never have to face such a dilemma with the brethren, would he? Well, Agatha just couldn't toss those girls onto the streets, certainly not when they were carrying new life within them. But the silly things would not confess nor name the fathers, and no other Believer would tell on them. And do you know what Agatha did? Took over a Union Meeting one evening! There we all were, sisters sitting across from the brethren, all set to discuss social events and theological concerns, and tiny Agatha stood up on a chair and told everyone they'd better listen up and tell her who was responsible for those babies or the Society would hear about it in every homily she ever gave for the rest of her life. The culprit confessed right there in the meeting. Between you and me, it was one man fathered the two little ones. Very popular with both the sisters and the brethren. No one wanted to lose him, but really!'' Josie shook her head and sent her chins jiggling.

Rose felt some of the tension in her shoulders relax. It was a comfort knowing that Agatha had taken drastic measures herself now and then.

''Josie, since we are discussing past times, what do you remember about a sister named Faithfull Worthington?''

Josie's head popped up. ''Goodness, what brought her to mind? She was one of my Infirmary sisters. It must be twenty years or more since she died.''

''Twenty-five,'' Rose said. ''Her name has come up recently. How did she die, do you know?''

''I must confess,'' Josie said, ''I've wondered a bit about that myself. I wasn't here, you see, I was getting additional nursing training. When I returned, I found that she'd died in her sleep in the Infirmary, and one of the other Infirmary sisters at that time said it was a heart attack. I was shocked. Faithfull was not more than thirty-five and fit as they come. She worked alongside the brethren every spring and fall in the fields, loved to work outdoors. She'd spent the night in the Infirmary being watched for a cough. Then she just slipped away in her sleep.''

"Do you think she could have been murdered?"

"Murdered? Goodness gracious, where did you get such an idea?"

Rose hesitated. Josie was reliable and trustworthy, so she asked, "Do you know of any way someone could make a death look like a heart attack, something that someone here would have been able to do back in 1912?"

Josie frowned. "Back then, I think it wouldn't have been too difficult. Just the Infirmary sisters determined how she died, and one of them was an inexperienced young sister called in to help because Faithfull was ill. I don't think they even called the doctor from Languor after they found her dead. Nay, my guess is it was pneumonia, and they just made a mistake." She finished putting away her newly filled tins and reached for her cloak from a wall peg.

"It's getting late, my dear. Let's run along to Samuel's burial."

Rose silently slipped on her own cloak and tied it shut around her neck, since the evening spring air had turned chilly. Samuel. Another unexpected heart attack.

Dusk shrouded the village as somber Believers left their evening chores and made their way to the cemetery for Samuel's burial. Rose and Josie scanned the village as they left the Infirmary to join the others, but they saw only other long, dark Dorothy cloaks and work jackets. No world's people hovering about.

The new cemetery had been in use since 1882, when the village's first cemetery had filled. Except for its location in flat open space on the east side of North

Homage, the new cemetery looked much like the old one. A slatted wood fence enclosed the square of land containing precise rows of graves. A small rounded metal marker, listing only the Believer's name, age at death, and death date identified each grave. Simplicity and humility prevailed in death as in life.

The sweet scent of wild plum and apple blossoms blended with the moist smell of newly turned earth as Rose joined the others around Samuel's gravesite. The plain pine coffin holding Samuel's body lay on the ground. His grave marker, still clean and shiny, glimmered in the final rays of the setting sun.

Rose and Wilhelm moved to opposite sides of the hole dug for Samuel's coffin. They'd agreed that each would deliver a short homily. Rose was pleased. At least for the moment, Wilhelm seemed willing to treat her more as his equal than as an upstart to be quelled. Had standing up to him earned her some respect?

As the Believers gathered, brethren in one group, sisters in another, Rose studied their faces. Elsa Pike, always vying for center stage, stood in front. She swayed dreamily, her eyes closed. Rose's antennae for trouble tingled. Elsa was known for her tendency to fall into trembling trances whenever she had an audience. Rose would not have minded had she believed the trances were truly inspired.

Wilhelm stepped forward and led the group in prayer. As the prayer ended, he raised his arms and his face toward the darkening sky. He held his pose for several minutes, as though waiting to hear the spirits of long-dead Believers that elders and eldresses had often reported hearing at funerals. But for all his zealotry, Wilhelm admitted never hearing the voices of Mother Ann or falling into trembling trances, which he explained as his own lack of perfection. He admired anyone who had the "gifts," even if those gifts were suspect. At every opportunity, he opened himself to receive them. As before, after a time, he lowered his arms without any sign of being blessed.

"Brethren and sisters," he began. Rose noted his inclusion of the sisters for once. "This night we cheer the soul of our brother Samuel to the arms of our Mother and the protection of our Father, where he will flourish forever, safe from the wretched tongues of the world."

The moon had risen in the night sky, shining its pale light on the faces of the Believers. Elsa still swayed and nodded as she listened to Wilhelm, but she seemed under control. Though she felt sad for the loss of Samuel, Rose's mind wandered from the homily to thoughts about who might have killed him, if his death was neither natural nor a suicide. Surely one of the apostates.

Yet Sarah concerned her, too. She seemed gentle and devoted to the Society—and, true, she had been attacked. But she was the only link to the apostates, as far as Rose could tell. She always seemed to be present when an incident occurred. She disappeared at times, maybe just to meet Caleb, maybe because she played a role in the incidents. Sarah seemed nervous as she listened to Wilhelm's powerful voice. She stood aside from the sisters, as if she didn't feel part of the whole. Her protruding eyes darted from Elsa to Wilhelm and back to Elsa.

". . . as we bury the body—now mere flesh and

bones, soon to be dust—of our brother, we will have a moment of silent prayer.''

Rose realized she had missed most of Wilhelm's homily and must begin her own in just a few moments. She rushed her silent prayer and pulled her thoughts together. Ending the silence, she stepped forward.

''Sisters and brethren,'' she began, ''Samuel was a good man, a devout Believer, and our friend. Though the world has judged him harshly, we must remember his life with us, which he filled with hard work and love, for us and for God.''

A low moan came from the sisters group. The sisters surrounding Elsa stepped away from her. Elsa's body quivered, and clipped nonsense syllables seemed to force themselves from between her lips. She began to bob forward in a stiff nod from the waist. Her lips moved again, but this time no sound came from them. A familiar foreboding washed through Rose. She glanced sideways at Wilhelm. He watched Elsa with expectant hopefulness.

''We are all sinners,'' Rose shouted, ''despite lifetimes of reaching to perfect ourselves for the greater glory of God. Samuel tried, too. It is now for Mother Ann to intercede for him, and for God to judge him. And He will surely be merciful.''

Elsa released another moan, this time rising to a haunting crescendo. Her cloak shook with her convulsive trembling. Rose berated herself for not being better prepared for this. It was just like Elsa to wait until Rose was speaking to go into one of her performances. Rose knew they were performances, yet they were so well executed that she, along with everyone else, felt a thrill of anticipation as if they were real. Throughout their history, Believers had heard their dead predecessors joining them in the funeral celebrations of one of their own. They expected these messages, welcomed them, cherished them. But those voices had been real communications to Believers who were truly open to them, not skilled bids for importance from a woman who wanted more power than she deserved.

Elsa's arms began to float upward until she had reached the same pose Wilhelm had used to listen for spirit messages. Wilhelm thrust his head forward, eager not to miss anything Elsa might say or do. He never quite gave up his belief in her apparent gifts.

Rose searched her mind for a way to interrupt what was sure to come next. A distraction, anything. She sought Josie in the group, but it was too dark to catch her eye. Finally, she took the only course she could think of—she breathed deeply and raised her voice to a volume equal to Wilhelm's at his most powerful.

"Samuel's worth will be reckoned by God," she shouted. "We are here only to send him to Mother Ann's arms with our love, not—I say again—not to judge him!"

All heads jerked toward her, including Wilhelm's. Elsa stopped moaning, but her arms still reached skyward. Rose thought she saw a glint in those hazel eyes, but she told herself it was a trick of the moonlight.

"For we cannot know the truth of his death," Rose continued, maintaining the power in her voice. "We know only this—that the world lies when it defiles our brother."

She saw Elsa's eyes glide shut again and her body begin to sway. In desperation, Rose took a chance.

"Samuel did not die gently!" For a split second, Rose wondered why that phrase had come to her mind. Then she remembered the journal page in Caleb's room. She glanced at Sarah. Despite the dimness, she could feel Sarah's intent stare. Each Believer now was still, even Elsa, though her eyes remained closed. Rose pushed her advantage.

"We abhor violence. Yet within our walls, violence was done to one of our own beloved brothers. Samuel did not die by his own hand—"

Rose had lowered her voice. It was a mistake. Elsa's moan slid upward in pitch, then resolved into rapidly babbled syllables. Rose sucked in her breath to deliver another shout. As if sensing Rose's intention, Elsa jabbered louder.

Without pausing for breath, Elsa shouted, "Mother Ann, I feel thy presence. I am thy willing vessel; speak through me." When she sang or spoke from a trance, Elsa seemed to lose the normal coarseness in her voice and sound almost British, as Mother Ann had been. Even Rose, who was convinced of Elsa's insincerity, could not explain this phenomenon.

"Yea, yea, I do hear thee," Elsa said. "What is thy message? I cannot hear clearly; I cannot believe thy words, but—what? Oh, nay, nay, I do not doubt thee. I am but a weak vessel, with flawed understanding. I will do thy will, without question. I will convey thy message that . . . that Samuel is not with thee."

Both sisters and brethren gasped. Rose held her breath.

"I hear more, but it is so faint. Samuel . . . Samuel

broke his vow. He . . .'' Elsa scrunched her flat features in a grimace, as if she were using all her strength to make out the words coming to her. "He . . . fornicated! Ah, Mother, can it be so? More yet? About Samuel? Oh, nay, nay.'' Elsa's face shifted to anguish. Rose swore she could see a tear glisten in the moonlight. "There . . . was . . . a . . . child!'' Elsa crumpled to a heap on the ground. The sisters around her bent to help. Out of the corner of her eye, Rose saw Sarah run into the darkness.

EIGHTEEN

ROSE BARELY STOPPED HERSELF FROM SLAMMING the front door of the Trustees' Office. How did Elsa continue to ferret out information before Rose or, apparently, anyone else? Who was her source? *All right, Rose*, she thought, *unclench your teeth. You don't have time to worry about Elsa right now.* She lifted her long skirts and ran up the stairs directly to the records room. She ripped off her cloak and tossed it on a wall peg before scanning the shelves for the right volumes. She had to guess at 1904 to 1909, since she had no intention of questioning Elsa and being fed whatever sensational half-truth she cared to spew.

As Rose had already discovered by going through the 1910 to 1912 volumes, Fiona had sprinkled her journals with chat and gossip about the Society. Rose hoped she'd find enough information to piece together what really happened between Samuel and Faithfull.

She decided to start with 1909 and work backward. Her determined curiosity pushed her through the first volume quickly, despite her tiredness. 1909 had been an uneventful year, and 1908 turned out to have been equally uninteresting. In the third volume, 1907, Rose began to see intriguing references to Samuel and Faithfull. In a February entry, Fiona had written:

187

Samuel is dragging his feet about adding cities to his sales trip this spring, and I'm more than a wee bit suspicious about his reasons. He was surely willing last year, seemed he couldn't wait to leave the village and travel for weeks on end. But now we have hundreds of extra tins of herbs and seed packages and jars of preserved fruits and vegetables, which we can't use, Heaven knows, and Samuel doesn't seem to care if they stay here, wasted. We have orders to fill in those cities, but Samuel wants Klaus or Caleb to go in his stead. It's all since Faithfull came back last summer that Samuel has gone through this mysterious change. I told Agatha, but you know Agatha, dear girl that she is, she just nods solemnly and looks stern and otherworldly. Oh, I'm being churlish now, and truly, Agatha is a Heaven-sent eldress, but sometimes I do wish she'd interfere a little more!

Intrigued, Rose turned the page. The rest of the volume contained a few more references hinting at the relationship Fiona suspected between Samuel and Faithfull, but nothing new. Going backward to the 1906 volume, Rose read:

Samuel seems distracted, poor lad. It's the winter, no doubt. He is trapped indoors, helping to package seeds and pining to be out selling again. He is my best salesman, but a trial to keep busy in the winter. Elder Obadiah asked him to be trustee, alongside me, and Heaven knows I could use a partner, but Samuel refused,

*as he has refused every other position offered
him. Thinks he isn't worthy or some such twad-
dle, and yet he is smart as any lad I've known,
but there you are. There's no explaining people
sometimes, which is why I like numbers! We're
talking of adding Knoxville and Nashville to his
sales trips to keep him better occupied. He
would make quick stops in the spring to meet
new customers and take orders, then deliver in
the fall. It would mean harder work to ready the
products, but we Shakers know how to work!*

Rose skimmed quickly, eager to reach the summer
entries and find some reference to Faithfull's return.
She found it in mid-July.

*Sister Faithfull came back to us today. I must
say I was surprised, though perhaps that's my
suspicious nature talking. She had seemed unhappy when she left to help care for her sister.
I thought then she was just taking the excuse to
get away from us, but now she has returned, and
with what a surprise! Her sister's baby! Now I
see why her sister needed her help. One can see
the family resemblance, though Heaven knows
who the father is. The sister couldn't raise the
child alone, so Faithfull brought her back to us.
It's lovely to have a tiny one around again.
We've had so few since the orphanages began
taking so many of them. It brings back sweet
memories of my days as a young sister, helping
the deaconess in the Children's Dwelling House.
I'd be up half the night with those little ones,*

and I didn't mind one bit. Those children have all grown and gone to the world now. You're rambling, Fee, my girl! Well, perhaps little Sarah will grow into a fine young Believer.

Sarah. Rose flipped over the open journal to keep her place while she puzzled through what she'd just read. Sarah was about the right age. Baker was the surname of the woman Sarah had lived with in the world, the woman she called her mother. If Fiona's information was correct, Sister Faithfull Worthington was Sarah's aunt. Yet Samuel's confession suggested that Faithfull could have become pregnant during the time before Sarah was born. What if Faithfull had left the Society not to tend to her sister, but to give birth herself? Much as Rose disliked the admission, Elsa's self-proclaimed message from Mother Ann made sense. There was a child, Samuel and Faithfull's child. Sister Sarah Baker.

Rose knocked on the door of Sarah's retiring room, and it swung open. It was after 10 P.M. Sarah should have been preparing for bed, after the long day they'd all had, but a quick look around assured Rose that Sarah had not been back since Samuel's funeral. Her curtains were open to darkness, and her bedclothes stretched smoothly across her narrow bed.

Back in the hallway, Rose listened for sounds of murmuring voices coming from any of the other rooms, but she heard only faint snoring. In any case, Sarah, though liked well enough by the other Believers, had never formed a close friendship. It was unlikely she had run to another sister for comfort this night. Rose tiptoed downstairs and checked the kitchen, which was empty.

Alarm shivered through Rose. It was not unheard of for sisters or brethren to flee the Society under cover of night, sometimes with each other. If Sarah believed Elsa had revealed her parenthood, might she have decided to escape, perhaps meeting up with Caleb Cox? The fear of such a disaster sent Rose flying out the front door of the Center Family Dwelling House. One more place to check—the Sisters' Shop. Sarah had been there in the early morning hours the day she was attacked. Perhaps the sewing room was her haven, her place of comfort when she felt troubled.

Rose groaned with relief as she came in sight of the Sisters' Shop and saw the faint light through the second-story window. A shadow moved across the illuminated curtain. Rose slowed to a brisk walk and caught her breath.

Rather than frighten Sarah, Rose closed the outer door of the Sisters' Shop with a loud click. "Sarah, it's just me, just Rose," she called out as she climbed the stairs. To her surprise, Sarah did not appear to greet her at the top of the staircase. The door to the sewing room was closed, so perhaps she hadn't heard.

Without knocking, Rose pushed open the door. The single light from Sarah's sewing desk created eerie shadows from piles of dark wool stacked nearby. Sarah was not sitting at her desk. From the doorway, Rose peered around the room but saw no one. Then she heard scuffling sounds coming from a dark corner at the other end of the room. Remembering the previous assault on Sarah, Rose hesitated only a second before tiptoeing to the large cutting table and grasping a set of shears. The thought of using the weapon was abhorrent to Rose, but she had to protect Sarah from harm. To preserve an element of surprise, she did not turn on more lights. She crept toward the sounds.

She saw Sarah lying on the floor, a man pinning her down. She was moving, struggling, thank God, not dead. Rose raised her scissors in the air, aimed at the shape of Sarah's attacker.

"Get away from her!" Rose shouted. "I warn you, I have a weapon."

The man rolled away from Sarah and scrambled to his feet. He stumbled past Rose in the dark, leaving behind the unmistakable odors of sweat and whiskey.

"Dammit!" Caleb cursed as he crashed into the worktable. Before Rose could take more than a step in his direction, he recovered and staggered out of the room. Rose turned back to Sarah, who had pulled herself to her feet and stumbled to her desk chair.

"Sarah!" Rose dropped her arm and the shears clattered to the floor.

Sarah's fine brown hair hung to her shoulders, free of its thin cotton cap. The white kerchief that should have crisscrossed her bodice was hanging loose over one shoulder. The top of her dress was unbuttoned. Her hands shook too much to rebutton them, so she grabbed the fabric and held it shut.

"Sarah, did he force himself on you?"

"Oh, Eldress, I . . ." Her brown eyes seemed to overtake her face, which was drained of color. "I've been so foolish."

"What was Caleb Cox doing here? Did you agree to meet him?"

Instead of collapsing, as Rose feared she would, Sarah drew in a deep breath and steadied herself. She buttoned her dress and recrossed her kerchief over her chest, tucking the edges into her apron at her waist.

"I've met him here before," she said quietly. She slid wearily onto the chair at her sewing table. "But he never acted like this, truly. It's my fault he was here. Samuel's funeral upset me so, I called Caleb's boardinghouse, just to talk. I guess I knew he'd been drinking, but I didn't want to admit it. He said he'd come over so I wouldn't be sad anymore." Sarah's shoulders rolled forward in a gesture of shame. "I should have known better, but I promised to meet him here," she said.

Rose felt a wave of exhaustion as the fear drained from her body. She pulled a spare chair next to Sarah's table and sat down. "How does he get here?" she asked.

"He can borrow a friend's car whenever he needs to. He parks it a ways outside of the village and walks in, so no one hears."

"What friend? Another apostate?"

Sarah's eyes grew wary. "I don't know. Just a friend."

"Sarah, this has gone far enough. I want to know what is happening here. Frankly, whether you can stay with us depends on whether you are now willing to be honest with me."

Sarah closed her eyes. Rose waited, letting Sarah draw her own comparison between life as a Believer and life with a violent drunk. She had faith that Sarah would make the right choice, but just to be sure, she said a silent prayer.

Sarah opened her eyes and gazed directly at her, and Rose knew Mother Ann had heard her prayer.

"I will tell you what I can, but I don't know much." Sarah's voice faltered, but she rushed on as if she had to say it all in one breath. "Caleb lied to me some, I know that now. He seemed really scared for me after I was attacked, and he kept saying he'd find out what happened, but he just gets drunk instead. He isn't going to change, is he?" Her body seemed to lose the support of her bones, and she slumped in her chair.

Rose shook her head. "Nay, Sarah, I think it unlikely. I believe it would take God's direct intervention; yours will never be enough." Sarah nodded.

"Now tell me," Rose said, "what you know about the threats to our village."

"Caleb said that a Shaker killed my mother." Anger lent force to Sarah's light voice. "He said a friend told him, and this friend cared for my mother and wanted to punish the Shakers for protecting her killer."

"And you believed this? Sarah, how could you? You know we would never break our vows by harboring a killer."

"I didn't believe it at first, but . . ." Sarah squared her shoulders. "I know it's true. Caleb brought me proof."

"What proof?"

Sarah lowered to her knees on the floor and removed the second drawer of her sewing desk. She turned it over, dumping out the contents. Several sheets of paper were secured with a tack to the underside of the drawer. She pried off the tack and handed the pages to Rose.

Rose recognized one sheet as the handwritten journal page she had read in Caleb's room. The other two were written by the same hand.

"So Sister Faithfull was indeed your mother," Rose said, after she'd skimmed the pages.

Sarah nodded.

"These pages claim her death was not natural, that someone killed her. Yet all the records indicate she died of a heart attack. Who wrote these?"

Sarah shrugged. "I don't know. Caleb didn't tell me, and I guess I didn't try too hard to find out. I was afraid he'd stop bringing them to me if I pushed too hard, and I so much wanted to know about my mother."

"Whoever wrote these was in love with Faithfull. Who is this friend of Caleb's? An apostate?"

"Yea," Sarah said. "There's more than one, but I never met them. I do know that the leaders were all Believers right when Caleb was, and they all left in the same year."

"Did they all leave for the same reason?"

Sarah's face was just beyond the center of light from her lamp, and her puzzled frown created dark furrows on her forehead. "I'm not sure, but I do know that Caleb left for his own reasons. He had no calling to be a Believer. He wanted to be out in the world and do all the things the world's people do—you know, marry and suchlike."

"I suspect there were more reasons than that for Caleb to leave. I've been reading Agatha's journals, and she seemed to feel that Caleb was having serious difficulties even as a youngster. Several Believers watched over him and tried to guide him into the light, but he was unable to follow. Sarah, my dear, I believe that several of the threats we've been experiencing—the rats, the smashed preserves—are very like events our village lived through twenty-five and more years ago. I believe Caleb is responsible for these evils, both then and now. He blames us for the weaknesses woven into his own character.''

Sarah's face crumpled in pain. "I had begun to fear so," she said, "but I wanted to believe in him. He seemed to want to help me find my mother's killer, and he needed me so. I've never been loved before." Her voice trailed off.

Sarah twisted a lock of her long hair around one finger. "I'm so deeply ashamed of my part in this. Mostly I smoothed the way—brought Caleb a set of Shaker work clothes when he asked for them, took the preserves from the storage cellar, and . . ." She slumped against the back of her chair. "I'm the one who fed the meat to Freddie that made him go to sleep. I didn't know it had anything in it, truly I didn't. I just thought I was supposed to keep him busy for a while."

She leaned forward, her hands almost touching Rose. "I left the *Languor County Watcher* for you and Wilhelm. I made Caleb bring them to me as soon as he picked them up to deliver them. He didn't want to, but I told him to or I'd leave him. They scared me. I never wanted anyone to get hurt." She sounded like a pleading child.

"Yet people did get hurt. Why didn't you come to me directly?"

Sarah pulled back her hands. "I was so happy here as a child," she said. "I thought Faithfull was my aunt, and the sweetest aunt on earth. She used to slip me pieces of candied angelica root and give me hugs when the other girls weren't looking. When she died, my world ended. I went to live with her sister, who everyone thought was my mother. She told me soon enough that Faithfull had been my real mother. My aunt resented having to feed me; she only wanted me as a servant. My uncle was fond of me, but he was hardly ever sober."

"You allowed yourself to be used by these apostates so you could learn whether your mother was killed?" Rose asked.

Sarah nodded. "And who killed her. I didn't want her killer to go free after taking away my mother's life and my happiness."

"And have you found the killer?"

"Nay."

Rose stared hard at Sarah. "Did you know that Samuel was your father?"

"I only found out a few days ago from Caleb. I wanted so to talk to Samuel about my mother, and I managed to get a moment to ask him to meet with me. He looked very sad, but he agreed. He died before I could talk to him. To think that my own father was so close, all these years . . ." This time her eyes filled with tears. Rose relented and reached out with a comforting touch.

"When were you to meet?"

"Just past midnight."

"Wait a moment. Are you saying you went to meet with him that night? And he was dead already?"

Sarah nodded. She shifted in her seat.

"And you said nothing? You just left him there? How could you do such a thing?"

Sarah's long fingers fidgeted in her lap. "I was frightened."

"Were you afraid you would be accused? Why? You had no real reason to wish him silenced, did you? Your birth wasn't your fault."

"I know, but . . . I told Caleb I was going to meet with Samuel. Caleb got so upset, I was afraid . . ."

"That Caleb might have killed Samuel?"

"Yea. So I just went back to my retiring room. But I couldn't sleep at all, and I stayed dressed. When I heard the ruckus in the kitchen, I knew the sisters had found him, and I couldn't stand it. I came running down. That's when Gertrude sent me to get you."

Rose felt a chill settle over the room, despite the many bolts of densely woven wool. "I have two more questions for you, and then I'll walk you back to your retiring room. We can collect some of your clothing. I want you to stay in the Trustees' Office for a while, so I can be sure you're safe."

"Safe from what?" Sarah's eyes seemed to pop out from her face in sudden alarm.

"Just a precaution," Rose assured her. "Until we can bring these apostates out of the shadows." She did not add that Sarah's mother and father had both been killed, and she didn't want Sarah to be next.

Instead she asked, "Do you know where Samuel's journals are? Did you take them?"

"Nay, I did not. I don't expect you to believe me, after all that I did, but I'm telling the truth. I do not know where they are."

Rose studied her for a long moment. After all her admissions, Sarah had no reason to lie.

"One more question, Sarah. How did Elsa know that Faithfull and Samuel had a child?"

Sarah's jaw tightened in the first show of anger Rose had ever seen from her. "Elsa is evil," Sarah said, her voice hushed. "I truly believe she is in league with the Devil."

NINETEEN

AFTER ASSURING SARAH THAT SHE COULD BE FOR-
given and remain in the Society, Rose sent her to bed,
tired but grateful, in the empty retiring room next to
hers in the Trustees' Office. Rose was relieved to be
bidding her good night rather than striking her from
the rolls of Believers.

It was past midnight. Rose crept back to her own
retiring room and settled at her small desk. She knew
sleep would be difficult. She tried to force her tired
mind to go over what she had learned from Sarah.

An unidentified brethren, now an apostate, had con-
fided to his journal his belief that a Believer killed
Sister Faithfull, after which the Society sheltered the
murderer from paying for his crime. Other apostates
have joined with this man to threaten North Homage
with a series of attacks. To what purpose? Was the
so-called murderer still among the Shakers? Did the
apostates hope to bring him or her to justice? Or did
they wish to drive the Shakers from their village as
punishment for protecting the killer? Most puzzling:
Why was all this happening now, twenty-five years
later?

Rose sensed that danger lurked very close. Caleb

may have been drunk, but once he returned to his comrades—assuming he didn't drive into a tree on the way back—they would suspect that Rose had pressured Sarah to reveal what she knew about them. It was quite likely that Caleb had either killed Samuel himself or reported back to the other apostates about Sarah's appointment with her father. Rose was nearly certain that Samuel had died at the hands of an apostate.

Might as well check on Sarah, she thought. At least she'd be moving, doing something. She stood in the hallway, straining her ears for unusual sounds—the click of a door, a soft footfall on the stair. Besides Sarah, Rose shared the floor with just two other sisters. She eased open Sarah's door and peered inside. The room was darker than the dim hallway. Once her eyes adjusted, Rose watched Sarah long enough to see her turn and hear her sigh in her sleep. All was well.

She turned back to her own retiring room, trying to ignore the large wavering shadow her moving figure made on the wall. She entered and left the door to her sitting room slightly ajar. After taking Agatha's journals from her recessed cupboard, she pulled her rocking chair up to her desk. She smoothed a soft brown wool blanket on her knees, more for comfort than warmth.

Maybe she had missed something in Agatha's journals. Maybe there had been some event that drew these apostates together into bonds of hatred. She selected the 1912 volume, determined to read it through page by page. When she had skimmed it the first time, several days earlier, she had been interested mostly in references to Samuel and Faithfull. It was too bad that Agatha's sensibilities had led her to use so many initials; it made Rose's work much harder.

She came to the disappointing section about Faithfull's confession and Agatha's conference with Samuel. Both references were vague—deliberately so, Rose assumed. She continued to read and realized that everything sounded new to her. Of course, she remembered, she'd been reading this volume when she had drifted off to sleep, only to be awakened by Sarah telling her that Samuel was dead. She had never actually finished the journal.

After several pages of reports on how the crops were doing, despite the lack of rain, Rose came to an intriguing reference:

Now having the same difficulties with K. and E. as with F. and S. Can there be something in the spring air that afflicts these young people? It does seem to happen every year about this time. It is to be expected, I suppose. Not everyone answers the call with a complete heart. This problem is worse than most, though, as E. moons around and is becoming quite negligent in her work. Josie says she does little but sit and dream out the window. She stammers when K. is nearby, while K. pretends that nothing is going on. But he, too, stares into space more than a Shaker should, and somehow I do not believe he is praying. When I became eldress, I saw myself providing guidance for the spiritually perplexed, not discipline for the carnally inclined!

Rose chuckled as she placed the journal on her desk. Disciplining the "carnally inclined" seemed to be her own assignment as eldress as well. She tiptoed into the hallway and to Sarah's room again, but nothing was amiss. Perhaps she had overreacted. Perhaps Caleb was too drunk to report coherently to his apostate "friends." Back in her own room, she checked her bedside clock. It was 2:30 A.M.. Rose sat on her tightly made bed and longed to snuggle under the coverlet. *Nay*, she thought, *I mustn't. If anything happens to Sarah . . .* She couldn't take the risk of being so close to her enticing bed. She picked up her clock and took it with her back to her sitting room.

Settling again under the cozy blanket, she leaned back in her rocking chair. Placing the clock on the desk where she could easily see it, she allowed her head to roll back against the wooden slats and closed her eyes. Just for a moment, she told herself.

A scraping sound intruded into her deep, dreamless sleep. At first she didn't realize she was asleep and wove the sound into an instant dream image of the brethren scraping mud from their feet before entering the dining room. She clicked her tongue at the sight of so much mud caked on the outside stoop, and the sound she made in her throat brought her closer to wakefulness.

The scent of lavender brushed her nose. Something soft touched her face, pressed against it, then tightened. She no longer smelled lavender because the soft object smashed against her nose and mouth, cutting off her breath. It pulled her backward in her chair, but the chair itself did not fall. Fully alert now, Rose understood why. Someone stood behind her. She felt her chair stop, braced against her attacker. Something downy covered her face. She was being smothered with the pillow from her own bed. The lavender scent came from the final rinse used in the Laundry.

Rose was caught by surprise, but she had the strength and agility typical of young Shaker sisters, who worked as hard as the brethren. She flung her arms upward and clutched at the top of the pillow, but it didn't budge. She was losing time. She squirmed to pull herself down under the soft weapon, but she couldn't escape the suffocating pressure. Finally her fingers touched the wrists holding the pillow. Her fingernails were blunt but strong. As bright spots began to appear on the insides of her eyelids, she dug her nails into flesh and scraped. A moment before she blacked out, she heard a gasp of pain, and the pillow bounced away from her face.

A blast of cold water splashed on her face returned Rose to the light. She was carried a short distance and placed on a bed. A sea of worried faces with disheveled hair bent over her. The roundest face belonged to Josie, who cried out in relief as Rose coughed and opened her eyes.

"Ah, thank the Lord, you are back with us," Josie said. "I was a bit worried there when the smelling salts didn't work. We could see you were breathing, but you seemed determined to stay unconscious."

"What . . . How did you . . ." Rose's voice sounded faint and hoarse. She was regaining her focus, though. She saw she was in her own room on her own bed.

"Don't try to talk too much, dear. Just lie back and rest, and we'll tell you what we know first." Josie looked around at the other faces. "Gretchen, you found her. Tell her everything you saw."

Gretchen was a no-nonsense young woman, already Laundry deaconess at twenty-eight, but this turn of events brought an excited sparkle to her eyes. Now that Rose was all right, Gretchen seemed ready to enjoy herself.

"Well, I'm a very light sleeper, you know," she said with a touch of pride. "I hear all sorts of sounds at night, but usually it doesn't bother me because I know what it is, like if a sister needs to make a nighttime visit to—" She paused as Josie raised her eyebrows to quell any further digression. "Anyway, tonight I stayed awake for hours because there seemed to be an awful lot going on in the hallway. Once I peeked out and saw you, Rose, going into Sarah's room, and then you came out again and went back to your own room."

"Sarah!" Rose croaked. "Is she all right?"

"I'm right here, Rose." Sarah's soft eyes appeared near Rose's face. "I didn't know you were that worried about me." She sounded guarded, as if she thought Rose might not have trusted her. Rose did not reassure her. She nodded and relaxed again against the pillow that had so recently been used to attack her.

She looked toward Gretchen to encourage her to continue.

"Well, I was getting tired, as you can imagine," Gretchen said. "I was just drifting off when I heard an awful clatter. At least it sounded awful to me. I got all twisted up in my coverlet, so it took a while for me to run into the hallway. I didn't see anyone;

they must have gotten away. But your door was wide open, Rose, so I ran here, and there you were, out cold on the floor, and your rocking chair was turned on its side. Your pillow was off to the side on the floor, and at first I wondered if you'd been napping in your chair and it tipped over. Then I got really frightened—you looked dead! I thought you weren't breathing at all, but then you sort of gasped, and I could see you were just unconscious. I tried to bring you to but I couldn't, so I called Josie from the hall telephone, and she came right over," Gretchen finished, breathless.

Rose had been recovering rapidly while Gretchen spoke. She pulled herself to a sitting position, waving aside Josie's murmured objections.

"I must get up," Rose insisted, tossing off her blanket.

"Nay, my dear, the only thing you must do is rest," Josie said, gently pushing Rose's shoulders back toward the bed. But Rose had regained much of her strength.

"Josie, I insist," she said. "I know you are concerned for me, but this is important." She did not wish to alarm the others. Josie saw the intensity in her eyes, though, and understood.

"How can I help?"

"Stay with me for a bit," Rose said. "And the rest of you, I'm fine now, so run along and get ready for breakfast. I'm afraid we'll all be short on sleep today, but it can't be helped. There's no harm done; don't tire yourselves more with worry."

Reluctantly, the sisters left Rose's retiring room and scattered to their own. With Josie hovering, Rose slid off her bed and tried her legs. They were shaky but serviceable. She led the way to her sitting room and stopped so suddenly that Josie nearly ran into her. She stared at her desk, then scanned the room. The door of her built-in cupboard hung open. Agatha's journals were gone, every one of them. Rose yanked open her desk drawer. At least her attacker had not found Fee's journals and the anonymous journal pages Sarah had given her. She moved them to the back of a recessed dresser drawer in her bedroom, while Josie watched, silent and wide-eyed.

Taking Josie's hand, she hurried into the hallway and down the staircase to her office. The door was ajar. They entered the room. Both sisters stood in silence as they surveyed the devastation. Cabinets and drawers were open and the contents strewn around the floor, as if the intruders had tossed over their shoulders anything they didn't want. Ledger books were pulled off the shelves and scattered around the desk, some open with pages ripped or smeared with spilled ink.

"Oh, Rose," Josie whispered. "What is happening to us?"

Rose quickly closed the office door and switched on the light. "We must keep this as quiet as possible," she said. "I'll have to tell Wilhelm, of course, but I'll want to find out what is going on without spreading panic among Believers." She reached down and rescued a bent copy of Mother Ann's sayings that lay at her feet. "The intruders must have been very quiet," she said, "to have done all this without being heard upstairs, especially with Gretchen so wakeful.

They must have come up to my room when they didn't find what they wanted here.''

"What *is* going on? Do you have any idea at all?''

Rose nodded. "I have some idea, or maybe part of an idea, but too many pieces are missing. Someone tried to smother me with the pillow you all saw on the floor. I never saw who it was, but I did scratch them before I blacked out.'' Rose inched among the scattered papers and books, now and then lifting one and piling it on her desk. Josie had a faraway look on her face.

"Josie? What is it?''

"I was just thinking. When someone has been smothered, the death can look very much like a heart attack.''

The papers in Rose's hand drifted to the floor again. "So Faithfull could have been smothered,'' she said. "And Samuel, too. It would have taken some effort, some planning, but even someone smaller than Samuel could have done it, coming from behind. Maybe Samuel had fallen asleep. It would explain why he was still sitting in the rocking chair, and why there were no signs of a struggle. The cookies, though; I wonder . . .'' Rose sank into her desk chair, and Josie lifted a chair from a wall peg and sat at the other side of the double desk.

"If someone wanted it to look like a natural death,'' Rose mused, "they might have placed the cookies there, taking a bite to make it look more real. That would explain why there were no crumbs around Samuel.''

"Then surely it could not have been a Believer,'' Josie said, her eyes bright with hope. "Not everyone knew of his vow to avoid sweets—you didn't, certainly—but everyone had noticed that he never ate them. He was so thin, too. No one would think he sneaked into the kitchen at night to snack on cookies! Only someone from the world would set up such a ruse."

"I'm afraid I can think of at least one other explanation for the cookies," Rose said. "I doubt they were poisoned, or they wouldn't have been left just so. But a Believer who hated Samuel might have placed the cookies there to shame him, even in death, with evidence of his broken vows."

"But is there anyone who would have hated Samuel that much?"

"That is what we must find out," Rose said.

TWENTY

AFTER SENDING JOSIE BACK TO THE INFIRMARY TO
sip chamomile tea and rest, Rose decided to contact
Deputy Grady O'Neal, rather than clean up her office
immediately. She placed a call to the Languor County
Sheriff's Office, and luck was with her; Grady was in
his office and promised to drive right over to North
Homage.

With a sigh of reluctance, Rose then placed a call
to the Ministry House. Keeping the news from Wilhelm would only further impair their ability to work
together as elder and eldress.

"I want to be there when you speak with that deputy," Wilhelm said, when she had filled him in. To
her surprise, he had not criticized her decision to call
in the police. "He is very much of the world, and I
don't trust him."

"Well, I do," Rose said. "He has been sympathetic
to us before. He is certainly a better choice than Sheriff Brock, who has never been our friend." She had
come to trust Grady during a previous investigation
of a young drifter's murder. Unlike Sheriff Brock,
Grady had been open-minded and fair with the Shakers.

Wilhelm grunted but did not object further. "I'll be right over."

Grady must have flown over the rutted road from Languor, because he and Wilhelm arrived at the same time, to Rose's relief. She had dreaded having to argue with Wilhelm about what to tell Grady.

They scanned the office silently for a few moments, as Grady made notes in his small notebook, and Wilhelm glowered.

"The world has a vicious heart," Wilhelm said, running his hand over a section of Rose's desk where the pine, aged to an orange glow, was dotted with splashes of ink. "What will the police do about this outrage?" he asked the room at large. "Nothing, probably. What do they care if we Believers are persecuted?"

Grady glanced at him but wisely said nothing. Rose relaxed. Grady was a self-possessed young man, unlikely to be drawn into a quarrel that would give Wilhelm an excuse to become even more self-righteous.

"Did you notice any pattern to the damage?" Grady asked Rose. "Did it seem to you that they were trying to destroy anything in particular?

Rose shrugged. "It seems random to me, but I can't be sure yet."

"Wanton is more like it," Wilhelm said. "The world is hounding us, hoping to drive us to extinction."

"What about this attack on you?" Grady asked. "Did you see anything at all?"

Again Rose shook her head. "The attacker was behind me. I thought I heard a gasp when I scratched the person, but I couldn't identify a voice from that."

"You scratched the guy? Did some damage, did you? Something we could see if we looked at a suspect's arms?"

"I think so." Rose wanted to confide more in Grady, but Wilhelm was likely to interfere at any time, so she kept quiet.

"Are these useless questions finished yet?" Wilhelm asked. "May we begin to set our house right again?"

"You really should put locks on all your doors," Grady said.

"Never!" Wilhelm's nostrils flared as if Grady had suggested eliminating Mother Ann from the lexicon of Shaker godhood. "We have always lived with our doors open to the world, welcoming, even when the world abuses our openness."

Sometimes Wilhelm's contradictory logic confused Rose. He seemed to invite the world to their door even as he pitted himself against it. The better to convert them, Rose supposed, though she had yet to see his approach succeed. Their numbers continued to dwindle.

"Sure, you can go ahead and clean up now," Grady said, his cheerfulness sounding forced. As Wilhelm bent to pick up some papers, Grady caught Rose's eye and flicked his head toward the office door. "I'll just be running along. I'll let you know what I find out."

"Wilhelm, I'll be back to help clean up in a few minutes," Rose said.

Intent on his task, Wilhelm grunted and ignored their departure.

*   *   *

"I know you, Rose; you've learned more than you're saying," Grady said. He leaned against the dusty black Buick that served as one of Languor's two squad cars. He studied Rose, concern in his open face.

Reaching into her dress pocket, Rose extracted her list of apostates. "These are names of people who might be involved in the incidents here lately," she said, handing the list to Grady. "They are all Shaker apostates who left North Homage about twenty-five years ago, angry with us, apparently. It seems they are living in Languor right now."

Grady's boyish face grew serious as he studied the list. "Richard Worthington? I didn't know he was a Shaker."

"He wasn't. He was brought up here and left as a young man, seventeen or eighteen, I believe. His widowed mother brought him here as a child. He left after she died."

"He's been mighty vocal in town against the Shakers, that's for sure. Any idea why?"

Rose shrugged. "None. Unless his mother's death . . ."

Grady's head snapped up. "Something suspicious about his mother's death, you think? What was her name, anyway?"

"Faithfull. And nay, I don't know anything for sure." She looked hard at Grady for several moments before continuing. "I'll tell you what I've pieced together, and what I suspect, and you can make your own judgments." She told him that both Faithfull and Samuel had died of apparent heart attacks, with no physical warning, and she reported Josie's observation that suffocation with a pillow could look like a heart attack—as it would have if Rose had died, too.

"Would have started to look like a whole lot of sudden heart attacks," Grady said, "but I can see how it might have passed by unnoticed. If you'd died, I'd have looked into it mighty carefully, though," he added. "Gennie would never have spoken to me again if I didn't."

"What a comfort," Rose murmured.

Grady cleared his throat and busied himself with the list of apostates again. "Okay, I'll check these folks out. Caleb Cox is a drunk, and we've had some suspicions about him setting some little fires and defacing a few houses when he's pie-eyed. Seems a decent enough sort when he's sober, but drink brings out the devil in him." He reddened slightly. "Sorry, I meant no disrespect."

"And I took no offense, I assure you," Rose said with a light laugh. "Remember, Grady, though I'm a Believer, I've spent a good deal of time out in the world, and there is little I haven't seen. Violence offends me, and cruelty, but never bluntness."

Grady nodded. "There's a couple of names here I don't recognize," he said, looking back at the list of apostates. "Klaus Holker and Evangeline Frankell. Don't recall hearing those names in town. Are you sure they live in Languor?"

"Nay, not certain, but Charlotte thought she saw a man and a woman last Sunday, driving away after someone threw raspberry preserves against the Meetinghouse during worship. Apparently those two are now married. They may be the couple who ran the public meeting at St. Christopher's. They introduced themselves as Kentuck and Laura Hill."

Grady shot her a stern look at her mention of the danger she'd put herself in, against his advice. "Okay, I'll ask around," he said. "Meanwhile, I'd feel a lot better if you all would put locks on your doors."

"We'll think about it," Rose promised.

To Rose's relief, Wilhelm had left by the time she returned to the Trustees' Office. The defaced papers and books were stacked neatly on her desk. She looked them over briefly. The worst damage seemed to be in her loan-payment ledger, which was unfortunate but not disastrous, since the bank held duplicate records. She would try to decipher them, though it would take precious hours of her time.

She left the piles for later and set off for the Infirmary. She had missed her visits to Agatha and was concerned that her friend might have learned of the attack on her and be worried.

Josie's desk in the Infirmary waiting room was empty, so Rose made her way back to Agatha's room. As she reached the doorway, she heard Josie's encouraging voice. Agatha was no longer in a cradle bed. She sat up, without support, in a regular bed, while Josie guided her right arm in gentle exercise.

"Agatha! What a wonderful surprise!" Rose said.

At the sound of Rose's voice, Agatha's thin face softened. The right side of her mouth still drooped, but the left side curved into a greeting smile. She said something that came close to "Rose" and held out her left hand. Rose ran to her side and took her hand in both of her own.

"Agatha has been making wonderful progress," Josie said, beaming at the former eldress as if she were a prize-winning pupil. "Her will is powerful, and maybe all those prayers of ours didn't hurt either."

Agatha's face grew serious. She extracted her hand from Rose's and pointed toward the empty hanging shelf which had held her old journals.

"You asked me to take them and read them, remember?"

Agatha nodded lopsidedly. She said a few indistinct words—five words, Rose thought.

"Josie? Did you understand her?"

"Say it again, dear," Josie said to Agatha. Agatha repeated the five words.

" 'Did you' . . . I got that much. Did I what? Read the journals?"

Again Agatha repeated the sentence, this time with some irritation.

" 'Did you find the evil?' " Josie said. "She's asking if you identified some source of evil in those journals; is that right, Agatha?" Agatha gave her crooked nod.

"I read both your journals and Fiona's for the same years," Rose said. "I found the names of four apostates, and I found out about—" She hesitated to discuss Samuel and Faithfull's liaison and their child, Sarah, in front of anyone, even Josie.

"I've got piles and piles of work to do," Josie said briskly. "I'll just leave you two to talk, shall I?"

Again Rose hesitated. Could she understand Agatha without Josie, who had so much more experience interpreting the garbled language of stroke victims? She decided it best to try. "Thank you, Josie, that would be fine."

"Agatha, it may be difficult for me to understand you, so do be patient with me," Rose said after Josie left. "It is important that I learn what you know about what went on in North Homage twenty-five years ago. I know about Samuel and Faithfull and about Sarah, their child." Agatha closed her eyes and nodded again. She remained quiet for a moment; she seemed to be gathering strength. She refocused her eyes on Rose and said distinctly, "Others."

"Others? The apostates? I have their names from the covenant, and I believe they are all in Languor and are responsible for some strange incidents we've had here. Nay, don't be alarmed, everything is under control." She had no intention of disturbing Agatha with the full story.

"The names I have are Caleb Cox, Richard Worthington, Klaus Holker, and Evangeline Frankell. Is that all of them?" Agatha nodded.

"You were so careful in your journals, Agatha. You used only initials and never mentioned specifics when someone's reputation was at stake." She thought she saw regret flash across Agatha's face. "Some questions are left unanswered—such as: Was Faithfull's death truly due to a sudden heart attack?"

Agatha's sparse white brows drew together, wrinkling the paper-thin skin of her forehead. She said nothing, but her left shoulder hunched up and lowered.

"Were you not sure?" Agatha nodded.

"Did you . . . did you suspect she had been killed?"

Agatha took a deep breath and held it. On the exhale, she closed her eyes and nodded.

"Can you tell me who you were suspicious of?" Rose asked. "Even if you weren't at all sure," she added, as she noted the look of anxiety on Agatha's face. "You know you can trust me not to besmirch someone's name without adequate evidence."

Agatha's face scrunched as if she were in pain, and Rose regretted her question. Naturally Agatha would have qualms about voicing suspicions that could harm an innocent person, no matter how much she trusted Rose. Agatha fell back against her pillow as though her sinews had snapped. She began to gasp for breath.

"Josie!" Rose shouted. "Josie, come quickly." She touched Agatha's arm gently. "Rest now, don't strain yourself. Josie will be right here with something to help you sleep. Just forget about my question. We'll be fine."

Agatha's eyes shot open and she stared at Rose.

"Oh, dear, dear," Josie fussed as she bounced into the room. "Leave it to our Agatha to overtire herself first time out. Well, we'll just give her a sedative and help her get that strength back." She gave Agatha an injection. "Don't you worry, now, Rose, it isn't your fault if Agatha insists on pushing herself too hard. She always was like that, you know. So very conscientious. But she'll be back again tomorrow, you'll see."

TWENTY-ONE

"WELL?" WILHELM SAID AS HE TOSSED A COPY OF the *Cincinnati Enquirer* on Rose's desk. Since Cincinnati was the nearest large city and a major market for Shaker goods, the Society always tried to read their newspaper. It was open to a section containing guest articles and letters from readers. Rose had been so busy that she had not looked at a newspaper in days. She glanced over the headlines in puzzlement.

"What is it you want me to read, Wilhelm?"

Wilhelm's thick finger stabbed at an article on the right-hand side of the page. The headline read: "A Stranger in Our Midst." As she began reading the article, her stomach tightened.

The Shakers, also known as the United Society of Believers in Christ's Second Appearing, are a strange and secretive lot, the article began. Rose skimmed through it quickly, her sense of dread deepening. The byline said "Kentuck Hill"—the name used by the man who spoke against the Shakers at the town meeting Rose had secretly attended. She was certain he was also the author of the *Languor County Watcher,* though the style of this article was far more sophisticated. *A man skilled with language,* Rose thought.

The article continued:

What do we really know of these Shakers? Since, in my youthful ignorance, I was once a part of them, I will tell you about them—not out of bitterness but love for my homeland. Many of you know of the Shakers only through the goods they produce, such as exquisite pieces of fine furniture, tasty preserved fruits and vegetables, decorative seed packets, and aromatic herbs.

What few of you know is that these items, excellent though they may be, are produced under conditions of the vilest servitude. Defenseless children are little more than slaves, doing their masters' bidding until late into the night. Young people are enticed into the "Society" with promises of a spiritual life and everlasting joy. Once entangled, these innocents find themselves working day and night, with little rest and without the comforts of home and family, and without even the smallest recompense.

Moreover, these products are made by traitors who will not defend their country against any foe, no matter how wicked. Few of you know that during the Great War, these Shakers chose the coward's way, refusing to allow their young men to take arms against the Kaiser. They did this for the sake of their beliefs, they claimed—yet while the rest of the country suffered and died and sank into a Depression, these folks have become rich! Judge for yourselves whether their purposes are of the Spirit.

Perhaps vilest of all is the way these Shakers live, so different from other Americans. Their "families" are large groups of men and women living together in the same building. Children are wrenched away from their own families and sent to live in a separate building. Husbands and wives are put asunder. One can only imagine—and it is best not to do so!—what volcanoes erupt when natural human affections are so unnaturally suppressed. The fury is spent on the children and on unprotected young girls, held against their will. I will say no more, to spare the sensibilities of my readers.

If you are as alarmed as I am, you will agree it is time for action. Naturally we do not advocate violence of any sort. To harm these folks would make them into martyrs, a fate for which they no doubt long. No, we believe that the best way to rid ourselves of this pestilence among us is to destroy its source of support: REFUSE TO BUY SHAKER GOODS. Refuse to patronize establishments that insist on carrying Shaker goods. If we all pull together, as we always have in times of threat to our American way of life, we can drive this curse from our beloved countryside.

Rose let the paper slip from her hands onto her desk.

"I've had calls from friends in Lexington and Louisville," Wilhelm said. "Their papers carried the same article. This person intends to destroy us, attacking our livelihood. But he cannot touch our soul," he finished grimly.

"Nay, but he can pierce our stomachs," Rose said. "Do the others know of this yet?"

"I've told no one, but word will leak out soon enough. It is for the best. The Society must join together, stand up bravely to this persecution."

Rose saw the brightness of Wilhelm's eyes. "One

might almost think you were looking forward to this struggle," she said. "It could destroy us, you know."

"We have suffered too little; we have grown complacent. Adversity will strengthen us. If we do not have enough to eat, well then, we will understand with our own bodies what the early Believers endured." Wilhelm's thick white hair, in need of a trim, curled over the collar of his brown work jacket, giving him the look of a nineteenth-century brethren just back from a long journey to gather souls.

Rose sighed. Wilhelm was a zealous Believer and a powerful spiritual leader. But he had never been a trustee, never had to watch over the financial health of the Society. He did not understand that the Depression had indeed touched their lives, though they had rich land and hard-working hands to work it. They always had food on the table and extra to share with the less fortunate. But their financial condition had weakened steadily as this Depression wore on. Their businesses were essential to their long-term survival.

Rose's office telephone jangled. Wilhelm tossed it an irritable glance. "I have preparations to make," he said. "We will speak more about all this later."

Rose decided she would rather face whatever was on the other end of the phone line than know what preparations Wilhelm had in mind. She nodded to him as he turned to leave, then reached for the phone. She almost regretted her decision when the operator informed her that the buyer for one of the largest hotels in Cincinnati was on the line.

"You're canceling *everything*? All the herbs and jams and preserved vegetables? But you've ordered from us for years, and we've always delivered the best quality; surely you agree. I know this is because of that cowardly and false story in the paper, but I can't believe you would accept those lies. I thought we'd always respected one another.''

"I know, Miss Callahan, and believe me, this wasn't my decision. Just got dumped in my lap to call you, and I'm mad as—well, I'm not happy about it. I always could trust your products, and our customers love them, but we're under new management, and with this Depression and all, they think we can't afford to lose customers who might be mad at you Shakers. For what it's worth, the whole kitchen wished they could quit, said they never tasted cooking herbs half as good as Shaker ones, but then they'd be out on the streets, what with there being no other jobs around. So you see what a pickle we're in. Sorry, Miss Callahan, really I am. Maybe we can start up again with y'all once this blows over.''

"I understand," Rose said. "I certainly wouldn't want anyone to lose a job over this. Thanks for your words of comfort. As you say, maybe when this blows over . . .'' She hung up and leaned her forehead against her hand, which still held the phone.

"Rose? Are you unwell?''

Rose whirled around, her heart leaping at the sound of the familiar, much loved voice of Gennie Malone.

"Gennie, my dear! What . . . How . . .''

"The 'how' is the squad car with Grady," Gennie said, as she hugged Rose. "He had to talk with someone down the road and said he'd drop me off and pick me up later. The 'what' is some not very pleasant news that I couldn't bear to deliver to you over the phone.''

Rose nodded and lifted from a wall peg her smallest chair, to fit Gennie's diminutive body. Worried as she was, Gennie looked lovely, her eyes sparkling after the eight-mile drive alone with Grady.

"You've come to tell me what is happening with our Shaker products in Languor, haven't you?"

Gennie nodded. "It's gotten worse and worse all day, ever since that awful newspaper article came out. I've heard lots of people say they weren't even going to warn you; they were just going to show up with everything Shaker and demand their money back. Floyd Foster led the pack. He took some carrots and potatoes and just threw them out in the street, which made me really mad, because there are hungry people who could have eaten that food, but the cars and wagons smashed it to pulp before anyone could grab it off the street.'' A spot of color appeared on each of Gennie's cheeks, and her eyes flashed with anger. *Oh, what a Believer she would have made,* Rose thought. But at least she had learned compassion, which she could carry with her into the world.

"I have something else to tell you, too," Gennie said, covering Rose's hand with her own. "The flower shop I work in—the owners want us to return all the herb plants and even the sprigs and flowers I've been working into bouquets. I told Emily—remember Grady's sister, Emily?—I told her I would do no such thing, and I didn't care if they fired me!''

"Gennie, nay, you must return everything. Don't risk your job. It would be nearly impossible to find another these days.''

"Well, Emily wouldn't let me talk to the owners," Gennie said with obvious regret. "She called them while I was at lunch and told them she would handle everything. By the time I got back, she had taken all the Shaker herbs and hidden them from me. She said Grady would be terribly upset if she let me lose my job. So I suppose Emily will bring everything back, but remember, she's really doing it for me and Grady, not because she agrees with that stupid article."

"I know, Gennie. Many people in Languor have been loyal friends to us. I trust that God will work through those good people, and we will survive this. Somehow."

All day long, the cars and wagons arrived at the Trustees' Office, filled with Shaker goods being returned for refunds. Some Languor citizens made hurtful remarks about Believers, but most looked sheepish and regretful. Often the lowest-ranking employee had been sent because no one else wanted to face the Shakers with their cowardice.

Rose had no way to reimburse people for their returned products. The money had already been used to make loan payments and buy whatever supplies the Shakers could not produce themselves. She handed out IOUs, cringing as she wrote each one. Within the space of one day, North Homage slid from relative financial stability to impending ruin.

Rose had begun a clean ledger book to record the day's transactions. She had filled far too many pages when her office phone rang. She reached for it reluctantly. News that day was never good.

"Miss Callahan?" asked a brusque male voice.

"Jackson here, president of the Languor School Board."

Rose's heart pounded with dread.

"I am very sorry to have to tell you this, Miss Callahan, but the Board met in emergency session this afternoon concerning the North Homage School District. We decided to close the district, effective immediately. Given the unfortunate publicity you all have been getting, and the many calls we've received from alarmed parents and citizens, we thought it best to decide the issue immediately. The situation is simply too volatile, and we can't afford to allow children to be placed in danger."

"Mr. Jackson, I assure you, there is no danger—"

"We are the best judges of that, Miss Callahan. If there is even the slightest hint of impropriety, we must act immediately to protect the children."

"*Impropriety*. There is absolutely no question of impropriety in North Homage's school. I'm shocked that you would believe such a lie. We live our faith every moment of our lives. We would never allow—"

"Miss Callahan, whatever may be your intentions, and I'm sure they are good, the fact remains that we cannot risk our children while the truth works its way to the surface. The parents would never stand for it, and the publicity—well, you can understand the pressure we're under. Now, I really haven't time to talk longer. We will be in touch later in the month to discuss sending the children who live in North Homage elsewhere for school." Jackson hesitated a moment, then relented. "For what it's worth, I've always had great respect for the education North Homage has provided. I shouldn't tell you this, but you will shortly be receiving a call or visit from a child welfare worker, as well.''

''*What?*''

''I'm afraid so. Some citizens are up in arms about any children being in North Homage, and they are lobbying to have them removed from your care. From what I can gather, it's actually a woman behind this movement, a Laura Hill, or that's the name I've seen on some of the literature being distributed around town. Seems she wants the children put up for adoption. In fact, she expressed an interest in adopting them all herself. Now I really must go.'' The voice was brisk again, then gone.

Rose felt a wave of exhaustion as she hung up the phone. She sank back in her chair and let her head rest against the slats. No sooner had she closed her eyes than she heard footsteps on the pine floor of her office. Her eyes popped open to see Richard Worthington standing before her, a look in his eyes, something bright and cold like a winter day, that chilled her blood.

''Richard?'' she said and, not liking the weak tone of her voice, she added, ''What is it, Richard?'' She pulled herself straight in her chair. ''We are quite busy just now, as you well know.''

Worthington nodded slightly. ''Believe me, Rose,'' he said, his voice bland, ''this is a painful errand for me.''

Rose stared at the thin patrician face and felt the anger and triumph behind the words. ''I doubt that,'' she said quietly.

Worthington slid a ledger book from under his arm and placed it on Rose's side of the desk. He remem-

bered not to stand too near Rose. She was glad for
the custom; his presence disturbed her. He opened the
ledger book to a page labeled "North Homage Shaker
Village: Outstanding Loans." Rose leaned over the
book, confused about Worthington's purpose in showing it to her. After all, they had their own records.
Nay, she remembered, their records had been defaced
and were illegible. Her heartbeat picking up speed,
she ran her finger down the list of loan payments for
the past six months. For four of those months, the
spaces for payment amounts said "No payment
rec'd." Only two months listed payment amounts, and
those were much lower than the actual amounts Rose
had counted out and delivered herself.

Rose grabbed her own payment records, hoping her
memory was wrong, that there really were some leg-
ible numbers inside that would contradict the bank's
records. But the entire "Paid" column had been oblit-
erated with a long streak of ink that looked as if it
had started from a blob at the top of the page. Someone must have moved the book gradually upright so
the ink would spill directly down the page. Without
looking at Worthington, she could feel the sharp edge
of his gloating smile.

"How did you do this, Richard?" She met his eyes.
"I saw you write down the correct payment amounts
when I delivered the money to the loan officer and to
you. You must have spent nights copying over the
entire ledger book."

"I can't imagine what you're talking about."

"Oh, now I remember," Rose said, her own voice
hardening to match Worthington's. "Six months ago,
the loan officer took a job in Cincinnati. Did you get

it for him, by the way? Such jobs aren't easy to come by these days. So with him gone, you took over receiving loan payments—just until you hired someone new, you told me. You must have started a new ledger book then. Yea, I see by the date on the first page that you did. That would mean you only had to keep two sets of books for six months, and it could all be in your handwriting. Since we always paid in cash, there would be no other record of the size of our payment." She pulled open a small drawer where she kept loan payment receipts. It was empty. She was not surprised.

Worthington's face was expressionless, just a hint of satisfaction in his cold blue eyes.

"I knew you were cruel, Richard, and clever. But I miscalculated the depth of your anger. All I can ask you is, why? Why are you doing this to us?"

"You have spent too long away from the world, Rose," Worthington said. "You are spinning a fantasy in which the Shakers' failure is someone else's fault. The truth is, you people are irresponsible. You just don't pay your bills."

Rose swallowed her surge of anger. "Are you foreclosing, then?" she asked, her voice as steady as she could manage.

"Oh, that may not be necessary."

"What do you mean?"

"The bank is willing to be lenient, given your previous history of paying more or less on time. If you deed over certain parcels of your lands to the bank, we will forgive the payments you have missed. We will send you a list of the lands we will require. Nothing need be made public, so your reputation will be safe. Whatever reputation you have left, that is.''

"And I suppose these will be rich farmlands?''

"We really don't wish to take your homes away from you, Rose. Of course you may keep your buildings. Some of the farmland will be sufficient.''

"How are we to survive?''

"I'm sure you'll find a way. Unless, of course, certain others have their way and you are driven out of the county. But that has nothing to do with the bank or with me.'' He slammed shut his ledger book and settled it under his arm, being careful not to wrinkle the fine wool of his gray suit. "Anyway, we can discuss the details at a later date. Say, next week? In the meantime, we will send you our offer by messenger, and you can begin to make whatever arrangements are necessary.'' He left without bidding her farewell.

Rose massaged her forehead to ease the pounding that had steadily gained momentum inside her skull. For the first time in her life, she felt despair settle over her like a thick wool cloak drenched by the rain. She pulled the ledger book toward her again but did not open it. The contents would not have changed.

TWENTY-TWO

"TOMORROW I'LL EXPECT THEE AT THE MINISTRY dining room for an early breakfast," Wilhelm said. He had stopped by her office on his way to work in the fields. Someone had to plant the crops, he'd said, while the world tormented the Society. *Probably hoping to shout homilies to townspeople stopping by for their refunds,* Rose thought in a weak, uncharitable moment.

"I may be up late with the books tonight, Wilhelm. Breakfast may be sacrificed to sleep."

"Then clearly thy strength is not equal to the tasks of being both eldress and trustee." He raised his eyebrows at her, but she allowed the comment to pass. It was time to preserve her energy, not waste it on squabbles with Wilhelm.

"Our financial condition is deplorable," he continued, "and it is because of thy inability to do all the necessary tasks."

This time, his stab hit the mark. "Wilhelm, you cannot hold me responsible for this financial dilemma. Forces are at work that I could never have anticipated, nor controlled. Richard Worthington has tampered with the bank's books, our own records were purposely defaced and our receipts stolen—how could I control all that?''

"Excuses," Wilhelm said. "I will expect thee tomorrow morning, early," he repeated. "We have important topics to discuss. We'll talk more then." With a quick nod, he turned and left.

At midnight, Rose finally set aside her financial records and stuffed her own journal, in which she had unburdened herself, in the back of a drawer. The Trustees' Office was quiet and dark, except for the circle of light at Rose's desk. She had never felt less like sleeping, but the demands of the coming day would be great, and her community needed her at her best. Or at least as close to her best as she could manage after the day she'd just endured. She switched off the light and climbed the stairs to her retiring room.

The nights were growing warmer, so Rose dug in the back of her dresser drawer for her light cotton nightgown. As she prepared for bed, her weary mind continued to race, but no helpful ideas surfaced. She prayed longer than usual, despite her exhaustion. She needed more strength than she carried within herself.

Slipping between the cool sheets, Rose allowed the peace of prayer to relax her mind. But it did not last. She drifted into sleep only to encounter vivid nightmare images that clung to her even as they jolted her awake.

Finally she gave up and tossed off her bedclothes. Slipping a light shawl over her shoulders, she padded barefoot to her sitting area. She gathered on her desk some of the materials she had been researching— Fiona's chatty journals and the three powerful journal excerpts Sarah had given to her. They had been pushed to the back of her cupboard, and apparently her attacker had been too rushed to see and steal them. She regretted the absence of Agatha's carefully vague journals, but she would have to make do with what she had.

She had used small bits of paper to mark the important pages in the journals, and she read carefully through all those sections again. Nothing new emerged, but maybe she was just too tired. She took the three journal excerpts and placed them side-by-side in the order she guessed they had been written. The first page Caleb had given to Sarah implied that an unnamed man was implicated in or knew something about Sister Faithfull's death. The other two segments filled in earlier details, mostly with hints and innuendos.

She read through the pages quickly, one after the other. An idea tugged at her brain, a perception that wouldn't form into words. She reached farther back into her built-in wall cupboard and drew out the other papers she had placed there: the copies of the *Languor County Watcher*, the announcement of the anti-Shaker town meeting, and the article from the *Cincinnati Enquirer* that had caused so much devastation in the past day. She laid them on her desk, putting the journal pages aside. Gritting her teeth, she read through each one. Again it struck her that all the articles had been written by the same person, Kentuck Hill, yet the styles showed clever differences. Each appealed to a different audience. If Kentuck Hill was truly Klaus Holker, he was not only an apostate Shaker, but a skilled writer as well. She spread out the three journal segments again. The style was both angry and lyrical, the sort of journal entry a Believer with a poetic bent might pen.

What had Fee and Agatha said about Klaus? She checked Fee's journals again. She saw no mention of any particular interest in written expression, but hadn't Hugo said that he remembered an apostate who had worked for the *Cincinnati Enquirer* after leaving North Homage? Fee wrote that Klaus stared into space more than he worked, and she guessed that he was mooning around because he was in love with Evangeline, his future wife.

Rose walked to her east window and pulled back the light curtain. A faint glow signaled the awakening sun. She had been reading and thinking and rereading most of the night. Her eyes felt sore and gritty. She rubbed them lightly with her cool fingers. That helped little, so she splashed cold water on her face from the worn porcelain bowl in her bedroom. As she reached for her cotton towel, the fog in her mind yielded to one clear question: What if Klaus was not smitten with Evangeline, but with Faithfull? Yea, indeed, it would explain why Klaus, as well as Samuel, declined to go on sales trips once Faithfull had returned to North Homage. The fury in the journal pages would be understandable—his love had died suddenly, and he blamed his rival, Samuel.

If Klaus wrote those passages, then he must not have killed Faithfull himself. Did Samuel? Was that the real source of Samuel's endless guilt and inability to confess fully? But why? Had Faithfull refused him in the end? Had she turned to Klaus?

Rose's mind clamped shut again. It was nearing

breakfast time, and she would be no help to the Society if she didn't sleep at least a little. She wrote a quick note to Wilhelm, explaining that she felt unwell and would be glad to breakfast with him the following morning. When she slipped down the staircase, the kitchen sisters were already brewing a rose hip and red clover tea and slicing brown bread. She asked one of the younger sisters to run the note over to the Ministry and give it to the kitchen sister there, to be handed to Wilhelm at breakfast. Pleading a headache, she declined breakfast and collapsed in her own bed. Finally, she slept, and if the nightmares returned, she was too tired to heed them.

A firm knock on Rose's retiring-room door yanked her out of deep sleep. Josie entered her bedroom clattering two cups on a tray.

"Ah, Rose, I hate to wake you, but the kitchen sisters said you asked not to sleep past eight, and they didn't have the heart to rouse you, and it is nine now . . ."

"Nine! I've got to get up right away. I've got so much to do today." Rose struggled to a sitting position, still groggy and light-headed from lack of sleep.

"Well, I thought you'd feel that way, though I was hoping to convince you to spend the day resting, so I brought you a rosemary muffin and some pennyroyal and chamomile tea, to soothe your head—the sisters said you had a headache—and put you back to sleep."

"Nay, Josie, I can't afford to rest, not yet. I have so many questions to pursue today, and they can't wait. So much depends on the answers. I don't even have time to join you for tea this morning.''

"Oh, the second cup isn't for me," Josie said. "I know our Rose, so I also brewed a cup of rose hip and lemon balm, with a pinch of dandelion root, to help perk you up and give you strength.''

"Josie, you are a jewel," Rose said, reaching for the second steaming cup.

Josie placed her hand on Rose's wrist. "First you must promise me that you'll rest when this is over."

Rose laughed. "Yea, Josie, I promise, but it may not be today or tomorrow or the next day." She wriggled into her work dress and pulled on her sturdy black work shoes.

"Just so long as I have your promise." Josie nodded briskly, sending her chins into vibration, and handed Rose the tea and muffin.

"How is Agatha?" Rose asked. She bit hungrily into the muffin.

"Agitated, poor dear. She didn't sleep at all well last night. It's as if she knows what's been going on here, people returning our products and all, but I've made sure she heard nothing of it. She is terribly worried about something, though.''

Rose paused with the teacup halfway to her lips. "Has she said anything?"

"Nothing coherent since you talked with her. But maybe she's just overtired. She's had a string of visitors since she began to improve."

Rose drained her cup. "Thanks, Josie. You've been a godsend, as always." She raced toward her retiring-room door, leaving Josie in the bedroom.

"Wait, Rose," Josie called, "you be sure to eat more than just that muffin. Do you hear?"

Rose tossed back a noncommittal "uh-huh" and flew down the stairs. She went immediately to the phone in her office and placed a call to the Languor County Sheriff's Office, thankful that for once she would not have to talk to Sheriff Brock. Grady's gentle drawl came on the line.

"Rose, Gennie filled me in on the mess you folks are in. She's mighty riled, even sent off a letter to the *Enquirer* herself, denying everything that fellow said about you all."

"Bless her," Rose said. "Not that it will do any good. I doubt the world has hated us this much since the days of Mother Ann. But that's not why I'm calling. I've been digging into some records here from twenty-five years or so ago, and I think I'm beginning to understand these attacks against North Homage. I need your help."

"You bet," Grady said. "What can I do?"

"What have you discovered about the list of apostates I gave you? Could one of them have been the person who attacked me?"

"Well, I had a chat with Caleb—as best I could, anyway. He was drunk as a—anyway, it was easy to take a look at his arms. I did see some scratches above his wrists. Hard to tell, but fingernails could have made them. Good supply of booze, too, some of it good stuff. Wonder how he got it. It looked to me like he'd been drinking for quite some time. I've never seen him this bad before."

"I suspect an apostate has been supplying Caleb with money for alcohol in exchange for inflicting cruelties on us. Agatha's journals indicated that Caleb had a troubled history when he lived here, and at the same time she reported episodes that sounded similar to what we've been experiencing lately. Including a rat hung in the kitchen.''

"A rat, eh. Like in your schoolhouse.''

"Yea, I suspect Caleb was involved in that. What else did you find?''

"Floyd and Ned were easy. I saw both of them at work, with their sleeves hiked up enough for me to see they weren't scratched. You sure you got the wrists?''

"Nay, I can't be completely sure,'' Rose said. "I blacked out soon afterward.''

"Richard Worthington was trickier, of course,'' Grady continued, "but he's friendly to me because my father's such a good customer.'' Rose remembered that Grady's people were well-to-do tobacco farmers who poured money back into their farm and equipment. They had never believed in putting their savings in banks, so the Depression had barely slowed them down, but they were often good for a hefty loan.

"I caught Richard in his yard, playing catch with his son, so I joined in. I got him to play hard, but he's always the gentleman. Just wouldn't roll up his sleeves. I caught a glimpse of his wrists and didn't see anything much, but that's the best I could manage.''

"Evangeline Frankell and Klaus Holker?''

"No one ever heard of them.''

"Impossible. All of them lived here at North Homage together. Are you saying that even Caleb, inebriated as he was, managed to lie about knowing them?''

"Well, to be honest, Caleb was pretty well passed out by the time I got to asking about them. The other three looked me straight in the eye and said they'd never heard those names. I asked a bit around town, too, both about the Holkers and those other names you gave me, Kentuck and Laura Hill. A few folks had heard of Kentuck and Laura, but no one knows where they live. Of course, Languor's just big enough that in the right part of town a couple of strangers could pass without notice for a while. Especially if they had a secret place to stay.''

"Are there any empty houses around town?"

"Some foreclosed ones, scattered around."

"And Richard Worthington's bank is the biggest one in town. Can you manage to find out which houses his bank has foreclosed on and see if anyone is living in one of them, perhaps without the bank's knowledge?"

"Interesting," Grady said. "Yeah, I could do that."

TWENTY-THREE

ROSE HAD SOME POINTED QUESTIONS FOR SISTER Elsa Pike, who seemed to know too much about Faith-full and Samuel and Sarah. Elsa would be cleaning up in the Center Family kitchen by now. Rose would let her finish her tasks. Rose's stomach gurgled with hunger, and she decided a side trip to the Trustees' Office kitchen was in order. An interview with Elsa on little sleep and an empty stomach sounded too onerous.

She whipped into the small trustees' kitchen and snatched a leftover slice of brown bread from a tray on the counter, slathered it with butter, and took a generous bite. Only one sister had remained to do clean-up. Rose gathered up dishes to be washed, as-suring the sister that she was feeling better but would be unavailable all day, in case someone asked. Es-pecially someone like Wilhelm.

As Rose headed for the front door, she heard the phone ring in her office. She hesitated. It could be another Languor citizen asking for a refund, but it could also be Grady with the information she had asked him to get about empty houses in Languor. She rushed back to her office and grabbed the phone.

"Reckon I found it," Grady's voice said as he replaced the operator. "I checked at Worthington's bank, soon as it opened and before he got there. They listed three houses in town and one farmhouse they'd foreclosed on, and no one's bought any of them yet. The farmhouse roof is falling in, and one of the houses is fire-damaged, so I checked out the other two."

"Did you go inside?"

"Yeah, briefly. The bank vice president—I went to school with him—he lent me keys, and we agreed not to mention it to Worthington. One house was completely empty, but the other one—well, no one answered the door, so I had a quick look around. The top floors were empty, except for two rooms that looked lived in, had men's clothes in the closet of one and women's clothes in the other. But guess what I found in the basement—a printing press."

"Ah, that's it, then." Rose's exhaustion yielded to excitement. "No sign of the inhabitants?"

"Nope, but I didn't stay more than ten minutes."

"Grady, do you still have that key?"

"Yes," Grady said, sounding guarded.

"I'd like to take a look at the house."

"Rose, I don't know about that. Harry wouldn't like it much that I went in there at all. If I let you go, too, and he finds out, he'll give me—uh, heck."

Rose laughed. "The sheriff has given us both 'heck' before, and we survived the experience. The risk is worth it, believe me."

Grady sighed, and Rose could almost see him run his hand through his straight brown hair. "I can't let you go in there alone," he said. "We don't know how these folks would react if they came back and found you there. All right, look, can you meet me in about half an hour? The address is 42 Ginkgo Lane. Worthington isn't due at the bank until noon; I could still get the key back without having to explain myself to him.''

"I'll leave right now."

"You stay in your car until I see if the house is still empty," Grady said as he leaned down to talk to Rose through the open window of the Society's Plymouth.

He knocked twice, then used the key to enter. Rose felt her first tingle of anxiety as a couple walked toward her car, arm in arm. She resisted the urge to sink down in her seat; that would look odd. Yet she felt exposed in her woven sugar-scoop bonnet, so she slipped it off. She stared straight ahead, watching the couple out of the corner of her eye. They passed her car and the empty house with no more than a quick glance in her direction.

Rose released the breath she'd been holding in her chest just as Grady appeared at the front door and beckoned her inside. She hopped out of the car, picked up her skirts, and trotted to the house. Grady locked the door behind her and led the way down a dark corridor to the kitchen. Rose had become so accustomed to Shaker buildings, which were cleaned and aired daily, that she could smell the dust in the stale air. Grady had a flashlight, essential in this gloomy house where sunlight could not penetrate the heavy brocade curtains.

"The steps are rickety," Grady said. "Watch yourself." He descended the staircase to the basement. Rose followed him and stopped at the bottom of the steps, unable to make out anything but a large shape that filled nearly half the room. She saw a cracked stool pulled up to what looked like a typewriter, which was attached to a complicated machine as tall as a man. She took it to be a printing press. Grady lit candle after candle, until wavering shapes emerged: a ring of empty chairs, dozens more unlit candles, oil lamps, and a table covered with stacks of paper. Piles of books cluttered the floor underneath the table.

"They'll smell those candles and know someone has been here," Rose warned. "If they come back while we're here, what do we do?"

"Run," Grady said with a laugh. "What can they do? We'd hear them come in, and I'm the law. They shouldn't be living here. Chances are they're the ones who'd run."

"And then we'd lose track of them," Rose said.

"Well, that's one way to get rid of them. Do you want to leave?"

"Nay, I need to know what's going on, even at the risk of giving them warning."

Grady seemed fascinated by the printing press. "Old model," he said. "Linotype. I remember seeing one like this as a kid. My father was friends with the editor of the *Languor Weekly Advocate*, and he used to take me over to watch the paper go to press sometimes. It would take some determination for them to cart this thing here and set it up."

"Determination and knowledge and anger," Rose said. She had carried a large candle over to the table and was reading a page with printing on it. "Grady, look at this."

Grady took the paper she held out to him, and read:

CITIZENS OF LANGUOR COUNTY
The time is NOW!!!

The Shakers have kidnapped their last child!

The message ended in the middle of the page. "Strong words," Grady remarked. "Any idea what it's about?"

"It's more than strong, it's a horrible lie. They've got something planned, I suspect. My guess is it's coming up soon. Several of these pages are variations on this one, some longer, as if they were drafts. Yet there is no evidence of a final version."

"Being distributed, you reckon?"

"I'm afraid so." Rose scanned the room. "There's nothing here. I want to look upstairs in the bedrooms." She was up the basement stairs before Grady could blow out the candles.

They split up, Grady searching the man's room, and Rose, the woman's. The woman's dresser held a few underthings, not enough to hide anything underneath, so Rose moved to the large closet. Stacked neatly into a far corner, she found what she'd hoped to find.

"Grady, come in here and look," she called. "These are Shaker journals." Ignoring the dust and dirt, Rose scrambled on her knees on the floor of the closet. "I'm certain these are Samuel's journals," she said, opening one volume in the middle. "I don't really know his handwriting, but here he's talking about discussing his sales trips with Fee. Fiona, our late trustee,'' Rose explained when Grady looked puzzled. "I'm taking these back."

"Are you sure that's wise? I bet they'll notice."

"I'm afraid they will destroy everything. These belong to us, to all Believers. And these journals are the only way I'll really understand what has been happening in North Homage. Will you help me?"

Grady sighed. "All right, I'll help." He began gathering up the small volumes. "These look different," he said. "Different handwriting."

"That's Agatha's handwriting," Rose said, grabbing the whole stack. "These are the volumes someone stole from my retiring room." She held one volume to her chest.

"Rose, are you positive the folks involved are former Shakers? I mean, couldn't they have gotten plenty of information about you all from these journals?"

"Nay, the articles about us began before any of these were stolen. But they must have one more set of journals."

"Why?"

Rose told him about the old journal pages Sarah had given her.

"I'm fairly certain," she concluded, "that the handwriting on those pages does not match Samuel's." She stood and brushed the dust from her dress. "Did you find anything in the man's closet?"

"Just piles and piles of old newspapers. They contained articles with the byline "Klaus Holker.""

"Then it's certain. Klaus Holker and Evangeline Frankell are involved, and Klaus is almost certainly the author of the *Watcher*. Did you find any other Shaker journals in Klaus's room?"

"Nope, not a one."

Rose looked back at the closet. "I do want to take these with me."

"How about we just take the ones you're sure you'll need? Maybe then they won't notice right away that any are missing."

Rose nodded in sad agreement. She selected volumes for 1906 and 1910 through 1912 of Samuel's journals, along with his most recent one, and Agatha's 1912 journal. She carefully stacked the remaining books to look as they had originally.

"What time is it?" Rose asked.

Grady pulled out his pocket watch. "Just past eleven. We'd better get out of here. If Worthington and these folks are together, and he is due at the bank at noon, they may return soon."

They left the house quickly, relieved to find the street still deserted. Worthington had chosen the house well; it was on a remarkably quiet street. They stowed the journals in the small trunk of the Society's car.

"If my guess is right," Rose said, "and the apostates are planning something, can I find you quickly?"

Grady nodded. "Call me at the sheriff's office or my home, anytime, day or night. Harry won't be back for a few more days, or I'd have a hard time being so helpful. I'm hoping you won't have any need to mention this visit to him in the future? Good, thanks. Let me know if anything happens, and I'll be there."

A rattling Model A turned onto the street, and Rose slipped behind the wheel of her car. Grady strolled to his own Buick as if he had just finished admonishing someone for erratic driving. Both started their cars and drove off before the Model A had sputtered close enough for the driver to see them clearly.

Rose's mind churned with plans and with fears. She was convinced that Samuel's journals would fill in enough details to help her figure out what was going on in her village, but she didn't have time to pore over them just yet. She drove toward Richard Worthington's elegant mansion on the other side of town. Despite Worthington's coldness, Rose believed he was the only one she could approach. It was in character for him to threaten to call in North Homage's loans, but she could not envision him taking part in an angry mob. If he planned to be at the bank by noon, he might just be home now, preparing for work.

Worthington's estate covered several acres on the corner of the most exclusive street in Languor. The home had originally been built by his wife's grandfather with the questionably gotten profit from his railroad empire. The Depression had not touched the house or grounds. A high wrought-iron fence surrounded the property. Just inside, a thick wall of lilacs and golden forsythia obscured any view through the fence.

Rose parked the Plymouth around the corner from the entrance, hoping to attract as little attention as possible. She walked around the corner and slid through the gate, from which hung an open padlock. The Worthingtons might own a mansion, but they still lived in a rural Kentucky town, where locks were rarely used. Her feet crunched on the shell fragments lining the driveway, which split into two directions—off to the right, toward a carriage house converted into a garage, and to the left, toward the curving limestone stairs that led to the front door. Rose stuffed wisps of hair back in her bonnet, shook out her wrinkled dress, and approached the door.

A uniformed maid answered her ring and stared at her, her wide eyes moving from Rose's dusty black shoes and loose dress to her heavy bonnet.

"I've come to speak with Mr. Worthington," Rose said.

"He's not home," the girl said with a deep Southern drawl. No wonder she stared; she might never have seen a Shaker.

"Will he be home soon? It's important that I speak with him."

"Who is it, Abbie?" Frances Worthington's small, pinched face peered around the shoulder of the taller maid. "Oh, hello."

"Mrs. Worthington, my name is Rose Callahan, and I'm eldress of North Homage Shaker village."

"Yes, of course, I know who you are. Richard isn't home yet."

"May I speak with you?"

"Well, I suppose so." Her dark eyes registered an emotion stronger than discomfort. Fear, perhaps? "Come in. Abbie, bring coffee to the parlor."

"You needn't bother, truly. I'll only take a few minutes of your time, and we don't drink coffee." Her stomach was complaining again, and she longed to request a snack, but she decided against it. Best to make this a quick visit and get back to North Homage.

"Oh, yes, of course. I forgot." Frances rubbed her

arms as if she were chilled and led the way to the parlor.

Rose stifled a gasp when she saw the room. The size did not surprise her; Shaker rooms were large enough to accommodate groups. But Shaker rooms also gave a sense of openness and light, with their generous windows and sparse furnishings. The Worthington parlor looked as if its owners had begun to collect possessions during the Victorian era and forgot to stop when it was full. Small Persian rugs lay on larger ones, while furniture, paintings, and painted statuettes lined all four walls. Heavy brocade curtains, slightly open, allowed only a sliver of light. To Rose, the room felt as stale and unlived-in as the abandoned house the apostates were using.

Frances Worthington perched on the edge of a velvet wingback. "What can I do for you?" she asked, in a voice as small and sharp as her body.

"Mrs. Worthington—"

"Oh, do call me Frances." A quick, nervous smile flashed across her face. "I feel as if I know you all. I've always appreciated your kindnesses to others."

"Then I hope that you'll be willing to help me now," Rose said. "We Shakers are in some danger, and I am quite certain that your husband knows what the danger is. Were you aware that he is threatening to call in our loans, claiming that we have not been making our payments?"

Frances slid into the deep chair. "No," she said, "I didn't know. I'm sorry, but I really don't see—"

"Mama, Mama, where are you?"

"In here, darling."

Rose turned toward the sound of the young voice,

and Rickie Worthington bounded into the room. He stopped and stared at Rose, then giggled.

"It's one of the funny ladies! Why does she wear a funny hat like that, Mama?"

"Rickie, don't talk like that, darling, it's rude. Come here and sit on my lap."

Rickie ignored her and continued to stare at Rose, who longed to get him into a Shaker school and teach him some manners.

"Look what I can do, Mama." Rickie crumpled into a ball on the rug and rolled over in an awkward somersault, narrowly missing a delicately carved end table holding a glass-beaded lamp and several figurines.

"Sweetheart, stop that. Papa will be very unhappy if you break anything." Frances's voice verged on a whine. Clearly she was used to being ignored.

"When's Papa coming home?" Rickie asked, as he tried to stand on his head, bracing himself against a love seat.

"Rickie! Papa will be home very soon, and he won't like seeing you do that."

Rickie fell over and rolled to a sitting position. "Papa said he's gonna take me tonight."

"Where is your father taking you, Rickie?" Rose asked gently.

Rickie stared at her as if he had forgotten her presence.

"Yes, where, Rickie?" Frances asked.

Rickie shrugged his pudgy shoulders and bounced to his feet. "Someplace fun. He promised this time he'd take me along." The boy marched from the room, imitating a train whistle at the top of his voice.

Rose turned back to Frances, who lowered her gaze to her fidgeting hands. "What is going to happen, Frances? Please tell me. You've said that you respect us. Our lives could be in danger. Do you want to be a party to that?"

"No, no, of course not." Frances drew a ragged sigh. "You see, I don't really know what's going to happen, only that something is planned. I can't believe Richard would be involved in anything that would endanger your lives. He'd never take Rickie someplace dangerous."

"Perhaps he doesn't really intend to take the boy along?"

Frances sighed. "Rickie does tend to get his hopes up." Her voice deepened with bitterness. "Sometimes I think Richard tells Rickie more than he tells me. He has been getting phone calls from . . . those people. I don't know who they are, but they have squeezed the goodness out of Richard and made him angrier than I've ever seen him. They brought back old memories that I thought he'd gotten over."

"Memories of what?"

Frances shook her head and sighed again. "I don't know all of that, either. He always kept things to himself. I do know they had to do with his mother and with you all."

"His mother was named Faithfull, and she was a Shaker sister," Rose said.

"Yes, I know. And she died, I know that, too. When Richard was seventeen. He blames you all for her death. Once he even said that the Shakers killed her. I asked him what he meant by that—you know, if he knew that a certain Shaker had killed his mother. He wouldn't answer.''

''Is that why he hates us so much? Because he blames us for his mother's death?''

Frances stared at the rug, a sad droop to her eyes. She shook her head slowly. ''No, I know that isn't the real reason. You see, I know why he is involved in whatever is happening. He wants his family's land back—the land his mother signed over to the Shakers when she became a sister. When I said he blamed the Shakers for her death, I didn't tell you everything. What he really said was, 'The Shakers killed her before I could convince her to demand her land back.' All he really cares about is the land that he thinks should have been his.''

Rose made a hurried stop at the Languor County Sheriff's Office and left a note for Grady O'Neal, telling him what she had learned from Frances Worthington. She asked him to be available later in the day, in case trouble arrived at North Homage. She sped home as fast as the Plymouth would travel along the rutted road between Languor and North Homage, rehearsing in her mind her next steps.

By the time Rose parked next to the Trustees' Office, preparations for the evening meal were under way. She could borrow Elsa from the Center Family kitchen and have that long-delayed talk. However, she made the mistake of stopping in her office to place the recaptured journals in the bottom drawer of a spare desk, and two Believers accosted her as she emerged. Day-to-day problems refused to delay just because Rose needed to handle threats to the Society.

She assigned several unused rooms in the Trustees' Office for storage of all the returned jars of preserved fruits and vegetables. And she promised to find yet another place to move Elsa since the kitchen sisters found her impossible. By then, the evening meal was about to begin.

When Rose slipped through the outside door into the Center Family kitchen, three kitchen sisters were filling serving plates with baked chicken in a creamy tarragon sauce and grimly avoiding each other's eyes. Rose recognized the handiwork of Sister Elsa, who clumped cheerfully through the swinging doors from the dining room.

"Where is Gertrude?" Rose asked, as she grabbed a hot corn muffin from a stack ready to be carried into the dining room. Gertrude was kitchen deaconess and would normally be directing the work.

"Helping out in the Ministry kitchen," a sister answered glumly. "We offered to go, all of us did, but she thought she should go."

"Can you blame her?" mumbled another sister.

"Look alive, now, Sisters," Elsa chirped. "We got a pack of hungry brethren out there, been out in the fields all day." Elsa assumed power at the slightest opportunity.

"Elsa, I'd like a word with you, please," Rose said.

"Can it wait until after the evening meal? Somebody's gotta get the food on those tables."

"The kitchen sisters are very experienced," Rose said. "They will see that everyone is fed. Come along with me now."

The kitchen sisters shot Rose glances of pure love as she took Elsa by the elbow and led her through the outside door. The early evening air was warm and pleasant, so Rose brought Elsa into the kitchen garden.

"Walk with me awhile," she said. "I have some questions to ask you, and I want you to consider your answers carefully."

Elsa pursed her lips and crossed her arms over the loose bodice of her work dress, which had grown tighter over the winter. "Nothin' comes out my mouth that ain't considered careful. Elder'll agree, just ask him."

Rose let the challenge hang in the air. Elsa was a favorite of Wilhelm's, and nothing, not even her most outrageous behavior, seemed to change that. "At Samuel's funeral, you revealed some information about Samuel's past that very few people knew about," Rose said. "I want to know how you got that information."

"Well, I can't rightly say how it happens. Just a gift I guess I got," Elsa said, with a failed attempt at humility. "Leastways, Elder says I got it. I guess it's just sort of a mystery."

"I'm not asking how Believers receive messages from predecessors who have passed on. I want to know how you got the information you revealed— that Samuel had a child. I do not for a moment believe that the message came from Mother Ann. She would not be so gossipy nor so unforgiving. Tell me the truth. My patience is growing thin."

Rose let Elsa walk in silence for a few moments, hoping that she would tell the truth as soon as she realized she could deny it all later, to Wilhelm. Instead of pressuring her further, Rose enjoyed a mo-

ment of calm in the garden. The perennial herbs—
thyme, oregano, and sage—were already lush and
green. Stalks of lavender were turning from brown to
gray-green and would soon have fragrant purple buds.
Rose longed for quiet hours tending herbs, rather than
fending off threats to their peaceful way of life.

Elsa sniffed, and Rose snapped her attention back
to the present. "I might've heard something in town,"
Elsa said.

"From whom?"

"Can't say as I remember, not for sure."

"Try."

Another silence followed, and Elsa again sniffed.
"Guess it might've been while I was in the Languor
dry-goods store, picking up fabric for the sewing
room." Allowing Elsa a few trips into town—usually
in the company of other sisters—was one of Rose's
attempts to find work for her to do that wouldn't drive
the other Believers to question their vows of pacifism.
A few times, Elsa had been allowed to go alone to
pick up fabric that Sarah had called ahead and ordered.

"I do have a memory of talkin' a spell with a couple folks from the world, which I wouldn't've done
normally, naturally, but these folks were friendly
about us Shakers and said they spent some time living
here a long time ago. Seemed nice, and they was real
curious about some of the Believers they remembered
from the old days."

"Were they a man and a woman?"

"Yea."

"Did they give their names? What did they look
like?"

"Just said they were married folks. They looked to be like they was gettin' on, older than me," Elsa said smugly and not very accurately.

"Who did they ask about?"

"Well, Samuel, of course. The man said he'd been friends with Samuel. Then the woman said wasn't it sad about Samuel breaking his vows and having a child and all and feeling so guilty that he killed himself. Well, I never heard that before, so naturally I asked more about it, but all she said was the mother was a Shaker sister and how Samuel come to hate her and all. She wouldn't say no more. And then we just chatted a bit about the old days. I mean, I wasn't here in those days, and I was curious. They said they'd heard about Agatha being close to the end, and how sad that was, but I made sure they heard the good news. They were such friendly folks."

"You told them Agatha was better?" Rose's heart jumped in her chest. Clearly the man and woman were Klaus and Evangeline Holker. Why would they make a point of asking about Agatha's condition? "What exactly did you tell them?"

"Like I just said, the good news. That Agatha came around and can talk again. They seemed real interested to hear it."

"What do you know about the attacks on North Homage?" Rose asked.

"Not one thing." Elsa plunked her fists on her hips and glowered. "Listen, ain't no call to—"

"Did you steal Samuel's journals?"

Spots of pink gave depth to Elsa's flat features. "Why would I do that?"

"You don't deny it?"

"Nay! I mean . . . It was probably Sarah done that. Why don't you ask her? She was out roaming around the night Samuel died."

"How did you know his journals were stolen that night?" Rose asked, her voice a gentle skewer.

Elsa glared at her in sullen silence for a moment, then said, "I never stole nothin' in my whole life. I just borrowed them. I'm gonna bring them back."

"When?"

"When those folks are finished with them."

"The man and woman you met? You gave them Samuel's journals! What could have possessed you to do such a thing?"

"It wasn't like it sounds." Elsa began to whine. "They were fond of Samuel, just wanted to see what he'd been up to all those years, that's all."

"Elsa, that's ridiculous. I don't believe a word of it."

Elsa savagely kicked at a clump of rosemary that hadn't made it through the winter. "Well, that's what they said. When I promised to help them out, they told me all about Samuel and Faithfull and their baby."

"I see. So you paid for gossip with stolen journals."

Elsa's hazel eyes darkened. "You breathe a word of this to Wilhelm, and I'll tell him you're lying. He'll never believe you. He knows you want to kick me out." She spun around and left, trampling an emerging oregano plant as she stomped off.

TWENTY-FOUR

"NED, FLOYD, YOU LEAD EVERYBODY OFF THE ROAD, gather them together in that field over to the west." Klaus Holker leaned out the window of his muddy brown Ford and shouted to the men on horseback. "I'll want to have a talk with them before we move ahead."

"That there's Shaker land, Kentuck," Ned said. "Just plowed, by the look of it."

"It won't matter by morning."

Ned nodded and rode toward the cars and wagons crowding the road from Languor to North Homage.

"Klaus, we can still leave." Evangeline sat rigidly straight in the passenger's seat, staring out the front windshield. "We don't have to do this. You've taught the Shakers a lesson, and Richard will get his land away from them. Why do we have to stay?"

"Because, Evie, that isn't enough." Klaus' voice was edged with impatience. He watched the crowd gathering in the distance. "You don't have to be here, you know. You can leave anytime. You always could."

"I wish I could," she murmured, too subdued for her husband to hear.

"Anyway, I thought you wanted those children so desperately. What we'll do with them all, I don't know. In fact, it's because of them we've got to drive the Shakers away completely and get some of their land. No other way to feed all those mouths you want."

"Don't you blame me for this mess," Evangeline said. "You're the one who couldn't let go all those years—tracking Sarah down and finding out about her going back to North Homage, following her to North Homage." She glanced at her husband's profile. Excitement erased years from his features. "I used to wonder," she said, "if you'd fathered her yourself."

"She was useful. That's all." He reached for the door handle. "What made you change your mind and realize I wasn't Sarah's father?"

Evangeline said nothing. She watched as Klaus maneuvered through the clumps of freshly turned dirt, his eyes on the men and horses clustered in the west corner of the field. When he began addressing them, she slid to the driver's side, pushed the starter button, and pulled away.

Caleb, carefully sober, kept some distance between himself and the restless pack of men gathered on Shaker land. He loved crowds when he was drunk, but being sober always made him feel nervous around more than one person at a time. He'd felt that way all the time at North Homage; they never let him be alone. He watched Klaus approach and beam at the men, both calming and encouraging them.

"Now, friends, I know how riled up y'all are—" Klaus began.

"You don't know the half of it," a man shouted. "My little Amanda, she's getting rabies shots because of that Shaker rat that bit her. You got any notion what it's like watching your kid scream in pain and not be able to help her?"

Angry murmurs spread through the group, and Klaus nodded vigorously. "You can bet I know just how you feel. In fact, I'm glad Laura, my wife, went on home, because she'd feel it like a knife in her heart. That's why she wants to rescue those kids the Shakers have got hold of. They need to be in safe, clean, Christian homes, like yours and mine."

"So what are we waiting for?" growled a burly farmer named Clem standing in front. "Let's teach 'em a lesson."

Klaus's voice turned soothing. "Now, friends, I'm with you all the way, but we've got a way to do this—"

"Yeah, let's get rid of them for once and for all," Floyd Foster yelled.

Klaus shot Floyd an angry look, and Caleb cringed as he thought about what could happen to Sarah if Floyd had his way. Klaus knew how to work a crowd, and now was the time to bring them back to a simmer. Floyd had blurted out his assigned line at the wrong moment.

"Right, what are we waiting for?" shouted Clem. "They're no match for us. I got my hunting rifle, and I'm set to hunt me some Shakers. Come on!"

The others gathered up their weapons—from rifles to pitchforks—and surged around Klaus and Caleb. "Now, folks, we can do this without bloodshed," Klaus pleaded. "What if one of you got hurt? What would your families do?'' But men's angry shouts and the neighing of excited horses drowned Klaus's voice.

For Rose, the evening meal had passed uneventfully but with a rising sense of anxiety. She believed the apostates had planned a final onslaught, and surely it would happen soon, but she could not guess what was coming. She wished to avoid creating panic in the village, and she could think of no quiet preparations to make besides calling Josie to warn her of impending trouble and to ask her to begin preparing Agatha to be moved, if necessary. Otherwise, Rose could only wait. She barely tasted her corn chowder, or the baked chicken that followed. Finally, she gave up and slipped away from the table before the others had finished.

The Center Family Dwelling House had a small parlor for infrequent visitors from the world. Since it was empty, Rose decided to use the telephone to try calling Grady O'Neal. Not that she had anything to report. It was the only action she could think to take, and she badly needed action.

There was no answer at either the sheriff's office or Grady's home. Her call went unanswered, as well, at the Languor flower shop where Gennie worked. Dinnertime for everyone.

Rose wanted to hide in her retiring room and go through Samuel's journals, but she had yet to tell Wilhelm about her discoveries at the apostates' house in Languor. He would be in the Ministry dining room. She knew Elsa was right. He'd never accept her accusation that Elsa had stolen Samuel's journals. He wanted so desperately to believe in her gifts that he quickly forgot anything that revealed Elsa's duplicity. Yet she must warn Wilhelm about the potential danger to the village.

It was dusk when Rose left the Center Family house. Before turning toward the Ministry, she glanced down the center road toward the Trustees' Office. She saw a car drive into the village and park next to the Society's Plymouth. A tall figure emerged. With long strides, he reached the Trustees' Office front door and entered without hesitation.

Rose changed her mind about talking to Wilhelm immediately. Grady had probably decided to drive over, just to be on hand. Wilhelm could wait. He'd be safe enough—and safely out of the way—in the Ministry House at the other end of the village.

She suffered increasing doubt as she approached the building and the shape of the car emerged. It was not the dusty old Buick that Grady usually drove. But perhaps he had driven his own car. He came from wealth, after all. He could afford a car.

Rose's office was lit. She rushed in the door, Grady's name hovering hopefully on her lips. Richard Worthington sat in her desk chair, facing the door.

"Ah, Rose, I thought you would arrive soon." Everything about him—his teeth, eyes, even his shoes—seemed to glitter with self-satisfaction.

"Why are you here, Richard?"

"To help you out of a very nasty mess, as you'll soon see." A small stack of papers lay on Rose's desk, next to Worthington's elbow. He handed it to her. Rose paced the room, skimming the pages.

"You want us to deed over some of our richest farmland to you?"

"Not to me; to the bank."

"Which means you." Rose tossed the sheets back on the desk. "That land was given to us by your mother. She signed the covenant of her own free will."

"Of course you would know that," Richard said. "You were trustee. You know the history of every parcel of land you people own."

Rose longed to throw open the windows and let in fresh air, but night would only chill the room more.

"I can understand your sentimental attachment to that land, Richard, but—"

"Sentimental?" Worthington's voice sparked with anger. "You understand nothing. You never did. I thought you might have learned something when you left here, but then I heard you came back. You let yourself get fooled. But none of that matters." He gathered up the papers. "I want you Shakers to return to me what's mine—mine and Rickie's."

"Are money and land all that matter to you, Richard? Did we teach you so little?"

"You all taught me more than you'll ever know. You taught me that people can call themselves humble Believers while they steal other people's land. You taught me . . ." With a visible effort, Worthington released the rigid tension in his body. "Never mind. We don't have time for this. Some very angry folks are on their way to North Homage, and I'm your best hope for stopping them."

"What?"

"A mob, Rose. Just like the old days. Wilhelm will enjoy that, won't he? He'll probably want to face them alone. Maybe he can stage a dramatic death for himself.''

''Who are these people? Who is leading them?''

''We don't have time to—''

''It's Klaus Holker, isn't it? And his wife, Evangeline.''

''You've been doing your research.'' Worthington pulled a gold watch from his vest pocket. ''We have a few minutes,'' he said. ''I suppose you deserve to know your enemies.''

Rose pulled up a chair and faced him.

''Yes, you're right,'' he said. ''Klaus and Evangeline are behind these attacks on North Homage. Caleb Cox is their willing dupe, in exchange for good liquor and a chance to impress Sarah Baker.''

''What is your connection with these people?''

''We were all friends, of a sort, here at North Homage. We all hooked up again about a year ago, when Klaus showed up.''

''He came back to avenge your mother's death?''

Worthington blinked rapidly. ''You really have been busy, haven't you? Klaus thought no one knew of his feelings for my mother. I suppose Agatha figured it out? Yes, Klaus loved Faithfull, who loved only Samuel. More hypocrisy among the celibate Shakers.''

''Did you suspect that Klaus had killed your mother?''

''For years I was sure of it. Then he came back to town with this scheme to discredit you folks, and I wasn't so sure. He'd followed Sarah here, you know. He needed someone on the inside, and he knew she was an unhappy, pliable girl. He kept in touch with

Sarah's aunt, who raised her after her mother—our mother—died. I suppose it made him feel he hadn't lost Faithfull completely, watching her daughter grow up. But it kept his hatred alive, too. Another man had fathered her. Pathetic fool.

"Anyway, he got her to help by feeding her bits of information about her mother and about the identity of her father. It was pure luck that she and Caleb hit it off.

"Now, I'd suggest signing these papers quickly," Worthington said, nodding his head toward the desk. "Right now, Klaus is whipping that mob into an anti-Shaker frenzy. They are gathered just outside North Homage. He'll wait for me to get there—if he can hold them in one place that long."

"How can you possibly stop them?"

"By telling them that you've agreed to turn over your land and leave."

"But that isn't what you are asking us to do."

Worthington shrugged a tailored shoulder. "No, but they won't know that. Once we get them to calm down and go home, they will stay home. Unless somebody stirs them up again."

"Which Klaus could do tomorrow."

Worthington nodded and stood, his suit falling into place around his tall body. "But I'm sure that will give you enough time to destroy his influence."

"How?"

"By proving he killed Samuel—or had him killed."

"How do you know that?"

"I don't." He took a pen from Rose's desk drawer and held it and the papers out to her. She ignored them. "I do know what Klaus told me," Worthington said. "He came back after so long because he'd found out that my mother had loved him, after all. That she planned to break off with Samuel and run away with him."

"How did he find this out?"

"You'll have to ask him."

Rose went to her office door and held it wide. "I won't sign those papers, Richard," she said. "We will not be blackmailed."

Worthington's face flushed. He tossed the pen on her desk and strode toward the door. "Let's hope your precious Mother Ann intervenes for you," he said. "That's your only hope now."

"I pray she will help us save ourselves," Rose said, as Worthington passed. "And I pray you will save your own soul by coming to our aid—that, instead of more land, you will pass down to your son the compassion you witnessed as a child living among us."

※

TWENTY-FIVE

"WILHELM, FOR ONCE, DON'T ARGUE. WE HAVEN'T time."

"As elder, I should confront them. Let them do their worst to me." The sacrificial glee in Wilhelm's voice carried over the telephone wires, and Rose felt the knot in her stomach tighten.

"If the mob reaches the village, you'll have plenty of time to confront them," she said. "Right now, we need to work fast. We need to gather everyone in the Center Family dining room. It'll be safer with everyone together. Deputy O'Neal called to check on us. He got sent on another wild-goose chase thirty miles away, but he's heading back here." The apostates were well organized. Rose shivered as she realized how easily they had invented emergencies to get Grady out of the way on the evening of the meeting in Languor and again tonight. "If you get the children, I'll help Josie," she continued. "Agatha is the only one in the Infirmary right now. Between us, we can move her."

Wilhelm grunted his assent. Rose didn't have time to worry about whether Wilhelm would stay in the Center Family building once he'd herded everyone there. She called the Infirmary. She listened to the endless ring as she darted nervous glances out her office windows. Josie must be in Agatha's room. She'd run over there as soon as she had shooed out the few inhabitants of the Trustees' Office.

Bunching up her skirt to keep from tripping, Rose raced up the stairs. She found Gretchen in the hall-way. "Get the others from their rooms," she ordered, "and all of you get over to the Center Family house."

"What—"

"Now!"

"Sarah isn't here," Gretchen said, as Rose turned to run back downstairs. "She went back to the Sisters' Shop to catch up on some mending."

Rose knew several curses, and she said them silently before switching to a prayer. She ran back to her office. Never mind, she thought, maybe this could work out well, after all. She called the sewing room. Sarah answered promptly and agreed to help Josie bring Agatha to the Center Family house.

A glance out a second-floor window reassured Rose that the village was quiet. She swept through her retiring rooms and her office, gathering up all the journals she had been using for her investigation. She piled them in a worn basket from the kitchen and left.

The Center Family dining room had never held so much noise. Rose wove through the chattering Believers and children to the kitchen. She nodded to the kitchen sisters, who were preparing a snack to keep the children busy. She entered a pantry and hid her cache of journals behind stacks of preserved fruits and vegetables.

Back in the dining room, she wandered among the

Believers, allaying fears when she could and keeping her eyes open for Josie, Agatha, and Sarah.

Richard Worthington parked his new Ford on the road and walked to the crowd in the field, arriving in time to see Klaus grab the reins of Floyd Foster's horse and heave himself into the saddle. The horse, used to a lighter load, whinnied and bucked, but Klaus held on and brought the animal under control.

"Hold on, now, men," he shouted. "No need to push too fast here. We've still got some planning to do." A few men listened, but most seemed not to hear him through their own demands for vengeance against the Shakers. Klaus reached down and grabbed Floyd's collar.

"You're the one who got them too riled up," he said. "Help me get them quieted down before this gets out of control."

"But I thought you wanted—"

"I want them riled up, but not crazy. Just do it, talk to them."

Floyd gave him a hard look and walked toward a cluster of gesticulating men. Klaus rode to another group and tried to calm them with his neighborly style.

Worthington stood on the edge of the group, watching. The plowed dirt beneath the hooves and feet had hardened to a solid mass. The din of angry voices increased in volume. Klaus wasn't as powerful as he thought he was.

"What's going on here? I thought you was on our side," a man in overalls shouted at Klaus.

Another man, from Floyd's group, caught the fury

and yelled, "Yeah, what the hell are we waitin' for? You told us what they're doing to kids. Why are we standing around?"

"You said they hid that murderer all those years," Clem boomed.

Worthington took a step back, then another. The men went for their horses again. Klaus still tried to regain his control, but Floyd had changed sides. The battle was lost, Worthington thought, and war was about to begin. He turned to leave, oblivious to the black mud caking his shoes.

"Mr. Worthington, you gotta help me." Caleb Cox appeared at his elbow. "Please," he said, "I gotta get to North Homage fast."

For once the man didn't look—or smell—drunk. Worthington threw him an irritated look, but he paused. "Why? If I were you, I'd head the opposite direction," Worthington said.

"I'm worried sick about Sarah," Caleb said. "You can see what's happening here. I gotta get to Sarah, get her out of there."

Worthington saw a gleam of something—cunning or maybe just determination—in Caleb's normally blurred and guileless eyes.

"Can you drive me to North Homage?" Caleb asked. "You don't even have to drive me into the village. You can drop me at the entrance, and I can still do what I gotta do."

Worthington nodded briskly. "Hurry up," he said.

As she circulated through the dining room, Rose glanced frequently at the door, hoping to see Sarah and Josie arrive with Agatha between them. She pretended to be calm, for the others' sakes, but her mind restlessly prodded and pried at the pieces of information she had. The more she could figure out about Faithfull's and Samuel's deaths, the better prepared she would be to reason with the crowd heading their way.

What puzzled Rose most was why this was happening now, twenty-five years after Faithfull's death. Why would Klaus and Evangeline and Caleb and Richard Worthington all band together now? According to Richard, Klaus had recently discovered that Faithfull had planned to choose him over Samuel. Was this the truth? If so, Klaus would have had a motive to kill Faithfull, because at the time of her death he believed she was rejecting him. But why kill Samuel? It didn't make sense for Klaus to punish the Shakers unless he truly believed Samuel killed Faithfull, and North Homage had known it and protected him all these years.

Could Samuel have killed Faithfull, after she'd rejected him? Was that truly the sin he could not confess? Rose could not ignore the possibility, despite his seemingly heartfelt confession of falling into the flesh and planning to run away with Faithfull.

Yet Faithfull had been ill the day she died. She was being watched over in the Infirmary. The Infirmary had only one entrance, so Samuel would have had to sneak past the Infirmary sisters, as well as anyone in the sickrooms. Rose was doubtful this could have happened without arousing someone's suspicions. Agatha had been suspicious, though—of something, someone. A niggling fear surfaced in Rose's mind. What if one or more of the apostates left twenty-five years ago because Agatha confronted them with her suspicions? It would be like Agatha to ignore danger to herself, if it meant protecting her Society. If she hadn't enough proof to bring the guilty to justice, she may have hoped to keep them from killing again.

Rose stopped dead. Agatha, in danger. If she knew where the guilt lay, and if the apostates knew she could speak again . . . Rose scanned the dining room. Had Sarah and Josie arrived with Agatha yet? No sign of them. Rose ran to the hall phone. Still no answer at the Infirmary.

She flew out the door and down the path toward the Infirmary. Fine dirt coated her shoes and the rim of her dress, but Rose noticed only her racing thoughts. Just one person could easily have killed Faithfull, and that person could be with Agatha right now. Samuel must have known or guessed the culprit, and carried that knowledge in his heart for half his life.

At the Infirmary door, Rose paused with her hand on the knob. If what she feared was indeed happening, she must enter quietly, take them by surprise. If she wasn't already too late. Through an effort of will, she slowed her breathing and steeled herself.

She heard no sound from inside. Opening the door a crack, she peeked inside. The waiting room was empty. She entered and eased the door closed behind her. She held her breath and listened. A murmuring reached her from the hallway. Relieved, she tiptoed toward the sound. If they were talking, maybe nothing had happened. Perhaps it was all her imagination, and she'd find Josie and Sarah still preparing Agatha to be moved.

She reached the hallway. A distinct voice carried across the still air. It was neither Josie nor Sarah nor Agatha's halting efforts. Hoping to hear more clearly, she edged closer. The door to Agatha's room was partially open, and the voice issued from inside. The door opened toward Rose and hid her approach.

As she neared the room, she stepped on a creaking floorboard. To Rose, the sound screeched through the hallway and filled the building. The voice stopped. A jolt of fear shot through her legs. She froze, her foot still pressing on the board. Moments of silence. Rose imagined the voice's owner tiptoeing to the door, looking out, seeing her. Beads of sweat dampened the rim of her cap. But the voice began again, with no difference in tone. Rose raised her foot from the offending board before silence returned.

Why did she hear only the one voice? Were the others already dead? Rose clamped her teeth together to stop a grieving whimper from escaping. She reasoned with herself. If the others were dead, why would their killer be speaking out loud?

She took a chance and rushed the last few steps to the cover of the door. She slipped behind it and peered through the crack between the door and the jamb. She could see most of the room, and it became clear at once why only one voice spoke. Sarah and Josie were tied to ladder-back chairs, their mouths covered with layers of rolled gauze. Agatha lay still on her bed. Gauze covered her mouth, as well. Rose told herself that Agatha must be alive. Why silence her if she was dead?

A figure moved in front of the sisters, facing them. Rose recognized the rigid posture and gray curls, now

disheveled, of Laura Hill—Evangeline Holker. Rose
had been right. Evangeline was the most likely suspect, once Rose had remembered that Josie had been
in Cincinnati the night Faithfull died. Evangeline and
Faithfull were the two Infirmary nurses at that time,
with only one extra inexperienced sister assigned to
the Infirmary when Faithfull fell ill. It was Evangeline
who had determined the cause of Faithfull's death. It
would have been easy for Evangeline to give her a
sedative, while pretending to check on her condition,
then hold a pillow over her face until her breathing
stopped forever.

Evangeline seemed to be explaining to the sisters
how and why they were to die. "It's only fair that
you know," Evangeline said in her high, prim voice.
"You'll never be able to tell anyone. The only person
I really wanted to die was Faithfull, and even that was
a mistake, after all. If Klaus had been less deluded,
none of this would have happened. He had convinced
himself she would run off with him, and like a jealous, love-struck girl, I believed him. And there she
was, sleeping away in this very room, with only me
to keep watch. It was as if God meant for her to die,
as if He gave me permission." Evangeline stretched
out her arms in supplication, and Rose saw a flash of
silver in her right hand. No gentle pillows this time.
She had a gun.

"Still, I've never been sorry that she died. She was
a bad mother. She gave up both her children to the
Shakers—you, Sarah, she just gave you away, while
I've been denied children all my life." She began to
sniffle. She squared her shoulders and cleared her
throat. Rose could see the horror in Josie's and

Sarah's eyes, and she guessed what they must be thinking—what kind of woman kills two people and is about to kill three more, yet cries for the children she never had?

"Agatha must have been spying on us, because she suspected what I'd done and told me either to confess and face justice, or leave. I convinced Klaus to go with me. I told him Faithfull died a natural death, and he turned to me in his grief." Her voice held a sneer. "At the time, I thought I was in heaven and everything was perfect," Evangeline said. "But my life with him has been my punishment."

Evangeline turned toward the door, and Rose's heart missed several beats. She was afraid to pull away from the crack for fear Evangeline would see movement and come out to investigate. But Evangeline was looking at something on the floor next to the door. Her face was composed, free of compassion or remorse. She looked like a woman with a job to do. She picked up a can and carried it to Sarah. With an awkward movement, she hefted the can to her chest, while holding the gun in her other hand. She sloshed some of the contents of the can over a squirming Sarah, who closed her eyes and screamed in her throat. The acrid smell of gasoline permeated the hallway.

Oh, dear God and Mother Ann and Mother Lucy, Rose thought. *She means to burn the Infirmary, starting with its inhabitants.* In a flash, Rose realized it would be a mistake to charge into the room. She knew nothing about guns, but she feared a shot might spark a fire. She had to get Evangeline out of that room.

Before Evangeline began dousing Josie, Rose ran

on frantic tiptoe back to the waiting room. She hadn't time to make a phone call. Her eyes darted around the room as she desperately sought an idea. So many gentle Shaker healing products—tins and bottles of dried herbs, powdered roots, syrups. Her gaze lighted on the coatrack holding Josie's long Dorothy cloak, and the glimmer of a plan came to her.

The coatrack was solid pine, but Rose found she could lift it easily. She stuffed a bottle of rosewater in each of her apron pockets. Careful to avoid making noise, she lifted the rack and carried it to the end of the hallway. When she found a spot that seemed just far enough away, she eased the rack to the floor. Quickly she arranged the cloak so its back faced the hallway, and its top rounded over two hooks, creating the illusion of shoulders. With the hood pulled over the top, the rack could be mistaken at first glance for a person, or so Rose fervently hoped.

She crept back to Agatha's door. Peering again through the crack, she winced as she saw Evangeline douse Agatha's body with gasoline, then splash the remains of the can on blankets around the room. Rose knew she had only moments. She pulled one bottle of rosewater from her pocket and threw it against the wall, as near as possible to the coatrack.

She heard Evangeline cry out, heard the can bang on the floor. Rose positioned herself at the end of the door, still just behind it. Her peripheral vision told her when Evangeline rushed through the door. Rose expected her to be cautious, to pause before bursting into the hallway. She thought of bumping her with the door or grabbing the arm with the gun as it extended beyond the edge. But Evangeline was rattled. She fired a shot into the opposite wall before she'd even cleared the doorway, then ran into the middle of the hallway.

Rose grabbed the second bottle of rosewater from her pocket and raised it over her head as Evangeline's trembling hand aimed her gun at the coatrack. The dark blue cloak began to move.

Evangeline fired two shots before Rose brought the bottle crashing down on her arm. The gun hit the floor as the bottle smashed, splattering rosewater all over Evangeline. Her astonishment was short-lived. She saw Rose and fury distorted her face. As she lunged for Rose, a movement from the coatrack distracted her. With the strength of youth, hard work, and fear, Rose used the moment to grab Evangeline, pinning her arms to her side. Evangeline squirmed and kicked Rose, who winced as the sharp heel cracked her shin. But she held tightly to Evangeline's arms. With a suddenness that almost threw Rose off balance, Evangeline stopped struggling.

As they both watched, the coatrack tottered and fell toward them, as if wounded. As it hit the floor, Caleb Cox rolled from behind the cloak. He groaned and pulled himself to the wall before growing silent.

Deputy Grady O'Neal ran from the waiting room into the hallway, his gun drawn.

"What the—?" He knelt over Caleb quickly. "He's alive. Now what's going on?" he asked, as he took Evangeline from Rose's aching arms and handcuffed her.

"This is Evangeline Holker," Rose said. "Shaker apostate and murderess."

"Samuel?"

"And a Shaker sister named Faithfull, who died twenty-five years ago. In both murders, she used a pillow to smother her sleeping victim."

Grady grabbed Evangeline's hands and pushed up her sleeves. Both wrists showed healing scratch marks. "So she's also the one who attacked you."

Rose nodded as she knelt over a groaning Caleb. "Just a superficial wound," she said. "We can leave him for now." She sprinted into the room where the three sisters were still captive. Grady followed, shoving Evangeline into a chair where he could keep an eye on her. She seem resigned.

Grady and Rose untied Josie and Sarah, then reassured themselves that Agatha was breathing regularly, merely sedated. Josie pushed them aside and began to fuss over her.

Grady sniffed the air. "I can tell this is going to be an interesting story, full of interesting smells," he said, "but I'm afraid I'll have to wait to hear it."

Rose darted a questioning look at him.

"They're coming, Rose, just like you feared. I need to get back out there fast. You stay here."

Rose ignored him and raced toward the Infirmary door. "Why did you come here first?" she asked, as he caught up with her, dragging Evangeline along.

"Richard Worthington," Grady said. "He had a change of heart, I guess. He brought Caleb in to look for Sarah, then caught me as I got to North Homage. Told me a mob was coming this way and then came back with us to help. When I couldn't find you, I got worried. Gretchen said Josie, Sarah, and Agatha were still in the Infirmary, and she'd seen you race off in that direction. I still wasn't worried until I saw Caleb head that way, too. That's when I figured the Infirmary was the place for me.''

"So Caleb must have been looking for Sarah, to protect her, and heard she was with the rest of us in the Infirmary," Rose said.

"That's what I figure."

"I wonder why Richard decided to help us." They were close to the Center Family Dwelling House, and Rose broke into a trot.

"Something about his kid, doing it for him."

They reached the Center Family house as four men emerged from the west doorway and stood side-by-side. The group included Elder Wilhelm, Richard Worthington, the Reverend Sim, rector of St. Christopher's Episcopal Church, and the sheriff's department's third officer.

The cloud of dust at the entrance to North Homage resolved into a mob of about thirty men, most on horseback, a few in cars. One man in front yelled and pointed at the Center Family house as he spotted the small group near the door. The Reverend Sim stepped in front of Wilhelm as the mob moved in their direction. Rose and Grady, the latter pushing Evangeline ahead of him, joined the four men.

Horses, cars, and shouting men, many holding rifles, left the unpaved road and gouged through the spring bluegrass. A husky man in front seemed to have taken leadership. He pulled up about fifty feet from the dwelling house, and the others stopped as well. They seemed puzzled by what they saw. They recognized Languor's Episcopal priest, his feet planted apart and his arms crossed in a protective stance, in front of the Shakers' elder. Beside the Reverend Sim was one of the sheriff's men, and Richard Worthington stood next to him, impassive and stern. The presence of two women, one in handcuffs, and Languor's deputy sheriff further confused them. Moments passed in silence.

Klaus Holker, straggling behind on a defiant horse, worked his way to the front of the group. He slid from his mount and stared. "Evie? What's going on?"

Evangeline rolled her eyes and didn't bother to answer. It was Grady who spoke. "Mr. Holker, your wife's been arrested for the murders of Samuel Bickford and Faithfull Worthington," he said. "And for the attempted murders of four Shaker sisters."

Klaus's face sagged. He dropped his reins, and the horse pranced away to look for its owner. Confused now, rather than enraged, the men behind him muttered to one another. Their self-appointed leader poked Klaus in the shoulder.

"What the hell's going on?" Clem demanded. "You said your name was Kentuck Hill, and Brother Samuel killed hisself because of killing that Shaker a long time ago."

Klaus stood silent and motionless, never taking his eyes from Evangeline. Wilhelm stepped from behind the Reverend Sim. Aware that there was no peaceful situation Wilhelm couldn't stir into a frenzy, Rose intervened.

"He misinformed you," she said. "But it was not entirely his fault," she added, as an angry murmur arose from the crowd. "Mr. Holker's mistake was in trusting his wife, Evangeline. She lied to him for years."

"Why should we believe you?" cried a gruff voice from the middle of the group.

Rose turned her head toward Evangeline. Grady pushed her a step forward, holding her upper arm securely.

"Evie, is this true?" Klaus asked. When she merely glared at him, he approached her slowly. "Did you kill Faithfull?" Disbelief and grief choked his voice.

"It's been twenty-five years, Klaus. How dare you feel anything for her after all this time! God knows you never felt anything for me, ever, just cheated on me, year after year." Evangeline's high voice deepened as she spat the words at him. "At first I thought I could get you to love me, but I gave up, and then all I asked was a child. But you couldn't even give me that much." She released an angry sigh. "Yes, I killed Faithfull. I thought if she were gone, you'd turn to me. We'd run away together, marry, have a family . . . I did it for your love and our children, and I never got either."

Evangeline looked Klaus directly in the eyes. "She never loved you."

"You told me she did! After all those years of telling me nothing, you told me Samuel killed her because she was going to run away with me. Why would you do that if it wasn't true?"

"Because," Evangeline said wearily, "it was my one chance for children. You were so obsessed with Faithfull's death, with the Shakers being responsible somehow, with Sarah being her long-lost daughter. You wanted to punish them, anyway. I thought if I gave you a good reason, you'd just get Richard to foreclose, and we could have the land and the children, and . . .'' Tears trickled down her cheeks. "Now I'll never have the chance for children, and it was all for nothing. A stupid mistake.''

''What do you mean?'' Rose asked.

Evangeline drew in a jerky breath. "I killed Faithfull because I thought she really was in love with Klaus. Because he was so convinced of it. I thought it was the only way. If her death seemed suspicious to anyone, I assumed they would blame Samuel. But Samuel knew she was going to run away with him, so he figured out what I'd done. Then Agatha figured it out, too.''

''But why kill Samuel?'' Rose asked. "He never betrayed your secret.''

''He was going to confess, and talk to Sarah, too. Caleb told us. I knew Samuel would talk about Faithfull's death, what he'd figured out about me. So I had to make sure he didn't—and get his journals, too.''

''Why not simply disappear?''

Evangeline's face crumpled. Her square shoulders slumped, and her handcuffed arms hung loosely in front of her. Tendrils of her long gray hair fell over her eyes. She made no effort to brush them aside.

''I wanted the children,'' she said, her eyes softening.

''Evie, you couldn't have done all . . . *How?* You were home with me when Samuel died.'' Klaus stood before Evangeline, gazing at her as if he were seeing a stranger.

Evangeline's eyes sparked with anger. "It was your idea to have separate bedrooms,'' she said. "I could do anything I wanted, sneak out in the night, take the car, anything. You'd never notice. So I called Samuel and convinced him to meet me in the Center Family kitchen after bedtime.'' Evangeline shook her head, and a hank of hair swung loose from its pins and hit her shoulder. "I told him I could prove to him that I never killed Faithfull. I thought I could still make everything work out for the best. But when I arrived, I saw he'd fallen asleep in his chair, and his back was to the door. I got a pillow from the parlor, sneaked up behind him . . . it was so easy, just like with Faithfull.''

"Oh, Evie.'' Klaus's legs buckled, and he dropped to his knees. The subdued crowd shuffled their feet and exchanged chagrined glances, clearly aware of the enormity of their narrowly averted error. With Richard Worthington accompanying him, the Reverend Sim wandered among the men, speaking quietly, tapping a shoulder here and cupping an elbow there until they began to mount their horses or walk away.

"So pointless,'' Evangeline said, her high whispery voice barely audible. "If I'd just left everything alone, Faithfull would have run away with Samuel, Klaus and I would still have married . . . and I still wouldn't have any children. Everything would have been the same.''

TWENTY-SIX

"WE'LL NEVER GET THE FOUL SMELL OUT OF THIS room," Josie complained, as she scrubbed the pine floor in Agatha's Infirmary room with soap and water.

"I could break another bottle or two of rosewater, if you'd like," Rose said.

"Rose Callahan, how wasteful! I'll just scrub, thank you."

Rose smoothed clean sheets over the new mattress on Agatha's bed. Agatha herself slept in another room, tired but otherwise unharmed. Evangeline had allowed Josie to sedate the fragile former eldress, so she had missed the terror of the previous day. Rose had thanked God and Mother Ann and anyone else she could think of for that blessing. Someday, when Agatha was stronger, Rose would tell her what happened. But not now. The sisters worked in companionable silence for a time before Rose broached the subject that was on both their minds.

"Josie," she said, "could you bear to talk about what Evangeline said to you in this room? There are some details that still bother me, and she seemed to be confessing to you."

"It would probably do me good," Josie said. "Ask your questions."

"The cookies—the ones we found with Samuel. Did Evangeline explain those?"

Josie sloshed some cleanser full-strength on the floor and scrubbed vigorously. "Yea, indeed. The cookies were already there. I guess Samuel had put them out for Sarah, for their meeting later." Josie sat back on her knees. "I have to wonder if it was a gesture of love," she said. "Evangeline didn't know that Samuel never ate sweets. She thought she was clever to think of biting into one cookie to make his death look like a heart attack during a midnight snack.

"The poor tired man had dozed off with one of his journals open in front of him. Probably planning to show parts to Sarah. Evangeline took the journal, of course, after she saw that he had written down so much about his relationship with Faithfull. She had already convinced Elsa to steal the rest of his journals for her.

"She claimed she hadn't really planned to kill him. But she did, she smothered him, as she had Faithfull, just as though neither was a real, wonderful person with so much good to give to the world."

Josie wiped a sleeve across her cheek and slopped a wet rag into a bucket.

"Did Evangeline mention anything about some pages from an old Shaker journal that were given to Sarah?" Rose asked.

"Ah, yea, she did. The pages were from Klaus's journal, she said. He was playing a 'fool's game,' she said, stringing poor Sarah along with enticing tidbits about her mother."

"Did Evangeline admit to attacking Sarah in the Sisters' Shop?"

"Yea," Josie said. "Another 'mistake' was what she called it. The other apostates were at the barn, releasing our animals, and she followed Sarah over to the Sisters' Shop."

"But why?"

"From the beginning, she had been afraid that if Sarah figured out who her father was, she would approach him and piece together the truth about her mother's death. Unlike Samuel and Agatha, Sarah would surely make the information public. She was quite dangerous to Evangeline." Josie stood and arched her back. She grimaced with pain, but she did not complain.

"Do you need to rest?"

"Nay, not until this room is spotless." Josie lowered herself to her knees again, but before returning to her task, she tilted her face up to Rose. "Be gentle with Sarah, won't you? There's good in her."

Rose nodded briskly. "Sarah will be a better Believer for her experiences." She did not wish to reveal Sarah's struggle, even to Josie. Caleb had been wounded attempting to save her life, yet she had forsworn further contact with him. Sarah's faith was enduring a hard test.

Josie did not press for details. She turned again to her scrubbing. "I am glad to be old and near my time," she said. She shook her head. "I don't envy the young their emotions. Evangeline was always far too emotional. I noticed that when she was my Infirmary nurse. She'd get a notion, and no amount of reason could talk her out of it. I always thought she belonged in the world. Foolish girl."

Rose put her hand on Josie's shoulder. "More than foolish, I'm afraid."

Rose took an appreciative bite of chive-blossom omelet with its mild onion flavor. She marveled how the kitchen sisters could dress up simple eggs for dinner, so that for one meal Believers could forget what winter and the Depression had done to their larder. She'd had a peaceful night's sleep, the Society was safe from mobs and foreclosure—her contentment would have been perfect if she were seated with the other sisters in the Center Family dining room, rather than across from Wilhelm in the Ministry House. However, she had delayed the meal long enough, and she had no more excuses.

"Has Sarah confessed?" Wilhelm asked, as he slathered raspberry preserves on a thick slice of brown bread.

"Nay, but soon," Rose said.

"She should confess to the community, during worship. Her behavior warrants it."

Rose took another bite of omelet and chewed slowly. "Her confession will be thorough. I'll see to that."

Wilhelm darted her a stern glance, but he said nothing.

"She sincerely wishes to remain a Believer," Rose said.

"She'll need careful watching." He pushed a hunk of bread around his empty plate to capture every morsel. "Thy duties as eldress are too demanding—"

"Wilhelm, I assure you—"

"Too demanding for thee to continue as trustee," he finished.

He slipped a folded paper from his work-shirt pocket and handed it across the table to Rose. She opened it and noted the return address. Mount Lebanon, New York. The Lead Society, where the Shakers' central leadership resided. Her heartbeat edged up a notch as she began to read. The beginning held the usual fond greetings and blessings, so she skimmed to the second paragraph.

We've met and prayed daily and believe we now have a solution for you and Rose. Despite an uncertain start, we feel that Rose should continue as eldress, for now. Surely she will grow into the calling, as have others before her. We are in complete agreement with you, Wilhelm. It is too much to ask of her that she be both eldress and trustee, and being the only remaining Shaker village in the west, North Homage needs a strong trustee. We have such a person, and he has expressed willingness to accept the call, to come west and help you. His name is Brother Andrew Clark. He is a devout Believer and a diligent worker. We are certain he can be of service to you.

Rose read no farther. She folded the sheet and handed it back to Wilhelm.

"I phoned the Lead Ministry and accepted their offer, of course," Wilhelm said. "Brother Andrew can arrive within the month. Thy time for preparation is short. I'll expect thee here soon, in thy new home."

Rose put down her fork and leaned back in her chair. She gazed around the small bright dining room, her eyes lingering on the wall peg where Agatha's sugar-scoop outdoor bonnet used to hang. Now her own bonnet hung in the same spot. She was needed here, now. It was time. Her gaze returned to Wilhelm, who watched her in silence, eyebrows arched.

"Tomorrow I'll begin my preparations for moving," she said. "It won't take more than a few days." She picked up her fork. She bit into a whole chive blossom, and the rich flavor exploded in her mouth. It had been some time since food had tasted so good to her.

Murder Is on the Menu
at the Hillside Manor Inn

Bed-and-Breakfast Mysteries by
MARY DAHEIM
featuring Judith McMonigle

BANTAM OF THE OPERA
76934-4/ $5.99 US/ $7.99 Can

JUST DESSERTS 76295-1/ $5.99 US/ $7.99 Can

FOWL PREY 76296-X/ $5.99 US/ $7.99 Can

HOLY TERRORS 76297-8/ $5.99 US/ $7.99 Can

DUNE TO DEATH 76933-6/ $5.99 US/ $7.99 Can

A FIT OF TEMPERA 77490-9/ $5.99 US/ $7.99 Can

MAJOR VICES 77491-7/ $5.99 US/ $7.99 Can

MURDER, MY SUITE
77877-7/ $5.99 US/ $7.99 Can

AUNTIE MAYHEM 77878-5/ $5.99 US/ $7.99 Can

NUTTY AS A FRUITCAKE
77879-3/ $5.99 US/ $7.99 Can

SEPTEMBER MOURN
78518-8/ $5.99 US/ $7.99 Can

IRIS HOUSE B & B MYSTERIES
by
JEAN HAGER
Featuring Proprietress and part-time sleuth, Tess Darcy

THE LAST NOEL
78637-0/$5.50 US/$7.50 Can

When an out-of-town drama professor who was hired to direct the anual church Christmas pageant turns up dead, it's up to Tess to figure out who would be willing to commit a deadly sin on sacred grounds.

DEATH ON THE DRUNKARD'S PATH
77211-6/$5.50 US/$7.50 Can

DEAD AND BURIED
77210-8/$5.50 US/$7.50 Can

A BLOOMING MURDER
77209-4/$5.50 US/$7.50 Can